HER HUSBAND'S SECRET

EMILY SHINER

INKUBATOR
BOOKS

PROLOGUE

The night air is cool, and I shiver, running my hands up and down my arms in a bid to warm up. He's late. He's always late, so that really shouldn't come as a surprise, but the one time I ask him to be on time because this is easily the most important meeting in my life, he drags his feet like he has nothing better to do.

It's maddening, that's what it is.

If he weren't family, if the same blood didn't pump through our veins, if I didn't have memories of the two of us sitting in a kiddie pool in our grandparents' backyard while our moms chain-smoked cigarettes on the sagging porch, I wouldn't give him a second chance.

But he needs a place to live. More than that, though, I need someone to watch.

"Hey." He steps out of the shadow, and I wonder, just for a brief moment, how long he was standing there watching me. He drags his hand through his hair and exhales hard, the scent of weed on his breath.

Gross.

I wrinkle my nose. Hold out my hand. Wait impatiently for him to take the key.

"They need a roommate," I tell him, even though I'm repeating myself at this point. Who knows how many times I need to say these words to him to get this through his thick skull? "And you need someplace to stay. You'll go; be nice. Just keep an eye on her, but don't make it obvious."

"Right." He takes the key, and it disappears into his pocket. "Right. I can do that. And what else do you want me to do?"

Irritation eats at the back of my mind, and I reach up to rub my neck like that will get rid of the feeling growing there. *Does he not listen to anything I say?*

"I want you to let me know if she's doing anything weird. If she talks about moving out. I want you to keep an eye on her. And the kid." I swallow, unable to make myself say the little boy's name. This isn't his fault.

Collateral damage.

That's all he is.

"Right. I can do that." He scratches behind his ear, really digging at it, and I wonder if he has something living back there. Lice, maybe.

I take a step back. We're a long way from when we were little kids hanging out while our moms chain-smoked. A long way from when I was working at the bar and he was a cook and he would sneak me food after my shift.

"Great, I know you can." I put on an encouraging smile even though it's dark out and I don't think he can see my face. "Hey, this is all because of you, you know that, right? You're the one who saw them out together, who put all this in motion. Thank you."

"Yeah, no problem." He steps forward, into a beam of

moonlight, and I get the first good look at him I've had in a while. He's thin, thinner than I've seen him in years; his hair is greasy. His eyes jerk from side to side like he's looking for someone who might be sneaking up on us. But there's nobody, I'm sure of it.

Who would come to the park at this time of night? Who in their right mind would swing by here looking for — what? For an illicit encounter? That's hardly what's happening here.

"Hey, one more thing." I'm losing him, I can tell. "Well, two. I'm going to send you some paperwork on buying a house. I want you to leave it out on the counter. Can you do that?"

A stiff nod.

"Great. The other, and listen, this is really important." I wait until he turns to look at me. His gaze jumps around my face, landing first on my lips, then my ears, the necklace in the hollow of my throat — his gaze lingers there longer than I want it to — and then finally he looks me in the eyes.

"What is it?"

"She's not yours." I say the three words, hoping I'm going to get through to him. My cousin isn't a bad guy, not really. He's just a victim of how he was raised and the fact that our mothers didn't have a lot of money. When I look at him, I see the way I could have ended up if it weren't for one really fateful meeting that changed the entire course of my life.

This meeting with my cousin won't change his life. I know it won't. All it will do is help him out a little bit, get him off the street, give him a roof over his head. I already set up an account for him with some money in it for rent and groceries, and he promised me he'd spend the next few months looking for a job.

Six months, to be exact.

I gave him enough money for six months of living expenses. There's no reason why he can't make it all last, why he can't figure out how to change his life by the time this is all over. All people need is some help, right? I'm giving it to him.

He just has to play by the rules, or I'm going to rip the rug out from under him.

His exhale is explosive. Agitated. For a moment, he narrows his eyes, his gaze still locked on me, and I feel a tremor of fear shoot through me. *Do I know what he's capable of?* But then it's gone, and he gives his head a little shake.

"I know she's not mine. You don't need to worry. This is all for you."

"You get the money when this is all said and done. A lot of money, remember that?" I prompt, wanting to hear him say it. *Needing to hear him say it.*

"I get the money; you get her."

"Right." I reach out, pat his arm. It's the first physical contact the two of us have had in years, and he jerks back in surprise, staring down at my hand like it's burning him.

I pull my hand back, clasp my hands together in front of me.

"You don't need to worry, okay?" He takes a step away from me. Any softness around his eyes I thought I'd seen a moment ago is gone. His face is hard, impassive. He looks like he's carved from stone, all angles and hollows, his eyes sunken deep under his brow.

"I know I don't," I lie. "I just wanted to make sure you and I are on the same page. This is your chance at a new life, okay? I want to do that for you. I just want you to do this one thing for me in return."

He nods. His hands are shoved so far into his pockets that he's hunched over a bit. He kicks a loose rock, and it skids off the path and into the grass. "I know what you want me to do," he finally says, exhaling hard as he looks at me. "You don't need to worry about a thing."

I know I don't. I'm cleaning up one loose end and changing my life in the process. He knows the deal. He helps me do what I want and he's never going to have to worry about paying bills again. Hell, he's my cousin, but even if he decides to spend the money on drugs and kill himself in a dirty hotel room, I'm not going to complain.

Actually, that would probably be a fitting end for him. It would really tie everything up, wouldn't it? Trusting my cousin with the information I've given him isn't ideal.

But it's my only chance to get what I want.

Two people screwed me over. Only one of them did it knowingly. But both of them are going to have to pay.

I'm going to see to it. And anyone who tries to stop me? Who even thinks about getting in my way?

It doesn't matter who they are, I'll kill them.

1

TINA

I sigh as I sink onto the sofa next to Luke. My son turns and squirms into my side, and I loop my arm around him, pulling him close.

"Was dinner good?" I ask. It's an easy yes or no question, because I'm well aware his attention is trained on the cartoon on the small box TV across the room, and I'm going to be lucky to get much of a response out of him.

He nods, but his eyes never leave the screen.

"So the guy we're going to rent the third bedroom out to will be here soon." Paula, my roommate, perches on the edge of the recliner facing me. She twists her fingers together as she waits for me to respond, and when I don't, she continues, "I know you and Luke really wanted separate rooms, but we need more rent, and unless you get a raise at work —"

"No, I get it." I scoot forward, pulling my arm away from Luke. His bony little head pressing into my shoulder has made it go numb, and I shiver as the pinpricks begin, a sure sign that I'm getting my feeling back. "Really, Paula, I do. I mean, of course I don't want to share a bed with my son, he does kick a lot, but we have to do what we have to do." I throw her a smile to try to lessen the impact of my words.

But really, how can I be mad? Maybe if either one of us made more money, we wouldn't have to worry about finding a third roommate, but that just wasn't in the cards. I'm honestly grateful someone wants to live here. Paula had been telling people we were looking for a roommate, hoping word through the grapevine would help us find someone.

And the grapevine worked.

Most people don't want to move in with two adults and a three-year-old boy. I've felt so guilty over the fact that Luke is probably a huge part of the reason we struggled to find a new roommate, so there's no way I'm going to throw a fit about someone moving in now.

"I know, I just feel bad." She leans forward and gives my knee a little squeeze. "But you know what, this is an adventure. That's what Luke would say about it." She nods at my son, who's still mesmerized by the dancing blue bears on TV. "Just think, it will be nice to have a man around the place too, don't you think?"

"Sure will." And I'm being honest. I might try to hide how disappointed I am about having to get a roommate in the first place, but having a man around isn't such a bad thing. Not that I don't think women can do everything a man can. It's just that when someone knocks on the door late at night, this guy can be the one to open it. I don't mind playing the role of the damsel in distress just a little at two in the morning.

"Great. Cool." Paula looks down at her watch. "Well, he should be here any minute now. Ricky. And from what he said, he's willing to move in ASAP, like tonight." She eyeballs me. "That's still cool with you, right?"

"Of course it is." I try to sound braver than I feel right now. Not that there's anything wrong with the guy wanting to move in right away. Who knows what kind of living situation he was in? And while our apartment certainly isn't the Ritz, our ceiling hasn't leaked since the landlord kicked out the tenants above us who liked to plug their bathtub so they could try to create a sensory deprivation chamber in their bathroom.

Talk about weird.

"Great." Paula tends to repeat herself when she gets nervous. She brushes a lock of dark hair from her face, tucking it expertly behind her ear. She opens her mouth, obviously prepared to say something else, but then there's a knock on the door. "Oh, he's here. Ricky, remember?"

"I remember," I say, but Paula has already dashed down the short hall to the front door. Sighing, I push myself up from where I'm cuddling with Luke and drop a kiss on the top of his head. "New roommate moving in, Luke," I tell him. "Make sure you're as nice as you can be."

He nods. Still stares at the TV.

Guilt wrenches through me at the way he doesn't want to look away from the screen. I know I'm not a bad mother. I know that letting him watch TV when I need to get things done or need to shower doesn't mean I'm a terrible person. Of course I'd rather have the energy needed to play with him on the floor all the time, but I just don't.

But he's fine. There are millions of kids all around the world watching TV right now, and they're all going to be just fine.

The sound of voices yanks my thoughts from Luke, and I plaster a smile on my face to go meet our new roommate. *Ricky.* Sounds nice, sounds like the kind of guy who was really popular in high school and probably played at least two sports. Now he's not nearly as athletic, thanks to his office job, but he's still nice and friendly.

And then I'm standing next to Paula, my hand outstretched to greet him. He turns, two bags at his feet, and his eyes land on me. They're dark, a little sunken into his face like he doesn't get enough to eat or enough sleep or *something*, but they lock right on me.

"Hey," I say, reminding myself of what my momma always said about not judging a book by its cover. I'm sure, if I were to see a reflection of myself, I'd look less than my best, too. Especially if the guy has been moving from his old apartment, I need to give him a break. "I'm Tina."

He grabs my hand, his long fingers tight against my skin as he shakes it. When he speaks, he clears his throat first, the sound loud and rasping. "Ricky. Nice to meet you."

For a moment, he doesn't let go of my hand, and I pull back, a tickle of fear in the back of my mind screaming at me that he's not going to let go, but then he does, and I tuck my hand in my pocket.

Silence. We're all sizing each other up. Ricky wasn't the captain of the football team, I know that much just from looking at him.

Or chess club, for that matter.

Paula clears her throat. "I hate to be the one holding my hand out asking for money, but I do need rent before you move in. Do you want to see the room first, or —?"

"Rent. Right. I have it right here." Ricky plunges his hand into his pocket and pulls out a wad of cash that he hands to Paula.

She flicks through it deftly, the tip of her tongue peeking out as she does, then gives a nod and tucks it away.

He clears his throat. "Thanks for letting me move in so quickly. You know how things can change." He nudges the suitcase at his feet.

"Of course." I have to remember my manners. This guy is obviously down on his luck. I've been there, more often and more recently than I'd like to admit, and I'm not going to judge him for what he's going through. "Glad you're here."

He smiles at me, one corner of his mouth twitching up.

Remember your manners, Tina.

"I am too. I think this is just what I need." He runs his hand through his hair and peers around me to the living room. "Is your son in there?"

I stiffen, then relax. Of course he knows about Luke. Paula told me she was up front about who was living in the apartment when she talked to this guy. There's no way she could offer the room for rent without being honest about a child living here.

"Yep, he's rotting his brain in front of the TV. But I'm sure he'll want to meet you later after you get all moved in. Need any help with your bags?"

"No, I've got them." He speaks quickly, stepping forward a little, like he wants to block me from picking anything up. "I've got them; you don't need to worry about it. Let me handle it."

"Okay." I smile at him, then turn to Paula. I'm trying to be nice here, I really am. I'm trying not to be judgmental, but this guy is just a little weird. *Okay, a bit more than a little weird.*

She either doesn't notice how strange he's acting or doesn't care. Holding out a key, she waits for him to take it. "Ricky, welcome home," she says, giving him a triumphant grin.

I can just see the dollar signs in her eyes as he takes the key from her and pockets it. For Paula, getting a roommate is the most important thing. She was willing to do whatever it took to make sure we had someone else to help split the rent, someone who would help keep the place tidy, someone who might be willing to help out with the cooking.

But that's where she and I differ.

Of course I want someone who can help out around the place. That sounds amazing, and, likely, it will keep me from vacuuming every single day after work. But while Paula wants the convenience and the money a new roommate will bring in, I want something else.

I want to keep Luke safe.

That's the most important thing to me. I stare at Ricky, trying to read him, but it's impossible. He doesn't seem like a bad guy, just one who's down on his luck. I've been there, been desperate enough to move in with strangers, to hope someone will take pity on me and give me a cheap and warm place to live.

Ricky turns to me. Smiles. It doesn't reach his eyes.

A shiver races up my spine.

2

ELOISE

It's Saturday, the most glorious day of the week, which means I'll not only get breakfast in bed but Jared will have the day off and be around all day long. When we were first married, his being home all day meant only one thing — that we would fall into bed together and not get out until we had to get something to eat.

Now it means he spends a lot of time watching TV, reading the news, and answering emails that he swears just can't wait. I have to make my own breakfast in bed and bring it back up here to snuggle down deep in our king-size bed, but it's still a far cry from putting on heels and fixing my hair to go into the office.

I roll over, fully expecting him to still be in bed, but he's already out. The covers on his side are flipped back, the mattress cold. I sit up, grabbing my housecoat to wrap around me before heading downstairs. Our house is huge, much bigger than the two of us need, and I take my time going down the curved staircase, admiring the chandelier, the sweeping view down the front lawn, even the soft runner under my feet as I work my way to the kitchen.

I've learned, as I've gotten older, that it's nice to slow down and really enjoy the everyday things. You just never know when it could all be taken away from you.

As I get out my breakfast tray, Jared walks up behind me. He grabs me by the hips and pulls me to him, kissing me along the side of my neck.

My first response is to stiffen. I inhale hard and slowly force myself to relax, allowing my body to melt against his the way he likes.

"You didn't sleep in," he says, brushing some of my unruly hair out of the way so he can land a kiss right behind my ear. When we were first married, that little kiss would have driven me insane, but now I turn in his hands, forcing a smile to my face.

"It's Saturday," I point out, like he doesn't already know. "Time to get some breakfast going and maybe sit outside, walk in the gardens, that sort of thing." I pull away from him, wanting to make my point clear. I'm not interested in what he has on his mind.

He frowns, then kisses me again before finally taking the hint and stepping back. When he runs his hand through his hair, his shirt pulls up a bit, showing me the smooth lines of his stomach. I feel my heart beat a little faster, but I keep my eyes trained on his face.

"I have to head into the office," he says, and even though I wasn't expecting the words, I guess I'm not really surprised. "I have some work to do."

"Always working," I say, keeping my words as light as possible as I turn to the refrigerator. "You know, some people might think you're more committed to your job than anything else."

"Well, they're wrong."

Is that a note of frustration in his voice? Part of me can't deny that I enjoy it, but I know I need to be careful. Keep him happy.

At least for now.

"I know. I was teasing." Holding eggs and cheese, I nudge the refrigerator door closed with my foot. "I admire your commitment to your company, you know that. You've worked hard to make it what it is. A marketing company built from the ground up without any help? Pretty impressive, Jared."

He grins and gestures to the food in my hands. "You mind making me an omelet?"

What I want to do is head back to bed with my breakfast, but if he's here, then I need to have a meal with my husband. "Of course not. Why don't you get the coffee going?"

He does as I ask, and I move quickly, grabbing some ham and chopped peppers to add to our breakfast. In just a few minutes our omelets are done, and I plate them with some fruit salad and join him at the kitchen island. This early in the morning, the sun comes through the windows at just the right angle to bounce off the quartz countertop, sending rainbows dancing across the ceiling.

It's gorgeous.

"So, I was thinking," I say as Jared takes a sip of his coffee, his eyes already locked on his phone screen. "About work. I know I've worked really hard to get to where I am selling mansions around the area, but I want to change my focus."

He doesn't look up.

"And I need your help."

That gets his attention. He puts his phone down and looks at me.

"I want to start a program for underprivileged home-buyers to help them buy their first house." I make the announcement and stab an errant piece of red pepper. Yum.

"Those already exist." Jared takes another sip of his coffee. "What kind of program do you think you could create that would be any different than the half dozen ones offered by the government?"

I was ready for this. I've learned, over the years we've been married, that you have to be willing and able to plead your case with Jared. He loves the challenge of building something from the ground up, but he doesn't suffer fools who don't know exactly what they want.

"Yes, they do exist." I set my hands in my lap, where he can't see me twist my fingers together. "But they're not personal. There's no friendly touch to them. Homebuyers are put into a program where they're chewed up and spat out, just numbers in a system that's not really designed to actually help them. I want to be that personal touch."

"I don't fully follow."

I lift my chin. My nails are digging hard into my palms, but I have to make sure he gets what I'm saying. I have to ensure he not only follows my line of thinking, but supports it. "I've mentioned it before, but it's time. I want to stop selling to my current clientele and work with underprivi-leged buyers. Single moms, homeless vets. I want to learn who they are as people and fight for them to get a place to live. You know as well as I do that rent right now is exorbi-tant, and there are a lot of people who are renting who would end up paying less on a monthly mortgage, but they can't get the help they need to buy. They don't have someone in their corner."

"And you want to be the person in their corner?" He tilts his head to the side a little, examining me.

I feel like a specimen in a Petri dish, but that's okay, because I'm getting exactly what I want right now.

I can practically hear his thoughts. *This would be so good for optics.*

"Right, exactly." I exhale hard, force myself to stop twisting my hands together, force myself to take a sip of coffee. I didn't put enough sugar in it, and it's bitter, but I keep it down. "And I need your help."

"Doing what? I don't do real estate."

"I know you don't. But you know how to make people believe in causes, and you know as well as I do that my boss won't love me forfeiting the huge Realtor fees I make on expensive homes."

"Right, Harrison won't." He frowns and turns his attention to his breakfast. Even though I want to push him for an answer, or to hear what he's thinking, I wait. Jared will tell me what's on his mind when he's good and ready, and there's no benefit to getting antsy now.

It feels like the silence between us stretches on forever, but he finally breaks it, looking up at me, one eyebrow cocked.

"I know. You need someone to run an article on you, get the news of what you're going to be doing out there."

I nod. Yes, I know. I already thought about this.

"And you need someone who can smooth things over with Harrison."

"He's going to need some hand-holding," I say, giving Jared a hopeful smile.

He nods. Tossing his napkin onto the counter, he pushes back and stands. "You let me take care of Harrison. And I know someone at the paper who can run an article on what you're doing, Eloise. I'll give them a call, too."

Excitement bubbles in me, but I don't respond. When Jared starts talking and planning things out, he doesn't like to be interrupted.

"This is good," he continues, more to himself than to me. "This is good. It's good for you to show that you're willing to give back to the community, and people around here love that selfless spirit. I'll make sure the article mentions that you're my spouse. That will reflect on my company, as well."

A stab of irritation shoots through me. "Oh, Jared, really? Thank you so much." I stand too and throw my arms around him. When he hugs me, he can't see the scowl on my face. "I really appreciate you helping me out. And believing in me."

"You're welcome." His large hand rests on my lower back, but whatever thoughts of intimacy he had earlier are gone. Now he's got a task at hand, and his mind is working hard on that. "Let me get started on it. You need to be dressed and prepared for your interview."

I pull back, honestly surprised by how quickly this is all happening. "You think I'll be interviewed today?"

"I'm going to see to it. Get it in the paper this week. You let me take care of everything, Eloise. Just be prepared for what's coming your way."

Oh, I am.

3

TINA

Sundays are park days.

By Sunday morning, I finally feel like I can be a good parent, like I can play on the floor with Luke without my knees aching and without wanting nothing more than to pop a Tylenol and collapse into bed. Sundays are our days, and I pull on the small backpack I wear, ready to head out the door.

Snacks? Check.

Water bottle? Check.

Empty plastic spice jars in case Luke finds a cool bug he wants to bring home? Check.

We're ready.

"We're headed out," I call to Paula as Luke's little hand slips into mine. He snuggles up against my leg before grabbing the door handle and twisting it hard to let us outside. "Be back for lunch!"

"Have fun!" Her voice floats to us from the living room, where she's curled up for her version of church. She has nail polish, a trashy magazine about the Royal family in the UK, three bags of chips, and an extra-long phone charger I got her for Christmas last year. There's no doubt in my mind she'll be right where we left her when we get back.

"Let's go, little man," I say, helping Luke with the door. It's chilly out this morning, but the sun will be out soon, and then it's going to be nice and warm. Luke has a light jacket on, and he scampers ahead of me a few feet while I close the door behind me.

"Where are you going?"

I jump, pressing my hand to my heart. Turning, I see Ricky leaning against the apartment wall, a cigarette between his fingers. He looks casual, like he's posted upright there to hold the wall up by leaning on it, but his eyes are bright and sharp.

"Geez, you scared me," I say, hitching my backpack higher on my shoulder. I pause, giving him the opportunity to apologize for almost making me pee my pants, but he doesn't respond, so I continue, "We're going to the park. Luke and I go every Sunday."

He nods. Takes a drag of his cigarette; then he drops it, grinding the heel of his black boot onto it. There's a cigarette receptacle five feet away, but he either doesn't notice it or doesn't care. Either way, he leaves the butt there on the ground and walks towards me.

"I'll go with you." The proclamation feels like he's thought it out and it's not spur-of-the-moment.

I have one terrifying second where I think that maybe this was the plan, that he knew Luke and I go to the park on Sundays, but that's not possible. I'd have seen him around the apartment watching and keeping an eye on us, right?

Besides, maybe he's just friendly. Since he moved in on

Friday night, he hasn't said much, but some people just take time to warm up.

"Okay," I say, forcing the word from my mouth even though the thought of him joining the two of us is anything but. "Yeah, you can walk with us."

"Great." He falls into step next to me, his hands shoved in his pockets.

I try to ignore the thick cloud of smoke that still seems to linger around him. "Hey, Luke," I say, holding out my hand. "You know that when we're walking on the sidewalk, you need to hold my hand."

Luke nods, dropping the stick he was using to dig up one of the remaining patches of crabgrass in the yard, and runs back to me, dutifully taking my outstretched hand. I pull him close, walking in the middle of the two of them.

We're halfway to the park before I speak. I've been waiting, trying to give Ricky the chance to warm up, but he's just silent. His presence makes it hard for me to concentrate on Luke and the way he keeps jerking my arm from side to side as he looks at rocks, sticks, and bugs.

"So," I finally say, too uncomfortable to let the silence between us continue unbroken. "What do you think about the new apartment?"

"Much better than my car." He gives a short nod like that's a great assessment of the situation.

I turn to him, surprised. "You were living in your car?"

A frown, then it's gone. He nods. "Yeah, I didn't have anywhere to live. So when I found out you guys needed a roommate, I was game."

"Wow, that's hard." I've been bad off before, but I've never actually had to live in my car. I've slept in a friend's closet in a sleeping bag and spent more than my fair share of time on friends' sofas, but living in my car is something I've never had to do and something I never want to experience.

And it's not even an option now, not with Luke. He's everything to me.

"It was." Ricky nods, but now that he's started to speak, it's like his tongue has loosened up, and he's much more comfortable than he was even a moment ago. "But I have a bed now, and that's the best feeling ever."

It was supposed to be Luke's bed. I wish I could have afforded to pay more for us to have our own rooms. But Luke and I will be fine to share a bed a little bit longer. Ricky obviously really needed someplace to live.

"I'm glad things have worked out so well for you," I say, finally releasing Luke's hand as we reach the park. He darts away from me, heading straight for the slide. The bench I always sit on to wait for him while he plays is empty, and I walk to it. Instead of putting my backpack on the ground where I usually leave it, I place it next to me on the bench.

I don't know why. I just know I don't want Ricky sitting really close to me.

He doesn't seem to notice how I've blocked him off, and he drops right down on the other side of my backpack, stretching out and yawning.

I cast a glance at him and look away. He's my roommate, nothing more, but I can't help the fear that people might see us together and get the wrong idea. He just makes me uncomfortable.

"Do you have a boyfriend?" The question feels explosive, like it was held behind a dam, and now the dam has burst.

"What?" I turn to look at Ricky to make sure I heard him correctly, but he's not looking at me. His eyes are locked on Luke.

"A boyfriend? Surely you have one. You're pretty."

You're pretty. My stomach twists not only at the words themselves, but at how casually he says them.

"I don't have one," I say stiffly. "Luke is my priority."

He nods, and I think that's that. If someone can't take a hint that Luke is everything to me and nothing else matters, then I don't know how else to spell it out.

"Someone will come along." He makes the pronouncement like it's a known fact. Like he's Nostradamus and my future is written in the stars.

I clamp my lips together.

He continues, unfazed. "I'm surprised you never met anyone when you worked at the bar."

"What?" I turn to him, jerking back a bit as I do. I grab one strap of the backpack and yank it towards me a little bit. It's a shield. A bright blue and yellow shield with a puppy on it.

"At the bar? You didn't find anyone?"

"How did you know I used to work at a bar?" Fear tickles the back of my neck. I always thought people made it up, but I swear I feel the hairs there stand up. Even though the sun has broken through the clouds and we're sitting in a bright patch of it now, chills race up my spine.

He blinks. Shrugs.

"How did you know?" I wouldn't normally push something like this, but Ricky has me fully creeped out right now. We're in a public place, in the middle of the day, and there's no reason for me to back down, not when I don't like the implication of what he just said.

"Paula must have told me."

She must have told you.

I sag a little, some of the fight going out of me. I'm so

tired, but I'm not sure that makes sense. I force myself to nod. To smile.

"Of course," I say. He can't hear my heart racing. He has no idea how clammy my palms are. "Paula loves to talk."

Relief crosses his face. "Sure does." He turns from me.

I don't want to see what he's looking at, but I already know, even without following his gaze.

Luke.

I don't think Paula would have told him I used to work at a bar. That was years ago, before Luke. But maybe he just guessed. Assumed. I mean, if you were to throw a dart into a crowd of people, you'd be hard-pressed not to hit someone who has worked at a bar at some point in their life.

But something isn't sitting right with me.

I don't recognize Ricky. He looks like every barfly I ever served when I did work at a bar. But maybe he recognizes me. Maybe he remembers me? But then why not come right out and say that when he first moved in?

And why does he keep staring at my son?

4

TINA

Ricky stayed with me the entire time Luke and I were at the park. He didn't talk all the time, but I caught him staring at me.

Watching me.

It felt like he was keeping an eye on me, making sure I wasn't going to do anything. But what might he be suspecting? All I know is now that we're home and Luke is finishing his mac and cheese, I'm ready for bed. Usually Luke and I stretch out on the sofa in the evenings and look at books together. He's only reading a few words himself, of course, but he loves it when I read to him.

Sandra Boynton.

Richard Scarry.

Mo Willems.

These are classics to a little kid, but tonight I don't want to read in the living room. Wrapping my night robe tighter around my body, I hesitate, my hand on the bathroom handle. The apartment is quiet, like it's holding its breath. I exhale hard and step out, my slippers whispering against the old floor as I walk to my bedroom.

"Hey, Luke?" My voice is soft, but that's probably just because I'm matching the quiet of the house. "You want to read?" I wait a moment, giving him time to poke his head out from under the bed, but there's nothing.

No movement.

He must be in the living room already. I shiver and leave our room to head to the living room. Now that we have a third roommate, I'm going to talk to Paula about keeping this place a bit warmer. It's downright chilly in here, and while I can put on another layer of pajamas for bed, it would be really nice if it weren't so cold. Surely we can afford to turn up the heat a bit.

Sounds from the TV reach me before I make it into the living room. Pausing to look in the kitchen for Luke, I grab the popcorn I popped before my shower and carry it with me to the sofa.

"Hey, I wondered where you were, buddy," I say, but then I stop. Luke's on the sofa right where I thought he would be, but he's not alone. Ricky's next to him, scooted so close to my son their thighs are touching. While Luke's watching what's on the TV, though, Ricky's staring at me.

"Hi, Tina." His voice is raspy.

I look at him; then a scream from the TV pulls my attention. On-screen, a young woman clasps her hands to her cheeks, her eyes wide. She screams, then there's a flash, and blood fills the screen.

"What the hell are you watching?" I practically vault over the sofa to stand in front of Luke. He leans to the side, closer to Ricky, obviously doing everything he can to keep watching the show. "He can't watch this. What's wrong with you?"

"I didn't know," Ricky begins, fumbling the remote. "I'm sorry, I thought it was fine."

Anger washes over me as I yank it from his hand, then point it at the TV. It feels good to stab the OFF button and watch as the screen goes dark.

"Momma, no!" Luke's hands are in fists, and he punches them into the air. "No, Momma!"

"Luke, I'm sorry," I say, putting the bowl of popcorn on the sofa and bending down to scoop him up. He immediately goes stiff, his arms and legs straight out from his body, his back arching so it's difficult for me to lift him. "I know you want to watch that, but I don't want you to have nightmares."

As much as I want him to just let me pick him up and take him out of the living room, he fights me, pressing his hands right up against my chest and pushing me back.

I almost trip.

My foot catches on a toy car — *of course it's a toy car* — and I feel myself tipping backwards. Before I can land, though, there's a steadying hand on my back. I gasp. Look up. I fully expect Paula to be standing there, a smile on her face, almost ready to laugh at how ridiculous this is, but it's not Paula.

Ricky's face looms close to mine. When his lips split into a smile, I see his yellow teeth. His tongue, thick and probing, slips between them and runs along his bottom lip.

"You almost fell," he says, and I stiffen, getting my feet under me.

I stand, stepping forward. Luke, for his part, has gone

limp in my arms. He wraps his arms around my neck and buries his face in my shoulder.

"I'm sorry, Momma," he whispers, but I don't respond.

I'm too busy looking at Ricky. At how he's staring at me. His right hand flutters by his pocket like there's something there he wants to pull out, but his eyes never leave my face.

"Thank you," I say, doing my best to smile as though I'm unbothered. In reality, though, it's like I can still feel his hand on my back, the warmth from it spreading across my skin, and a shiver runs up my body.

God, does he notice?

"Do you want to sit and watch TV?" Ricky's words aren't as disjointed as they were when he first moved in. He's getting more comfortable here, and while that would normally be a good thing, while I'd normally be happy someone felt more comfortable around me, I don't like it.

I don't want him snuggling up next to my son. I don't want him to feel comfortable enough to touch me on the back like that, even if he is the reason I didn't just land on my butt. It's a strange feeling, to know I should be grateful to him but to also want to scream at him to never touch me again.

My head hurts thinking about it.

"Actually, I'm exhausted," I tell him, which is a lie. After my shower I felt rejuvenated, and now I'm even more awake. Adrenaline pumps through my veins, and I feel like I could lift a car off a child if the need arose, but I'm not letting this guy know that.

"Oh." His face falls, and he looks at Luke. "You can go to bed if you want, and I'll stay up with Luke."

"No, that's fine," I say, and I realize as soon as the words are out of my mouth that I answered too quickly.

He frowns, his thick eyebrows crashing together, his mouth flattening out into a line.

"I appreciate it," I say, the need to smooth things over between us driving me to keep talking, "but Luke and I could both use an early night."

I hold my breath, fully expecting my son to throw a fit over what I just said.

He doesn't make a sound.

"Well, that's fine." Ricky gives a nod like he's trying to convince himself of that fact. "Tomorrow, then."

"Yeah, maybe." Does my voice sound appropriately nonchalant and noncommittal? "Have a good night."

He doesn't move when I take a step forward, and I have to brush against his shoulder to pass him. My heart thuds in my chest, and I hold Luke as close to me as possible. Around the sofa I pause and look back at him.

Surely he'll have sat back down by now. He'll be watching whatever slasher flick he thought was okay to show my little boy, but he's still standing there.

Watching me.

He lifts one hand, the movement slow and almost too creepy to bear, and a shiver dances all the way up my spine.

I nod at him. "Goodnight."

"Sleep good, Tina."

I turn back, moving faster now. He hasn't moved, at least not that I can tell. I'd hear him coming, right? I'd hear the creak of the old floor under his weight. Sure, he's a skinnier guy, but he still weighs more than me, and I can't imagine the floor wouldn't creak if he were coming for me.

Sweat beads on my brow. Luke's slipping a little bit, and I hitch him higher on my hip but don't let him go. He's great at slipping out of my grip when he really wants something, but

I refuse to let him go back to the living room and watch that movie.

My room is second down the hall. I have to pass the bathroom first. Even though I really want to know where Paula is, I'm not going to bother walking to her room to look for her. I have a feeling she's not home, just Ricky and Luke and I are home, and I swear I can still feel his eyes boring into the back of my head.

I'm not going to turn around to look, though.

"Momma, my car!" Luke comes to life right as I reach our door. He arches his back, throwing himself away from me, but I tighten my grip, swinging my hip around to try to get him through the bedroom door.

If Ricky's watching, then he can see what's happening. He'll know Luke isn't happy. What if he brings his car, the one that almost tripped me? What if he takes that as an invitation to come to our room? The thought of him in my doorway, filling up the space, his eyes hungry on mine, gives me a burst of energy.

"Shh, Luke," I say, stepping into our room. He's dead weight on me now, doing his best to slither down my leg, and I grab the back of his shirt with one hand as I close the door with the other.

Throw the lock.

Sag against it.

Finally free, Luke drops to the floor and grabs the door handle, violently twisting it back and forth. "My car!"

"Shh!" I'm on my knees now, and I take him by the shoulders, forcing him to look at me. "Shh, Luke." Desperation courses through my veins.

There's a creak in the hall.

I know it's bad parenting, but that doesn't matter to me right now. "If you keep quiet, buddy, I'll buy you a new car tomorrow."

He eyeballs me and is about to shake his head when I interrupt.

"*Two* new cars. You just have to be quiet, Luke. You have to go to bed."

Another creak outside my door.

My shower was a waste. Sweat pours down my back, but I don't move from where I'm crouched in front of my son. I have to get him to see reason. Suddenly the thought of Ricky coming into our bedroom is enough to make me sick. I know it's probably my imagination, but what if it's not?

Women are trained to stay alert, to keep our eyes open, to trust our gut and not put ourselves in stupid situations where we might get hurt. At the same time, we're told not to hurt a man's feelings.

I can't do both right now.

"Two cars," Luke says, his lower lip trembling.

"Two cars," I agree, pulling him to me and kissing him on the forehead. At the same time, my ears strain against the silence in the hall.

Maybe I was imagining things. It wouldn't be the first time in history a woman got scared and thought a man was going to hurt her when he was really innocent.

But I know what I heard. I heard someone in the hall. Paula isn't home, and she doesn't walk past my room slowly. She bounds. Crashes down the hall. Knocks out a little rhythm on my door to let me know she's around.

It was Ricky, I know it was.

Not for the first time, I look around our small room and

wish we were anywhere else. If I could afford something better, I'd move us in a heartbeat. I'd yank Luke out of here and never look back.

I've never been afraid in my own home before.

But that was before Ricky.

5

ELOISE

I set the large cardboard box down on my desk with a sigh, then turn and lean against its edge, my eyes on the window. This. This is the type of view I wanted when I decided to become a Realtor. Sure, I knew corner offices with soaring views were mostly reserved for bigwigs high up in large companies, but I had a dream.

And that dream didn't involve board meetings all day long, it didn't involve schmoozing clients, and it certainly didn't involve the long evening and weekend hours that being CEO entail.

My phone rings in my pocket, the vibration startling me out of my thoughts.

Then again... my phone does tend to ring more than I'd like.

I pull it out and thumb it on to answer without paying attention to the name on the screen.

"This is Eloise Jones."

"Mrs. Jones, do you think you could help me find a house?" It's my husband, Jared, his voice warm like caramel.

I laugh, walking over to the large window and putting my hand up against the cool glass. "I could do that for you, Mr. Jones. Do you have anything specific you're looking for?"

"Just a house where I can love my wife. Somewhere I can watch her cook, keep an eye on her. A nice backyard in case there are ever kids, you know. The normal."

"I have the perfect thing." I laugh, then close my eyes for a moment. Everything I've worked for all my life is finally happening. I've never been the type of woman to just sit back and let life happen to me. No, I've wanted to work and have a family. I've wanted to bring money in and have time to play.

I wanted to be rich, if I'm being entirely honest.

And this step is going to help me reach that goal in ways I couldn't before.

"How's the new office?" Jared clears his throat, pulling me from my thoughts.

I glance down at my watch and realize he's probably in between meetings, just eking out enough time for a quick chat with me. He's always going from meeting to meeting, which means any time on the phone with him like this is something to value.

"It's incredible. I really wish you could see it, Jared. The windows are huge! And the view of the mountains, well, let me tell you, I could sell a place with this view in one show-ing. I have a huge desk and a door that — get this — locks. People can't just burst in on me."

"You're really moving up in the world." His words have an edge to them, but I know he's just thinking about the time someone burst in on me in my old office. I was eating lunch and spilled my tomato soup down my front, it took me so by surprise.

Let's just say that suit didn't make it home from the cleaners. There's no saving something that makes you look like you're Freddy's latest victim.

"It's funny, isn't it?" I pause, waiting to see if Jared will jump to fill in what I'm trying to say. He doesn't respond, so I continue, my words picking up speed. "For the company to be willing to give me such a nice office when I'm going to be working with... clients who don't have as high a budget."

I know Jared's the reason I have this new job, this new office, but I want to know if he's willing to admit just how much he was involved. He's known for a long time that selling multimillion-dollar homes tucked up in the tippy-tops of the Blue Ridge Mountains isn't what gets me out of bed every day.

Give me a struggling mom getting back on her feet and I'll hit the ground running. Show me grandparents trying to make the best of a bad situation after they lose their home to eminent domain, and I'm all fired up.

But for the company to not only *make* that position for me, but also give me a huge office right after I brought it up yet again?

Yeah, Jared did more than just *smooth things over* with Harrison.

Things don't entirely add up, and I know that when things don't add up for Jared, he usually just puts another zero on the end of whatever sum he's bandying about. It's always worked out in his favor.

And now it's finally working in my favor.

I hold my breath.

"Eloise, you're passionate. You're driven. You, more than anyone I've ever met, want to help people who are down and out on their luck. Have you stopped to consider the fact that maybe Harrison Realty just recognized that?"

"You're too good to me, you know that?"

"I love you, you know that?"

His words make me smile. I'm not about to look a gift horse in the mouth.

Or a gift office, in this case.

"Well, this place is amazing. I can do a lot of good here as the head of the new Homebuyers with Heart program. If someone were to have helped me out a little bit by pulling strings, I might have to thank them. Privately."

"Well, that changes everything." His voice is lower now, like smooth honey, and I close my eyes as I turn, then lean back against the windows. "But we're going to have to put a pin in it, Eloise. I have a meeting, but I'll be thinking about you."

Of course he does. What in the world would Jared Jones do if he didn't have a meeting to escape to? The man thrives on them the way some houseplants thrive on neglect. Not that I've found any that will stay green through my accidental months-long droughts, as evidenced by my black thumb, but I've tried every one the local nursery keeps suggesting.

I wonder if they know they're just sending plants to a slow death when they sell them to me.

"You have fun at your meeting," I say, dragging my thoughts away from the crispy peace lily in our main bathroom. "I'm going to get my desk all set up and see about finding my first clients."

"Brilliant. Love you."

"I love you," I say, gripping the phone tight like that's going to ensure he waits long enough for me to respond. But it doesn't, and he doesn't, and my words echo in my ears as he hangs up.

"I knew he'd help out," I tell myself, tucking my phone back in my pocket. I give it a little pat, then walk to my desk. There aren't a lot of things I brought with me from my old office two floors down, but I do have all of my notebooks, my favorite pens, and some books that talk about real estate law and what Realtors can and can't do.

Of course, I have them all memorized by now, but that doesn't mean I don't want to have them close at hand if I need to look something up.

That's the beauty of it, isn't it? This office? This space?

I'll be able to do so much good here. I'll be able to change lives for the better. I can help people find their forever homes and not have to worry about hitting a quota to stay with Harrison Realty. That was part of the agreement, and something I didn't think Harrison himself would agree to.

Nobody wants to keep on an employee who uses up more resources than they're bringing in, and that's exactly the risk of my job.

Low to no Realtor fees.

Improved rates thanks to an agreement Harrison worked out with the local bank.

Or did Jared pull those strings with the bank, too?

First access to new, low-cost homes before they hit the market.

And a personalized approach no other company can offer.

That's me. I'm the personalized approach, and I'm going to be amazing at my job.

You know why? Because you can't lie to me. I always find

out. That's why I'm so good at matching clients to the best home for them. I've had clients try to hide things from me before, but it doesn't matter how careful they are.

I always find out the truth. Now, whether or not I tell people what I know is up to me. It's up to my discretion. Sometimes I want them to know they were found out.

Sometimes I want them to stew in it for a bit. I want them to wonder if I know the truth or think they've gotten away with it all.

Like Jared. He thinks he's untouchable, up there in his ivory tower, protected by the company he built. He thinks making sure I have this job, the thing I've told him over and over I'd love to do, will ensure I don't dig deep into what he's done, who he is.

But he's wrong.

God, he's wrong.

6

RICKY

My new room is small, and the bed sags a little in the middle. There's a wooden dresser in the corner of the room, and when I put my clothes and diary in it, the drawers got stuck halfway, but I guess that doesn't matter, not really, not in the long run.

I'm not here to worry about how nice a place I'm living in. And anything is better than my car.

I lie down on the bed and stretch out, letting my fingers trail down the wall as I do. It was just luck that I got this apartment, I know that. Luck and a little string-pulling from family. How many nights have I spent trying to get comfortable in the back of my old Blazer? How long has it been since I've had access to a hot shower without having to try to sneak past the front desk workers at the twenty-four-hour gym?

Too long.

Groaning, I roll over and sit up, staring at the opposite wall for a moment.

On the other side of the wall is where Tina sleeps. *No,*

don't think about that, that's not important. She was so upset last night when I was watching that movie and Luke looked up.

I thought he'd like it. Horror movies have always been my favorite, but then she had to come out and get upset.

Today's been better though. I've been quiet and stayed out of the way, and she actually laughed a little at something I said earlier.

She seems happier. If I didn't know better, I'd think it was relief, but no, there's no reason for her to feel relief, it's something else. It's like yesterday didn't happen. She's moved on.

She's forgiven me.

I drag my eyes away from the wall. My room doesn't have a bedside table, so I have my empty suitcase set up there, creating the perfect place for me to charge my phone.

Phones.

One is old, something I won in a bet a year ago, something I scrounge around every month to buy enough minutes to last me for thirty days. I plug it in, wiggling the charger a little bit to ensure it connects. There's a soft *boop*, and I carefully put the phone down, making sure I don't knock the charger out of place.

Now my new phone. It's not the nicest model, but the screen is smooth and unblemished, and it holds a charge a lot better than my old phone. I'd like to use it full time, but I remember the warnings against that.

It's only for talking to me.

Right, I know, I know. I don't need to charge it, but I plug it in anyway, just in case, then stand up and turn around, taking in my room. It really is so much better than the back of my car.

Even though I'm exhausted and could pass out and sleep all night, I leave the room, slowly walking down the hall to the living room. Three bedrooms and one bathroom. The door to the outside. Then a small kitchen, almost laughably small, so small I can't imagine more than one person in there at a time. There's an eat-in bar on the other side of the counter, but no stools.

Then the living room. Old furniture, a tiny TV. A stack of little-kid books, the top ones almost sliding off and onto the floor, but teetering there like magic. Paula in the recliner.

Tina and Luke on the sofa. He's watching TV. Tina is looking at something on her phone.

My steps feel stilted as I walk across the living room and drop down next to Luke, not too close for anyone to think I'm accidentally touching him, but close enough that I'm not crammed up against the arm of the sofa; close enough to smell whatever shampoo or bubble bath the kid uses to clean up.

It's cloyingly sweet. I wrinkle my nose.

Nobody says anything.

"So what are we watching?" I turn to the adults, to Tina, really, looking right over Luke's head. He probably wouldn't respond if a bomb went off right in front of him, not when there's those stupid bears on TV, dancing around and singing about being friends and how to take care of the world. I notice Tina's mouth is moving —

"— but he loves it, so what do you do?" She shrugs and smiles at me, and I latch onto her smile, staring at her mouth.

It's so perfect.

Then I realize there's a silence growing. She's still

looking at me like she's waiting for me to respond, and I laugh, then shake my head. "You do what you have to do."

"Exactly." She nods grimly, then turns back to her phone.

I know I should just watch her and see what she's doing, that that's what I'm supposed to do, but I really like how it felt when she smiled at me. I like the way her eyes sparkled just a little bit, like she was holding back a laugh.

"What are you working on?" My voice is loud, and she starts, glancing up at me like she's guilty of something.

"Oh, nothing much." Her thumb mashes the side of the phone before she drops it in her lap, but I already saw the screen.

My skin feels tight. Uncomfortable. I feel a chill race through my body.

She's looking at houses. I just got here, and she's already looking to move.

I have to report this.

7

TINA

Did you know that most teachers are lying when they say your child is a pleasure to have in class?

Take a minute. Let that sink in. I know it hurts. Nobody wants to think their child could possibly be a pain in the butt. I know I don't want to believe that about Luke. He's so sweet, so precious. I bet every parent looks at their child, especially when they're asleep, and thinks the same.

How in the world could the teacher be right about what they're saying about my son? He's so perfect.

Wrong. He's not. No kid is, not when you get down to it. But that doesn't mean I don't love my job. I do! I just... do you know how much daycare teachers get paid? Not a lot.

My hand cramps from wiping down so many tables. We're out of disposable gloves, and I know the Clorox wipes are going to eat away at my skin a little bit. My fingers will burn and hurt for a few days, but as long as we get more gloves in soon, I won't have to worry about it.

It's just part of the job. Like dealing with kids who aren't potty-trained even though their parents promise they are, handling little playground altercations, and making sure every kid has enough to eat. It might just be goldfish crackers and an applesauce pouch, but I never let a single kid in my room go hungry.

Never.

I've been hungry before. When there's that gnawing in your stomach, it makes it impossible to think. You honestly feel like your body is going to curl in on itself, going to eat itself, and there is no reason for a child to feel that way.

Standing, I rub my lower back, then toss my used wipe into the trash. "Swish," I whisper to myself.

Time to pick up Luke from down the hall. Get home, maybe play a game with him. Make some dinner and go to sleep.

Then wake up and do it all again.

Before I can reach the door, however, it flies open. One of the pieces of art I hung there flutters to the ground, and I bend down to pick it up. Macy scribbled with marker on the paper, declared it *art*, then demanded I hang it up.

"Tina! How was your day?" Bethany is the director of Little Ones Daycare and has taken it upon herself to step into the role of a mother to me. I don't need a mother. Didn't really need one when she was alive, and I certainly don't need one now in my mid-twenties.

"Oh, it was great." I hold up my hand and wiggle my fingers at her. "But we're out of gloves. Do you think we can get more here by tomorrow?"

"I'll order some on Amazon," she says, pulling her iPhone from her pocket and typing away. It's the newest model, I see, and probably costs more than I pay in three months' rent. "They won't be here tomorrow, but you can last one more day without them, right?"

"Sure can." I swallow down what I was going to tell her about how bad my fingers hurt when using Clorox wipes and unlock the cabinet where I keep my purse. Actually, maybe it's not so bad Bethany stopped by. She can see how careful I am about keeping anything dangerous locked up and out of the kids' reach. I really need to keep this job so I don't have to worry about paying someone to look after Luke while I'm at work.

Not that there's anything dangerous in my purse. A maxed-out credit card. A bent key to my old Civic.

Okay, maybe working at a daycare is squeezing me tighter than I thought it would, but at least I don't have to worry about leaving Luke with strangers. I leave him with Debbie, right down the hall, a woman who smothers kids to her giant bosom when they're crying and cuddles them until they feel better.

Sometimes I wish I had someone like Debbie to pick me up, dust me off, and ensure that everything was fine.

It hits me Bethany is trying to be that for me, and I frown.

"How do you think Xena is fitting in? It's hard to move to a new country, especially when you don't speak the language." Bethany's phone is back in her pocket, her eyes locked on me as she waits for a response.

"She's going to be fine," I say, and I think it's true. "She's tough, and her parents really want her to be here so she can start learning English. We did a lot of rudimentary sign language, and she was laughing by the end of the day."

"Good, good. I knew putting her in your room was the right call. You have a big heart, Tina. Thanks for all you do."

Was that all this was? Just Bethany swinging by my room to tell me what a great job I'm doing? Maybe I don't hate the thought that this is all she wanted, but I am a little surprised. She usually comes with some sort of feedback to give or questions to ask, but this has been pleasant.

"Of course! I love working here, and Luke loves Miss Debbie." I swing my purse over my shoulder and dig in it for my key, pushing aside granola bar wrappers and a sticky sucker stick in the process. "Is there anything else you need?"

She takes a step forward, doing a great job at blocking the door so I can't scoot past her. It's silly, but it feels like the air in the room has been sucked out. I don't like being cornered.

"Debbie was going to talk to you, but I told her I'd come to you while she kept Luke a little longer." Bethany's mouth pulls down in a grimace like what she's about to say tastes unpleasant.

"What happened? Is he hurt? I know he bit someone last week, but you and I both know Tyler had been instigating it for a while now." God, I can't lose my job. And I can't handle Luke getting kicked out of here. There's no way I could afford to send him to daycare without the huge discount Bethany gives me for working here.

I close my eyes and take a deep breath, steadying myself for whatever Bethany is going to say.

"No, he didn't bite anyone." She laughs, puts her hand on my arm. "Tina, look at me. Let's sit."

We move to the table, perching ourselves in the laughably small, blue molded plastic chairs. My knees are up to my chest, and Bethany looks uncomfortable, but all I want is to hear what bombshell she's about to drop on me. Comfort can come later.

"What happened with Luke, Bethany?"

She reaches out, takes my hand. "I know this is going to be really hard to hear, Tina, and that's why I wanted to be the one to talk to you about it. He was asking about his dad in class."

My heart drops. There's also a sense of relief. Can you be both relieved and upset at the same time? It feels like I'm going to throw up, and I pull away from her, the feet of the chair scraping loudly against the tile.

"Tina, did you hear me?"

Of course I heard her. I nod. "Yes, thanks for letting me know. I'll talk to him." I move to stand, ready to get out in some fresh air where maybe I'll be able to breathe, but Bethany doesn't move.

"Tina, he was really upset. Debbie said he was crying, that he sees other kids with their dads, and he wants one for himself."

"Well, we can't just wish a dad into existence out of thin air, can we?" I snap to make a point.

Bethany blinks hard at me.

"Shoot, I'm sorry, Bethany. I just... what am I supposed to say to him? Sorry, Luke, I don't know your dad?"

She gasps. It's quiet, but I still hear it.

Yep. That was a mistake.

"You don't know his dad?"

Here we go. This is going to be great. Anytime someone finds out the truth about Luke's father, which is that he has one but I don't know who he is, they scrunch up their noses and start judging. Too bad women don't really wear pearls anymore, because I'd love to see how many would clutch theirs when they heard the truth.

"I don't know his dad." I say the words slowly like Bethany will need time to let them soak in.

She blinks at me, gives her head a little shake. "How don't you know his dad? What happened that you — oh." Realization dawns on her, and her mouth drops open a little bit before she snaps it shut.

This is what I hate about people finding out the truth about me. They always act like I'm some poor little kitten out in the street in the middle of a rainstorm. Then they either pity me so much that I honestly can't stand to be around them at all, or they cut me off.

They act like sleeping with someone and getting pregnant without knowing the dad's name is catching.

"It was a mistake. But Luke isn't." I stand, my face burning now, and walk towards to the door, hoping she's going to drop it. "Luke is the best thing to ever happen to me, and even though I don't know who his dad is, I wouldn't change a thing about how I got him."

"It has to be so hard." Bethany's right on my heels, practically fawning all over me. "Doing this by yourself, I mean. It has to be so hard."

I refuse to be her trauma porn. As soon as we're both out of my classroom, I turn and lock the door, then face her once again. "Sure, it's hard, Bethany. But I'm stronger than most people realize, and I'm not going to let something *hard* ruin the amazing experience I have of being a mother. Thanks for letting me know. If Luke brings it up again, I'll figure out what to say to him."

And then I turn. Each step down the hall is measured, careful. I need to get to my son.

I need to get to my car.

Only when I'm in my room tonight will I let myself break down.

8

ELOISE

I've just gotten everything organized on my desk the way I like it when there's a knock on my office door, and it swings open. Harrison Davis, the man who started this company in the living room of the tiny apartment he shared with his first wife, stands there, angling his body so he's blocking the entire doorway.

"Harrison," I say, standing and walking around my desk to greet him. "How are you doing?"

"Just came to check on you." His eyes flick around the room before his gaze lands back on me. "How's the new office treating you? You like the view?"

"The view is amazing." I turn to look at it, giving myself time to formulate what I want to ask him. *Why is he here?* "Is everything okay? There wasn't a mistake giving me this office, was there?" I smile like I'm not really worried about his response, but on the inside my stomach is twisting.

There's no way he's going to take the office back. I know Jared is the reason I have this office, and Harrison isn't stupid. He won't turn his back on a big donor.

"Oh, no, this is for you. I want our less fortunate clients to feel like they're getting the star treatment when they come to you. You know, this could be really good for Harrison Realty." He says that like he hadn't really considered the implication of setting up this section of the agency.

"Well, I appreciate it. And I appreciate you understanding that I'm not so keen on the huge multimillion-dollar deals." I shrug, like it's no big deal, when I know for a fact the agents downstairs are fighting, tooth and nail, to nab some of the clients I would have had.

I mean, really. A commission or two off of those sales will set you up for an entire year. Sure, the clients need a lot of hand-holding, and yes, they can be a bit whiny, but for agents who are desperate for some cash, those traits can easily be overlooked.

"It takes a special person to be willing to turn their back on that much money just so they can help the less fortunate." His brows knit together. "And it's wonderful Jared is so willing for you to take your foot off the gas."

Yes, yes. Nobody can look at what I'm doing and not recognize the fact that my husband will be picking up the slack. Except that's not really true, is it? Not when he makes multiple seven figures a year.

To be fair, I don't need to work. If I didn't want to be out of the house every single day, I could sit at home eating bonbons and watching TV, but that sounds miserable to me.

No, I want to work outside the house, and that's why I got my real estate license. It's always been my dream to have enough money to help people who are less fortunate. Marrying someone as rich as Jared wasn't something I planned, but it means I have extra time to volunteer and work.

And now I can marry the two things together.

And I can get what I really want.

I should feel guilty about how I kept dropping hints at the dinner table, telling Jared how badly I wanted a change, how much I wanted to be able to give back to society.

It wasn't until I came right out and told him what I wanted that I got just that. Honestly, I didn't think I'd end up in an office like this, but I'm certainly not going to complain. It'll just make the end result that much sweeter.

"Jared is a special man," I tell Harrison, who nods. "I'm just lucky I get to work for someone like you who understands how important it is for me to be able to give back."

"Right. About that." Harrison exhales hard. "How do you plan to find your clients? We're known for working with... a clientele of a higher caliber than who you're looking for."

"Oh, I have a plan." I hurry behind my desk and open the top drawer, pulling out a thick file and putting it on the desk between us. "Have a seat," I say, already flipping the folder open.

This should impress him. When I found out this position was being created, I immediately leaped into action, doing my best to figure out exactly how I was going to find the clients who needed me the most.

Oh, fine, some honesty? I had my plan ready to roll before I even started dropping hints to Jared.

But now that I have Harrison's attention and the job title I need to help people down on their luck, I'm ready to roll.

"Okay," I say, turning the folder so he can see what I'm looking at. "My first step is to get word out in the community that I'm here to help people who don't have a huge down payment, or those who won't be able to get a conventional loan because of credit problems in their past. Jared has already helped with this. I had an interview with a reporter who's going to write an article for the paper and run a series of ads."

"Ads on TV or in the paper?"

"Both. I want maximum reach. There's even that billboard out on Highway 64 that's been empty for a while. I think if I called the owner and told them what I was doing, I might be able to get my poster up there for less than the usual price." I sit as I wait for him to think about what I just said.

In fact, I *know* that will happen, because I've already called the billboard owner. Once I explained what I was hoping to do, he was more than happy to cut me a deal on the rental. Not that Harrison can't afford it, but the man is cheap. He's not going to want to spend much of the money Jared paid him for me to move up here.

"Okay, that's good. Once you have your name out there, do you think you'll get enough interest?"

"Absolutely. I'm also going to talk to some of the librarians downtown. They know everyone and can easily point people in my direction if they're in need of a little extra help. I'm going to put up flyers at the hospital and grocery stores. The need is out there, Harrison, and I know you see it too or you wouldn't have given me this new position. I just have to be willing to go out there and meet people where they are. And I am."

"Great." He leans back in his chair, stretching as he does. "Sounds like you've got things under control."

I nod. "I do. My plan is to finish settling in here and get my office all set up for my first clients. I've already got the copy written for the ads I want to run so I'll send that out once you approve it, and I'll swing by the library to talk to the librarians and drop off my business cards."

He nods. Taps his chin. "You'll send me the copy first?"

I just said I would, didn't I? "Of course." I smile. It's fake, but I doubt he can tell that. Harrison honestly thinks everyone sees him as this amazing person who walks on water. I, on the other hand, know the truth — he's just a man. A middle-aged man who has never been told *no*.

Charming.

"Great." Now he raps his fingers on my desk. Stands up. Looks around. "Great. Well, let me know if you need anything." There's a long pause. "This is a nice office."

"It is, thanks." I remain seated and lean back in my chair, getting comfy. "The view is incredible."

He looks over at the window. His jaw tightens. Envy is scrawled all over his face.

God, Harrison, would you just leave?

"Well, Eloise, I guess you'd better get to work. I don't want you to sit around and not get things done. It's easy to get distracted when you don't have someone keeping an eye on you." He laughs and points at me. "But I'm watching."

I force myself to laugh too, but not with him. At him. I didn't see it before but now I can't unsee it. Harrison wanted this office, didn't he? He wanted to be up here with the amazing view, with everyone whispering in low tones about how great his office is.

But he wanted Jared's money more.

Not gonna lie, it feels good.

Harrison is just like every other mediocre man. He's so used to having whatever he wants handed to him on a silver platter that he forgot the very important rule of getting ahead.

Never let them see you coming.

9

Looking for a new home and a little extra help?

Homebuyers who might not meet the qualifications for conventional loans now have another option that will help them achieve their goals of homeownership.

Eloise Jones, wife of Jared Jones, of JJones PR and Marketing, has started a new venture, one that will allow her to help almost everyone who wants to own a home. "I believe it's important that people are allowed to achieve their goals of owning a home," she says. "I think everyone should have that opportunity, especially people who are so often overlooked by the system, and that's why I started the Homebuyers with Heart program at Harrison Realty."

And there are many people who are overlooked. Statistics vary, but most first-time homebuyers have to save up for a lot longer than buyers who are selling an existing home to buy another. This saving for a down payment can put a lot of stress on anyone who is already pushing themselves financially.

Enter: Eloise. Driven by the desire to help others who might not have the support they need to have the home of their dreams, she's willing to put in the long hours to help any homebuyers reach their goals. While she's best known for helping the "home buying elite" buy multimillion-dollar mansions outside of town, she's completely changed her focus.
And at the best possible time, too. While home prices are soaring and more and more people are being turned away thanks to the rising closing costs, Eloise has come up with a plan to help buyers get the home they want without all of the stress.

She calls it her four-prong approach to homeownership. First, Eloise plans to dig through listings to not only find homes priced at a reasonable price, but also to see if there are owners who are willing to take a little less for their listing to help someone in need.

Next, she's going to offer a personalized financial review for every one of her clients. This allows her to find any money needed for the purchase and monthly mortgage payments, and her personalized approach is much more focused than simply running numbers through a computer.

The third step of her approach is custom care. Instead of handing everything off to a mortgage banker and hoping for the best, Eloise will remain focused and in constant contact with the banker, ensuring nothing is overlooked and any problems can easily be dealt with.

Finally, Eloise promises to help with any unexpected problems that arise after closing. Unlike traditional mortgage services, where the Realtor and the mortgage banker are both completely hands-off after the home has been bought, Eloise wants to be there for her clients. She wants not only to be present at closing but will provide information about various services that might be beneficial.

These services include discounted moving services, coupons to various home furnishings companies, and even a promo code for a free pizza on move-in night from Marino's on Main Street.

By doing everything she can to provide million-dollar care at a lower price, Eloise is prepared to help homeowners from all walks of life. She said it best when she said "everyone deserves to have a place they call home. Someplace they feel safe, where they can let their hair down and be happy. I want to help people find their home so they not only have a place to rest after a long day at work, but a place where they can be who they were meant to be."

For additional information regarding the new program Eloise is starting, prospective clients can reach her at Eloise.Jones@HarrisonRealty.com.

10

TINA

Luke's sound asleep in the bed we share, but I can't seem to keep my eyes closed long enough to let sleep take over. Every time I think I'm relaxed enough to catch some Zs, my eyes spring back open.

Through the window, the waxing moon is so bright it feels like a full moon. Down the hall, I hear one of the roommates in the kitchen. Paula, maybe. She tends to like a snack in the middle of the night.

Or Ricky.

I shiver.

I don't trust Ricky. Don't trust the way he looks at me, and I really don't trust the way he looks at Luke. He stares at me, watching me, sizing me up. No matter what I'm up to, his eyes are on me like he's trying to memorize what I'm doing.

My momma always told me there are some men out there who are just plain dangerous. I always promised her I'd do whatever it took to live somewhere where I didn't have to be around dangerous men.

And look where I am now.

To be fair, I was here first. When Luke and I moved in, Paula told me that she'd be looking for a new roommate eventually. I just never thought it would be someone like Ricky.

Frustrated, I roll over, resting my head on my arm so I can stare at Luke. He's on his back, his arms and legs splayed out like a star. If I were to scoot over to try to take my half of the bed, he'd wake right up. He's a light sleeper.

We need our own place.

I push that thought from my mind. Worrying about how to find our own place to live isn't going to do any good right now. Until I either make more money or find some place that isn't worried about my lack of credit, I don't see a way out of the roommate situation. I guess I should be happy.

We could always be living in my car.

I saw how expensive homes are when I was checking listings the other night. We'd need a miracle to get out of here.

Luke snorts in his sleep and turns a little, his face shifting right into the moonbeam. I hold my breath, sure the light on his face is going to be enough to wake him up, but he doesn't move again.

So I just stare at him. Bethany was shocked I didn't know who Luke's dad is. I should feel ashamed of that, I guess, or should at least wish I knew him to tell him how amazing his kid is, but I don't.

I did for a while. I looked for him, desperate to find him, desperate to not have to do this on my own, but now I don't worry about it. He didn't want to be found, that much is obvious. But there's more to it than that.

I'm a great single mom. No, we don't have the nicest

clothes. And no, Luke doesn't get to pick out new toys every time we go to the store, but don't the kids who do end up a little spoiled? I like Luke, like that he's thoughtful and okay with borrowing books from the library every single week.

Sure, he's only three. And things might not be as easy when he leaves daycare and goes to public school in a few years, but maybe by then my luck will have changed. Maybe I'll have a little extra money I can use to get us a better place. Maybe I'll be able to afford the new shoes he wants.

Or maybe we'll still be right here, in this lumpy bed, wondering who's awake in the next room and if I locked the bedroom door.

Tears burn my eyes, and I allow them to fall, but I don't allow myself the luxury of making a sound. It's one thing for me to be upset about my lot in life, another to make Luke suffer for it.

My choices aren't his fault. I met a guy. Got drunk with him when I got off work at the bar. Slept with him.

Fell for him.

We dated for months before he told me he had to end it, that his company had an image to maintain, that he couldn't keep running around with me.

It's not Luke's fault his dad gave me a fake name and that I couldn't find him after I found out I was pregnant. I looked for him, I swear I did. I looked on Facebook for any pictures he might have been tagged in at the bar.

I tried all the places he'd taken me, sure someone at a restaurant would know him.

But he was a ghost. Damon Rhodes — the fake name he gave me — was gone like the wind, and I didn't know he'd left me a parting gift until a few weeks later.

There was one more last-ditch effort to find Damon. For months I spent all of my spare time at the Upsidedown Spoon, the bar where we met, where I worked, hoping to run into him, but it was like he'd disappeared into thin air.

So I did the only thing I knew to do. I buckled down. Became a mom. Changed jobs so I could go to work and not have to worry about paying for childcare. And now I need to buckle back down and figure out a new place to live.

Luke shifts towards me, rolling onto his side and scooching his little butt into my stomach. Instinctively, I wrap my arm around him. Pull him close.

This little boy is everything. He even smells good tonight thanks to me spending extra time washing his hair. He smells like bubblegum, and I breathe him in before my eyes finally close.

The last thought that runs through my head before sleep finally takes over isn't a new one. I've had it before, multiple times, probably like every other mother in the world has had.

How far am I willing to go for Luke?

If it were just me, I wouldn't worry so much about where we were living. No, I wouldn't want Ricky stopping outside my bedroom door, wouldn't want to know he tries the handle every evening just to see if I left it unlocked on purpose. Or accidentally.

I could live through it. But with Luke, everything is different. It's like my entire focus has shifted, and now he's the most important thing in the world.

"I'm going to get us out of here, buddy." I whisper the words under my breath. My lips press against the back of his head.

He shifts but doesn't wake.

Tomorrow. Tomorrow is Saturday, and I'm not working. I was already planning on getting out of the apartment with him, and now I have a really good reason to leave here. I'll head to the library and see what kind of rentals I can find online.

I'm getting us out of here. No matter what.

11

RICKY

The sofa sags under my weight, a spring pressing into my ass, and I shift. The furniture smells.

Or I do.

I look around for Tina. She's not here where she's supposed to be. Every evening she comes to the living room with Luke, but not tonight, and I need to know where she is.

Grabbing the front of my shirt, I pull it out and up, then drop my nose to it and sniff. It's me. I stink. Sweat and beer and the stale smell of cigarettes. Not from inside the bar, no. A few years ago North Carolina made a rule that you could no longer smoke inside a bar, like the assholes sitting behind their desks in their suits and ties have never enjoyed the feeling of switching between beer and a cigarette, sucking down first the biting taste of Natty Ice, then switching to a good burn, a smooth burn, one that lights you up from the inside.

No, they've never had that, have they? They've never had to spend the entire day at the bar because they don't have a job, because just showing your face outside the bar is enough to get dirty looks.

I shift again. Drain my beer. I'm half sunk into the damn cushion, and I fight to sit up and put the dead soldier on the coffee table by the others I've had before I sink back into the sofa.

Four.

No, five. Five beers, one, two, three, four, five, one right after another, each one chasing the previous one, each one filling me up and calming me down and soothing the roaring sound in my head, the sound telling me to —

Five is fine. It leaves one more for the morning when I need a little something to get my head thinking straight. Everything's fuzzy, especially since I talked to my cousin.

Especially since moving into the room next to Tina's.

Tina. Tina, Tina, *Tina*, even her name sounds pretty, hard and then soft, just like her, all angles, but with some meat on her bones, right where it counts.

My phone buzzes. It's between the dead soldiers, and I have to fight to sit back up to answer it. Maybe it's a friend; maybe he found something good for us to get into; maybe I'm going to be pulled out of the never-ending boredom of sitting here in the same apartment as Tina. Tina, who makes it impossible for me to think about anything else, and not just because I'm supposed to watch her.

No, there are other reasons I can't stop thinking about her.

But it's not a friend.

It's the wrong phone.

It's Eloise, hoity-toity Eloise, who married way above her raising, who looks down at me over the tip of her perfectly carved out little nose, like we don't all know she had some plastic surgery as soon as she married Jared so she could fit in with his life better.

> Did you put the newspaper article I sent you out on the kitchen counter for everyone to see?

No, no, I didn't, because I don't want Tina to move. I don't want her to leave me.

I look down at the glowing screen in my hand and frown before looking towards where Tina sleeps. She's right there, so close I could just go to her, so close I can almost taste her, I can imagine the way her lips would feel when I pressed mine against hers and finally let her know how much I love her, how much I want her, how much I —

> Ricky, did she see the paper?

I scowl.

> oh, i forgot. i thought about it

There. Let her worry about it herself. She moved me in here to keep an eye on Tina, that was all. I'm not her gopher. I'm just supposed to keep an eye on Tina, I'm not supposed to —

> You forgot? You know that was part of the plan.

Was it? Was it part of the plan because right now I can't remember. All I can think about is taking a drag from a cigarette and the way the wind whips the smoke away when you're outside, and how good another beer would feel right now and what it would be like to see Tina's lips wrapped around a cigarette, her thin hands shaking as she holds it, her cheeks hollowing as she sucks on it —

> Ricky.

I shake my head. Clear the vision.

> right. i forgot.

> can you fix it?

> she goes to the library a lot

> hello? can you fix it

I send a flurry of messages although I don't really care what Eloise does. She can fix this all she wants, all that matters is that I'm living right next door to Tina, and I don't want her to move right now. I like having her there, like knowing she's breathing softly, her body curled on its side like a comma while she sleeps. I saw her once, when I first moved in. She was sleeping, and I opened her door because it wasn't locked. I just wanted to know what she looked like while she slept. I found out, and it was more beautiful than I could have imagined, but then she must have heard me or maybe I didn't close the door all the way because now she locks it at night, now she keeps me out, but she doesn't know that I'm patient.

I have the money from Eloise. Her name makes me scoff, and I push out of the sofa, leaving my phone on the cushion. There's another beer in the fridge, and I want it, want it so I can stop thinking about my cousin and what she wants me to do. Instead, I can think about Tina and how pretty she is when she's playing with Luke.

How happy she is.

I don't want to stop thinking about her. I crack open the last Natty Ice and press it to my lips, but while I'm drinking it down, I'm thinking of Tina. I'm thinking of you, Tina, about how pretty you are and how happy I could make you.

I could make you really happy, do you know that? You need someone; Luke needs someone, needs a man, needs a father figure who can take care of him and raise him, teach him to be a man and be a good person. Even though I've never been a father and didn't really have one, or didn't have one that mattered, I can do it, I know I can, and you just have to let me prove that to you.

But that's not what Eloise wants.

I frown. Lean against the refrigerator. Take another sip.

I don't mean to drain half the bottle, it's just that I sometimes get so focused on what I'm doing I don't really pay attention and then it's gone. I don't really have any recollection of doing it, of drinking it, of punching that guy or whatever they said it was I did, or stealing or running from the cops.

I take a deep breath. My fingers wrap tightly around the bottle, and I drain the rest of it. Set it in the sink.

Eloise would tell me to get my head on straight, that I need to stop letting my mind wander, that I need to pull myself together. She'd tell me she's the person who's helping me right now and that I need to remember the plan and stick to it.

I'll do it. I'll do it for Eloise because she found me someplace to live even though the doctor said I wouldn't ever find somewhere to live if I didn't see him regularly. Not if I wasn't taking little tiny pills that make it really hard for me to think straight about things, pills that make everything fuzzy and soft instead of bright and hard and exciting.

I'm not taking those pills.

I'll do it for Eloise.

I just have to remember what it is she wants me to do.

Grabbing the sides of my head, I squeeze as hard as possible, my fingers pressing into my temples, the pain shooting through my face, down my jaw. I imagine it like a lightning bolt striking the top of the head, my thin hair standing up like I'm scared, making its way down through my nervous system, branching out from my spine like fingers that worm their way through my body, worms that eat me alive and then leave me empty, but I'm not empty.

Because I have Tina.

"No." I whisper the word. Turn. Slam my forehead into the refrigerator. It's old and hums and doesn't move when I hit it, even though I feel the pain radiate out through my skull like someone pressed a gun right there and pulled the trigger.

"Because I have Tina."

No, that's wrong. It's not Tina I'm loyal to, not Tina I'm supposed to be helping.

"Eloise." I whisper her name.

I slam my head into the refrigerator again. There's a dull thud. It stops humming for a moment but then picks back up, the sound like wasps in my head.

Something warm trickles down my forehead.

"Eloise." I step back from the refrigerator. My head swims. Too many beers after a long afternoon at the bar. I need to tell Eloise I need more money. She'll tell me to stop drinking it all, that it's for rent and food, but she's not in my head, is she, she's not living in my mind. She doesn't know all the things I know, nor want what I want.

It's sticky when I wipe my hand across my forehead. Without really thinking about what I'm doing, I wipe the blood out of my eyes, then rub my hand on my shirt to clean it.

I stumble back to the sofa. My phone falls between the cracks in the cushions, but I don't reach for it. Instead, I stretch out, then curl into a ball, grabbing an old blanket and yanking it up to my chin.

I have to remember Eloise. Remember what she wants me to do.

God, my head hurts.

Why does it hurt?

It has to be the beer. I try to think about whether or not I got in a fight at the bar. If I did anything to hurt my head.

Nothing comes to me.

Nothing but Tina. Helping Tina. Loving Tina.

No. Not Tina.

Helping someone else.

Eloise.

12

ELOISE

"Can I fix it?" I mutter to myself. I've been grinding my jaw so much my teeth ache, but I can't seem to stop. "Of course I can fix it, you useless sack of crap, but I shouldn't have to clean up your messes."

It's too early for this. Saturday mornings are supposed to be relaxing.

Closing my eyes, I take a deep breath.

Count to ten.

Better. That's better. Not perfect, but improved.

There's something about the smell of freshly printed paper, isn't there? It smells like promise and future and the hope that things are going to change for the better. I press the stack of information flyers I printed up to my nose and inhale, trying to catch the last whiff of magic the paper contains before it disappears.

After sniffing them once more, I tuck them in my satchel and throw it over my shoulder. It's a quick drive to the library this morning. Even though the weather is nice, I'm surprised at how few people are walking downtown. They'll be out in their droves later, sitting outside the bars and restaurants, having a beer, eating nachos.

For the people who don't live in the mansions up on the hill, it's a simple life here. It's where Jared wanted to live when we first got married. He said we could afford it — and we could have, multiple times over. He said it was fitting for a man of his position in the community and for the wealth we had.

But I fought it. I love Jared, I really do. He's everything to me, especially since we don't have children. When a beautiful home tucked in a cul-de-sac in a quiet, private neighborhood off the end of Main Street went on the market right as we were looking for a place to live... well, it was fate.

At least in my eyes.

It's huge, much bigger than I would like. Jared wanted something even larger, but I didn't want to be sequestered in a gated community that felt like something royalty would live in.

And Jared loves me enough to have bought the home I wanted, forgoing the huge mansions perched precariously up on the mountain. Ours had been the original estate manor in our neighborhood, and then when the family needed money, lots were sold off for other people to build on.

Still, it's the nicest home in the neighborhood. Tucked on a hill, with a gorgeous view off the back deck, there's a lot to love. Not that I don't see him sometimes look up there like he wishes he could change where we live.

I notice everything.

The library parking lot is half full, so I easily find a spot, parking between an old farm truck and a new Prius covered with bumper stickers. See? That's what I love about this place and what I would miss living in a private gated community. People here are real. They don't worry about how much money they have, they've all just come together to create this amazing life in town.

I shut the door of my car, a newer model Lexus Jared bought me for Christmas last year even though I told him my old car worked just fine, and silence my phone before entering the library.

This is where all the magic happens, isn't it? It's like on that MTV show *Cribs*, where rich celebrities are made to feel even better about themselves by showing off their homes and all the gadgets they own. They always lead the way into the bedroom, a cheeky smile on their faces, like they just can't wait to show off their beds.

Like everyone in America doesn't know what happens in a bed. Give me a break.

The children's section is tucked away in the back right-hand corner of the library, far enough away from the checkout so that people who don't want to run into kids while they're grabbing some light reading don't have to. There's a large wall of computers thanks to a recent grant, and a librarian hovers there, making sure everyone who needs help using the internet has it.

To my left as I walk in are the movies, all the DVDs lovingly arranged by the cinephile who works here. The first time I stopped by to ask for recommendations on what to watch on Netflix, I ended up walking away with half a dozen movies for the weekend.

I didn't even own a DVD player.

But I do now.

Jared made fun of me for that purchase, let me tell you, but I had a wonderful weekend watching movies that were handpicked for me. Georgina, the cinephile librarian, waves at me, and I wave back.

This is home. I can't remember how many long days I spent in the library when I was younger, when the weather was bad and I didn't want to go home. The librarians never kicked me out, and I stayed warm and safe.

I check the hold shelf to make sure I don't have any books I need to grab before I leave, even though I'm pretty sure I picked up everything last week. I might as well kill two birds with one stone. Once I'm satisfied I don't have any to take, I walk up to the main counter and stop behind an older couple checking out.

They scan each book slowly, talking about the author, and I can't help but listen in. *Hurry up.*

Jared doesn't read, which was the one red flag I noticed about him right away when we started dating. Maybe I should have dug into it more, should have thought more about what it would mean for my future when my husband wanted to watch sports and I wanted to read, but we've made it work.

For the most part. I mean, who doesn't read? It's concerning, that's what it is, but at least he doesn't judge me for loving to read.

Three years ago he even had another room added to the house and turned it into my own personal library. We may not always see eye-to-eye, but I can't say he doesn't care in his own way, especially if he can just throw money at the problem.

Maybe I'll miss that part of him.

"Eloise." The couple have stepped to the side, and Agatha, my favorite librarian, smiles at me. She's older, with deep creases around her eyes, but those eyes are sharp and bright blue and don't miss a trick. "You forgot to grab some books to check out before coming up here."

I laugh and lean against the counter. "You're in charge here, right, Agatha?"

She nods, her mouth pressing into a firm line. *Business mode activated.* "Yes, I am. Is there a problem?"

"Nope, not at all. It's just I know that you know everything about everyone." I open my satchel and pull out the stack of leaflets I had printed. The only regret I have right now is that I don't have any new business cards to hand over now, but they're on order, and I'll bring a stack by as soon as I receive them.

I dip my hand back into my satchel and pull out a copy of the paper with the article about me. It's not the best one I've read, but the reporter was new and hungry for something to write and promised me it would be in the paper ASAP.

And it was.

"What's this?" Agatha's knuckles are thick with arthritis, but her fingers still seem nimble as she plucks the top paper from my stack and turns it to read it. "What have you gone and done, Eloise?"

I don't answer. This is the type of thing that is often best explained by itself.

She reads quickly, her eyes flicking back and forth across the page. By the time she reaches the bottom, her mouth has relaxed, the edges curved up into a smile.

When she speaks, it's in a low voice. "Tell me how you got Harrison on board with something like this when I know he loves bringing in huge stacks of money over everything else." She holds the paper up to her face, using it like a shield to ensure nobody watching us can hear what she's saying.

"You know I'm passionate about helping people." I don't keep my voice down. I don't need to. I want anyone walking by to hear what I'm saying and know I'm on their side. "This is the best way for me to do that in my current career. Selling huge houses is great, but I want to help people."

Am I laying it on too thick?

"And, let me guess, you think I know enough about everyone here in town to pass these out to the people who really need your help." Her brows knit together in a frown, but I know it's all just an act.

Agatha knows everything about everyone, and it's not a secret.

I laugh, and she does too.

"Yep, that's the plan, my friend. Do you think you could help me out? I also thought I'd stick a few on the bulletin board in the lobby. When I get my business cards, I'll swing some by to you so you can hand those out, too. I want to help. Will you support me as I do that?"

I lean over the counter to her, trying to make sure she sees just how important this is to me. It's one thing to say you want to help people who are less fortunate. Anyone can do that. Talk is cheap.

But it's another thing entirely to be willing to put in the work. I'll lay it on as thick as necessary to make people think I really believe in this.

"You know I will. But don't get mad at me when your phone starts ringing off the hook and you don't have time to pick your nose without someone interrupting you."

I laugh harder and slide the stack of papers over to her, but not before I take a few off the top to tack on the bulletin board. "I knew I could count on you." I pause, wondering how much I can push this without making her suspicious.

"Single moms, Agatha. That's who I really want to help. My mom was a single mom and —" I let my voice crack.

She smiles at me and taps a short fingernail on the stack. "This is good stuff, Eloise. This is the type of thing people in town need. I can only imagine where I'd be if I'd had someone helping me when I was younger. Not a handout —"

"A hand up," I finish for her, nodding. "Right? I know I struggled when I was younger. I thought I had it all figured out, and in the long run, I got pretty lucky."

She raises an eyebrow.

"Really lucky," I amend. "And I want other women to feel that same way. It's the least I can do."

"Well, bless you for being so willing to go out on a limb and try something new to make a difference. I still don't know how you got Harrison to agree. That man is tighter than a mouse's —"

I clear my throat. "Agatha, no swearing in the library."

She grins, her blue eyes flashing. Then, quick as a wink, the stack of papers disappears below the counter. If I didn't know they were there and that I'd handed them to her in the first place, I might wonder if I'd imagined it.

"It's a hard habit to break." She leans on the counter. I notice immediately that her sweater sleeve is a little worn around the elbow. There are loose threads around her wrist. It sags a bit, stretched out, like it was put through the dryer one too many times.

I refuse to ever end up in a situation like that again.

"Among others." I grin at her and pat my satchel back into place on my hip before gently rapping my knuckles on the counter between us. "Anyway, my number is on there, and so is my email. Anyone who needs my help or thinks they might want to just talk to me, send them my way. That goes for everyone. I don't have any reservations about who I'm going to work with."

"You're an angel." Her hand snaps out faster than I expected, and she grabs mine. Her skin is cool. Dry. "I'm serious, Eloise, for you to be willing to do this, to meet people where they need help instead of just standing back and sending thoughts and prayers? It means a lot. This world needs good people like you in it."

Ouch. That one hurt. If Agatha ever found out how selfish I'm being with my new altruistic endeavor, I can only imagine how shocked she'd be.

But she'll never know. Nobody will. That's the beauty of it.

I squeeze her hand back and let it go.

"I'm just really glad I'm in a position where I can help. It would be terrible of me to have this life I didn't ask for, a life many women want, and not help. I've been here," I say, tapping the counter above where she tucked the stack of papers. "It's not easy."

"It's not. Thank you."

I nod. Nothing about what I've done to get to where I am has been easy. This looks altruistic, I know it does.

If people really knew my reason for helping, I'm sure they'd have something to say about it. Only one person knows.

And he wants the money as badly as I do.

13

TINA

Whoever came up with the idea of toddler time is both a genius and sadist.

First of all, I love it. I love getting to bring Luke to see other kids, to let him have some fun in the library so he doesn't grow up thinking it's a stuffy old building for stuffy old people, and I love that someone else is reading to him for once.

But let's get real. Whoever thought you could put a dozen squirming kids in the same place at the same time without snacks that will keep them entertained obviously hasn't ever tried to herd cats, because it's about the same experience.

I don't even remember what story was just read to us. I'm cranky and hot, and by the time I grab a few books and stuff them in my bag to take home, Luke is ready to hit the road. He's so energetic this morning compared to how exhausted I am that I just want to cry.

And then I remember the real reason we came to the library, and I feel hot tears spring to the corners of my eyes. I need to find us someplace new to live, and I need help. Looking online hasn't yielded anything we can afford.

We have to get away from Ricky, away from the threat he brings, away from the silence of my heart when I hear footsteps stop right outside my bedroom door.

Luke deserves more. He deserves the world, and all I've given him so far is a shared lumpy mattress and plenty of microwavable mac and cheese for dinner when I'm too tired to cook anything else.

"I'm a failure," I whisper. I don't even realize I'm speaking until the words spill from my lips, and by the time they're out, it's too late to take them back. They hang there, deadly and true, like icicles above a person's door. One wrong move and they're sure to come crashing to the ground.

One wrong move and someone might hear me.

Luke pulls my hand as I lead him to the checkout. We just have to get these six Gerald and Piggy books checked out, and then maybe I can bribe him for ten minutes of quiet at the computer. I just need to sit down and compare some of the different housing options I have.

Not that there are a lot. Not for a single mom, but maybe a librarian can help me. That's what they're there for, right?

"Luke, if you're good, we can go to the park after this." He loves the park. What kid doesn't? It's the perfect place for them to go completely feral and run around screaming. He does that in the library and I'm a terrible mom. He does it in the park and everyone gives me a knowing smile, telling me they're also part of the club of tired parents.

"Is this it for you?" The librarian helping me is ancient. She smiles at me, though, then produces a roll of stickers from somewhere. I watch in surprise as she rips the paper and hands a strip of them to Luke. "Don't stick them on books," she warns him as she makes the roll of stickers disappear. "Or your furniture. Or your mom's car windows."

She looks at me. I swear, she's seeing inside me, to where I'm trying to hide just how exhausted I really am, and gives her head a little shake.

She pulls out a notebook. From where? I don't know, but she might be a magician.

"Here," she says, handing it to Luke with a flourish. "Stick them in here. One for each book you read. Bring the notebook back with you every time you come with your mom to the library, and I'll give you more stickers."

He takes it from her, his mouth and eyes wide.

"What do you say?" I nudge him in the shoulder.

"Thank you." His voice is soft, but the librarian smiles.

"That should buy you a little time to get to the car." She taps something on her screen. "Go ahead and scan your card and books."

I do, fumbling my card from my wallet. She smiles as I drop it and pick it back up, not saying anything about how messy I seem right now.

"I really appreciate it," I tell her, taking the stack of scanned books back from her when she's finished. "I need to use the computers, and the stickers will help keep him entertained."

"What are you looking for?" She doesn't look at me as she asks the question. She's looking past me, and I turn to make sure there isn't someone waiting on me to get out of the way.

I have a distinct feeling she already knows what I'm going to look for on the computer but doesn't want to mention it outright.

Some women are like that, aren't they? Especially older

ones. It's like they already know what's going on in your head, like they can feel your pain and put a name to it even when you can't. I've met a few women like this in my life, and before I answer her, I glance down at her name tag.

Agatha.

"We're looking for a new place to live." I straighten myself up, drawing my spine as firm and solid as I can. Even though the words feel fake in my mouth, like I'm playing a part, I still want to believe this will happen for me. I don't want to be the cautionary tale, the story of the woman who thought she could do better for herself and her child but just couldn't.

I want to be more than that. Surely that isn't too much to ask.

"A new place?" Now she is looking at me. Her nose is a little pointed, like a bird's beak. Her eyes are fast and quick, a bright blue that take me in and make me feel like she can not only tell exactly what's going on now, but what I've faced in the past. "So you already have a place to live, and you don't like it?"

I hesitate. Glance down at Luke. He's plopped himself down on the carpet and is carefully sticking stickers in the little book she gave him. For a moment I feel bad that he hasn't started reading the books yet like he was supposed to before using the stickers, but I have a very good feeling Agatha wouldn't care. What matters is that he's busy right now and not listening, although even if he were paying attention to me, I doubt he would understand the implication of what I'm saying.

Little kids might feel the undercurrent of danger in adult conversations, but that doesn't mean they really understand it. He won't know what I'm talking about.

"Where we live isn't safe." I keep my voice low anyway, not only because I don't want Luke to hear me, but I want to ensure nobody else is listening in. People are nosy. "I want to let him grow up someplace where I don't have to worry about him getting hurt."

She doesn't answer right away. I feel my cheeks start to flush.

"I just need to look online. See if there are other apartments available. We have roommates, and that helps keep the costs down, but..." My voice trails off. How can I look at a little old woman named Agatha and tell her what I'm really afraid of? How can I look her in the eyes and let her know the danger I think lurks in the room next to mine?

It's my fault for getting into a position where I have to live with Ricky. I don't expect pity.

"Do you have a job?"

Agatha's question surprises me. I straighten even more and look her in the eyes when I nod.

"I do. I work at a daycare." I reach down, ruffle Luke's hair. "It means I can be around him, and I don't have to worry about hiring a babysitter. I can keep an eye on him."

"Good." She nods, then pulls a piece of paper out from under the counter. A newspaper follows. They appear so quickly it's like she's a magician. First there's nothing there, just an empty counter; then there are two things there.

It's upside down to me, but I see the exclamation points.

She drops the newspaper on top.

Homeowners Get The Help They Need in New Program

"I want you to call Eloise," she says, spinning the papers

around and pushing them towards me. "She's a good person. She can help you."

I take the papers without thinking about whether or not I want to. "I can handle it on my own," I tell her. "I don't mind doing the work, really. Using your computers will make it easier than trying to read everything on my phone screen. It's really just a simple internet search to see if anyone needs a new roommate, and I thought maybe the librarian over there would know of another website."

"I can't imagine it's easy finding people who are okay with living with a toddler." There's truth in her words, and I wince, but she's not trying to be unkind.

She's right.

"I was really lucky to find the apartment we're in now," I admit. Shame rushes through me. What's the possibility of me finding someplace where Luke will be accepted and I will feel safe?

Is that too much to ask?

"Call Eloise." Agatha's voice is kind. Gentle. "She's a good person, okay? She'll help you, I can pretty much guarantee it."

I look down at the papers, my eyes skimming the words, trying to get the gist of it without standing here for too much longer. "She's a Realtor," I say, and my voice sounds flat. "I can't buy a home." I chuckle at the absurdity.

"She's amazing." Agatha holds her hands up when I try to return the papers. She shakes her head. "You have to have some faith that sometimes things might work out the way you want them to, okay? Just call her."

"I will." I stuff the papers and the Gerald and Piggy books into the bag I brought and slip it on my shoulder. Gone are any thoughts of using the computers to try to find a new place. Right now I just want to get out of here. I need some fresh air. Maybe the park will help. Anything but here.

I won't cry here. Not in front of this woman.

"Call her." Agatha waves at me as I tug Luke up from the floor and turn him, my hands firm on his shoulders, away from her, away from the counter. "Trust me. She might just change your life."

"Change my life," I mutter to myself as we walk through the pneumatic doors and into the sunshine. "Right." The last person who told me he'd change my life left me pregnant and gave me a fake name so I couldn't hunt him down.

He changed my life all right. He gave me Luke.

And I wouldn't give my son up for anything. But I also don't trust people who promise miracles like that.

"I hafta pee." Luke tugs on my hand, pulling me away from the parking lot and back towards the library. "Mama, I hafta pee."

"Okay, let's pee." I put a smile on my face even though right now I feel like screaming. Instead, I let him lead me back into the library.

There's a billboard with flyers right inside the door, and I pause long enough to see another one from Eloise.

She's everywhere. Maybe this is a sign.

We turn before reaching the check-out station, and I take him with me into the women's bathroom. I just hope we're not too late. Potty training hasn't been easy, but he's determined.

Nobody else is in the bathroom, and he scurries into the first stall, closing the door on me before I can join him.

I stiffen, trying to peer through the crack between the door and doorframe so I can make sure he doesn't have an accident.

When I hear the sound of him peeing in the toilet, I sag against the door with relief. *Okay*. You know, I was feeling a little like nothing was in my control there for a bit.

But I can handle anything.

While I wait on Luke, I pull the paper Agatha gave me out from my bag.

Eloise. It sounds like a nice name. And, from scanning the article really quickly, it looks like I fit the criteria of people she wants to help.

Maybe I reacted too harshly to Agatha trying to help me.

Maybe I will call Eloise. I don't expect anyone to change my life. That's something I have to do for myself.

But I wouldn't mind a little help right now.

14

ELOISE

Even though I talked a big game to Harrison, telling him I was sure to have people ringing my phone the moment they saw the article and heard about how I want to help homebuyers end up in a house they not only love, but can afford, I don't get my first email until almost a week later.

Jared sits across from me at the dinner table, his phone face-up next to his plate, his eyes flicking down to the screen every few seconds. At least I have the manners to turn my phone upside down and put it on the counter. I'm itching for it to ring or beep or something to let me know my idea wasn't in vain.

But so far, nothing.

And I just feel like I'm coming out of my skin.

"So how's work?" I ache to fill the silence between us. Jared doesn't talk a lot. He never has, and I hate to admit it, but that's one of the things that drew me to him when we first met. The silent type, you know. So quiet, so introspective.

So unable to hold a conversation.

"Work is work." He double-taps his phone screen quickly, making it light up. Whatever he sees there — or doesn't see — is enough to cause his eyebrows to crash together. "You? How's your new project going?"

My new project. Like it isn't something that's going to change my life. *Hopefully.* I hate how, in just three words, Jared can diminish something I want to do to the point that it's almost laughable.

"I haven't gotten any phone calls yet," I admit. "But I'm hopeful. I gave Agatha at the library a bunch of information so she can pass it on to people who might need it. Hung up some flyers around town. Hopefully the newspaper article will have gotten my name out, too."

"And you really think this is a need the town has?" Now I have his full attention. His dark brows are still knit together like his face has frozen in an expression of surprise. I used to love the way I could make him look at me like I'd shocked him. Now I'm not sure I do.

It's not a good surprised. It's more like he's surprised I pulled one over on him, and he's trying to figure out his next step.

"A need for someone to help people find affordable housing?" I take a sip of my Riesling. It sits on my tongue for a moment before I swallow it. "Yes. I know there's a need." Of course he wouldn't see that.

"But no calls." He stabs a piece of steak and points the fork at me. "You said it yourself. No calls. So maybe it's a perceived need, not a real one. What do you think about that?"

My hands are in my lap, so he can't see the way I twist my napkin into a knot.

"I think," I say, then pause to clear my throat. "I think sometimes it takes people a little while to work up the courage to call. It's not easy to ask for help, Jared. Haven't you ever struggled to reach out for help when you needed it?"

I ask the question without really thinking about who I'm talking to. The man sitting across from me has never wanted for anything in his life. There's no way he's ever struggled to ask for help, because when there's a problem, he just throws money at it until it disappears.

"You know the answer to that question." His mouth is quirked up in a smile. Before I can respond, he looks back down at his plate and stabs another piece of steak. "How long are you going to give it? More importantly, how long will Harrison give you to make this work?"

That's the question, isn't it? I guess it all depends on how much money Jared has given Harrison recently.

"It's not even been a week." My phone beeps on the counter behind me, but I ignore it. Probably spam, considering my luck. Besides, Jared and I need to finish this conversation. "Sometimes you have to wait for good things. Remember when we first started dating?"

I've steered the conversation back into safer waters. His mouth relaxes, the lines around his lips disappearing.

"You were so adamant you weren't going to go on a date with me." He laughs and takes a sip of his wine. His glass is almost empty, and I stand, bringing the bottle with me, to top it off. After I do, he reaches up and pulls me down to kiss me. "And now look at us. I love you, Eloise."

"And I love you." I pull away from him before he can kiss me again.

He drains half the glass of wine before tossing his napkin on the table and standing up.

"What are you going to do now?"

"I think I'll take a shower and then work in my office. If you need me, you know where I am, but I'm sure you have things to do."

Yeah, like clean up the kitchen. Clear the table. I know Jared would hire a chef for us if I asked him to, but that's not the point.

It's not how I was raised.

Jared gives me another kiss, this one on my cheek when I turn my face away; then he's out the door, his mind already on whatever work he's going to do.

I sigh and turn back to the table when I remember the beep my phone made. Leaving the dishes where they are for the time being, I snatch my phone off the counter and thumb it on. It takes just a moment for it to recognize my thumbprint; then my screen blinks to life.

"Just an email," I mutter, disappointment growing heavy in my chest. As much as I want it to be from someone who needs my help, it looks like that will have to wait for another day. Still, it is a work email, and maybe someone did reach out to me. Maybe they just didn't feel comfortable giving me a call.

You never know with people.

I tap the little icon and gasp, leaning back against the counter as I start to read.

"Dear Eloise," I say, my voice quiet enough that even if Jared were to come back in the room, he wouldn't be able to hear a thing from the doorway. "I was given your informa-tion at the library last week and wanted to reach out to you to see if you can help me buy a home."

Yes, yes I can.

Excitement courses through me, and I take a deep breath, then continue reading. "My name is Tina Miller, and I have a son, Luke. We've been living in an apartment with some roommates and it's time for us to get our own place. I do have a job, although it doesn't pay a lot. You can send me an email at this address or call me to talk."

It's happening. I want to run to Jared and shove the email in his face to show him that things are working out just the way I told him they would, but I stop myself. He's not in the mood to hear about my plan coming together. Right now he wants to be right, and he wants me to be wrong, and even though it's going to kill me to let him think that's how it is, I have to play his game.

And more importantly, I don't want him to realize whom I'm working with.

"Tina," I say, tapping my finger on her name to open a response email. My fingers fly over the little keyboard as I hammer out my reply.

Hello! I'm so glad you reached out to me. Yes, I can help you and your son, Luke, find a new place to live. If you let me know a little bit about you two and what you're looking for in a home, I'll start finding some places that will work for you. Why don't you come by my office on Monday and we can talk?

I hit send, then hold my phone up to my chest.

Monday isn't that far away. Letting her think about the possibility of a new home over the weekend is sure to make her dream that much more exciting. Living with roommates sounds miserable, especially with a little kid.

But I can change her life. Tina needs me, and I need her, and there isn't any reason why the two of us can't work together to get exactly what we both want.

Well, that's not entirely true, is it? *I'll* get what I want.

Tina will be... let's call her collateral damage.

Of course, she won't know how much she's helping me. The last thing I want is for anyone to figure out exactly how I know her. This plan has been a long time coming.

But when it all works out, everything in my life will be better.

I hear the shower click on upstairs, the water rumbling through the pipes. Jared hates this house. He wants something bigger, something that will make people realize just how much money we have, but I love it here.

Walking across the kitchen, I lift the curtain and look out the front window. There's a small house across the street with a huge oak tree in the front yard. It has faded blue shutters and a small front porch, but good bones. Most people will probably look right past it when on the hunt for a house.

But I think it's time for some new neighbors.

15

RICKY

The text Eloise sent me earlier today is still making me scowl.

> You need a job if you're going to keep spending so much money.

Right, like she isn't already asking so much of me today by having me keep an eye on Tina. Yes, my cousin is paying for the apartment. And yes, she gave me money for food. For going out. But that's running out, and now I need more, I need more or I'm not going to be able to keep an eye on Tina, and that's what she wants, isn't it? For me to keep an eye on Tina, to make sure she's safe, to protect her and make sure nothing bad happens to her, to watch her while she —

No, *that's* not what she wants.

I shake my head, lean against the outside brick of our apartment building. There are weeds popping up in the flower beds, choking out whatever plants were planted there. I squint, then kneel to get a better look. Daffodils. Well, there were daffodils, but they're mostly gone now, choked out, and nobody has ever come by to weed, nobody has ever done anything to clean it all up.

I pull my phone from my pocket. Thumb it on. Open my text exchange with Eloise.

> i need more money not a job

Her response is almost immediate. I wonder what she's doing in that giant house of hers, if she's just sitting around in a fluffy bathrobe, eating ice cream, and waiting on me to text her to tell her what's going on, because she answered way too quickly for her to be involved in anything productive, anything that will help people, anything that will —

I shake my head. Read her text.

> I gave you more than enough.

Exhaling hard, I stand up. Sag against the building. Beer and liquor make my head swim and my legs feel weak, but in a minute I'm going to walk upstairs to the apartment because I don't like going to bed without seeing Tina. I have to text Eloise and let her know if there have been any developments.

> it's more expensive than you know

My thumbs fly across the keyboard without giving me a chance to consider what I'm talking about. What is more expensive? Bar food? Alcohol? This phone Eloise bought me so I wouldn't miss out on any of her calls or texts?

I'll transfer some in the morning, but you
need to stop spending so much.

I grin. I won. I always win; that's the thing my dear
cousin isn't thinking about. She's so caught up on getting the
one thing that she wants that she's not realized there may be
something I want too, and that I may be willing to work hard
to ensure I get it, and that it isn't fair that she always gets
what she wants and I don't.

How is Tina tonight? Everything still good?

Stepping away from the building, I look up at the
window to our apartment. We're on the third floor, a damn
long way to walk when you've been at the bar all day long.
There's a soft glow through the window, but that's all I can
see. I'm going to have to make it up there before I can tell
Eloise what's going on.

"Getting ready to report on Tina, sir," I say, giving a
sloppy salute with the hand gripping my phone. I have to
hold it tight, tight, tight, make sure I don't drop it, not just
because it's the only way Eloise said she'd communicate
with me and I have to be able to tell her what's going on, but
because I've taken some pictures of Tina on it. Only because
I need to do reconnaissance, only because it ensures I don't
forget my target, and I don't want to lose those photos.

I can't lose them.

The stairs are empty, and I lean forward, crawling up
them more than walking up. Each time I lift my foot to take
another step, it's so difficult that I'm almost out of breath, but
I make it, and my key slips into the door after I stab it once,
twice, three times. It slips in and turns, and I'm in the apart-

ment, locking the door behind me, remembering how Paula crawled right up my ass that one time I didn't, telling me we had a child living with us, and it was up to all of us to keep him safe.

God, she's exhausting.

My phone is still in my hand as I walk down the hall, only bumping into the wall once as I stumble a bit. That boy left a toy car out in the hall, and I kick it. It spins away from me, metal slamming into the wall, and the voices from down the hall go silent.

I stop. Steady myself. Take a deep breath and put a smile on my face. I'm handsome, my mom told me I was handsome when I was younger, and I see the way women look at me from across the bar, almost afraid of not getting a chance to talk to me.

There she is. My mark. Tina's on the sofa with Luke, the two of them snuggled together, her arm looped around his shoulder, his little body buried right up next to hers. They're reading a book, or they were, but now she's stopped and is staring at me like she's not sure what she should do now that I've walked into the room.

I smile.

She returns it.

Good. This is good. Even though I want to talk to her and see how she's doing, I remember that Eloise needs information about her, needs me to learn as much as possible, and I swallow down whatever I was going to say and stare at her.

She's fine. She's healthy. Luke looks happy. He taps the book impatiently and squirms against her a bit more, like that's going to get her to pay attention to him. But she can't, can she? She's too busy staring at me to notice that Luke wants her to keep reading, and the fact that she can't take her eyes off me sends chills down my spine.

Just like the women in the bar.

Only here she doesn't have to be afraid of coming up with something to say to meet me. I'm right here, all ears, ready to talk about whatever she wants.

But she doesn't say anything.

I swallow hard, willing words to come to me, looking for something that will be brilliant and witty, something that will make her stay out here with me. Maybe she'll put Luke to bed and come back so we can talk, so I can find out what Eloise wants to know and make sure everything here is working the way it's supposed to, but no words come.

She stands, her mouth in a firm line. Luke claws at her as she swings him up onto her hip, settling him there like a sack of potatoes, and even though I hear sounds coming from him and see his mouth moving, I can't make out what he's saying.

A slight nod like she's afraid not to acknowledge me at all, then she pushes past me, scoots around me, practically knocking the recliner out of the way in an effort to be polite and not bump into me, and she's down the hall. Luke's still talking about something, but what, I don't know.

She ducks into their room. I freeze. She's going to come back, I know she is. She's just putting Luke to bed so the two of us can spend some time together, can talk and get to know each other better, and then she'll come back.

My ears hurt I'm so quiet. I'm standing completely still. In my chest, my heart thuds, beating like it's hard to pump blood through my body, like there's sludge in my veins and not blood, and I feel each pump hard, like someone's thumping on my chest. Then, even louder than that, impossibly loud, the click of the door lock, even though it doesn't really make sense, does it, that the little sound from down the hall would be so loud.

She's going to bed.

I don't move. I stare down the hall, wavering a little on my feet until I finally reach out and hold on to the back of the recliner for support, still waiting for her to come back, for her to realize it was a mistake to leave me here, that she wants to be out here with me but she just had to put Luke in bed first — *you understand, don't you, Ricky?* — and of course I do, I understand whatever it is she needs me to.

But she doesn't come back.

My phone vibrates.

> How is she?

Frustration shoots through me as I tap out my response.

> in bed tired she's fine

She's fine, right? I have to assume she is since she didn't say anything to me, but that just means she's tired and needs sleep. Tomorrow, I'll get to try again. And tomorrow Eloise will send me more money so I won't need to worry about that.

I stumble down the hall. Trace my fingers along the wall.

Stop outside Tina's door.

Carefully, so she can't hear me, I lean over to it, pressing my ear against the wood, listening for any sounds of her still awake.

There's silence.

My breathing is too loud.

I hold my breath.

Still nothing.

She must be in bed. Exhausted. Taking care of Luke and working has to be a full-time job.

I press my hand against her door and look down at the knob. She locked it, I know she did, but I still reach down, still take it in my hand, twist it first to the right, then to the left, just to check, just to make sure I wasn't hearing things, to make sure she didn't really want me to come to her and cuddle her and tell her that she wouldn't be here much longer, tell her that there is a house waiting for her and Luke, that I'll join her there because I see how her eyes widen when she looks at me, that everything will work out —

But the knob doesn't spin under my touch, and I drop my hand back to my side.

Shuffle next door to my room.

16

TINA

Luke looks at me from the safety of Debbie's arms, his eyes wide. I'm officially off work, and the two of us are supposed to be on the way home. On Mondays we usually stop off at the park and let him burn off a little extra energy. Sometimes, if I have some extra money after our grocery shopping over the weekend, we swing by the bakery and each get a cookie.

So I totally understand why he's looking at me like I just threw him to the wolves.

"I really appreciate you keeping him while I run this errand," I say to Debbie, ignoring the pleading expression on my child's face. He'll be fine. Better than fine, actually. Now that the daycare is officially closed for the day, Debbie already told me she'll bring out the good snacks for my son. He might not want to be here right now, but as soon as she hands him a pack of Dunkaroos, I'm sure he'll forget all about my betrayal.

"You know I'm happy to keep this little peanut anytime you need to do something." Debbie coos at him, shifting how she's holding him, but not letting him worm out of her grasp. She's good, I'll give her that.

"I might be taking you up on that until I get this all settled." We're speaking in coded language, but Debbie knows exactly what's going on. I called her yesterday, all in a tizzy about my upcoming meeting with the Realtor. I just don't want Luke to catch a whiff of what's going on.

The thought of how disappointed he would be if everything fell apart and we didn't get a new home eats at me. I need to keep him in the dark for as long as possible, and only when I have the keys to our new place in my pocket will I tell him what I've been up to.

And if Eloise can't really help me? Then I guess he'll never know the truth. It seems harsh, but I think it's a much better option than breaking his heart. Normally kids tend to bounce back pretty quickly, but Luke is a big softie.

"You be good for Miss Debbie, okay?" I plant a kiss on his forehead, then scoot away from him when his arms swing out for me. Little kids are like octopi when they want to snag you and keep you from leaving them.

"Momma, no." His voice is sad, but then he turns and buries his face against Debbie.

She laughs. I don't.

"He'll be fine, Tina, don't you worry. Trust me, when all this is said and done and you have some good news to share with everyone, this will be just a memory. Now, you go have a great meeting, okay?"

"Thanks." I nod and exhale hard before smoothing my hands down over my pants. As soon as all the kids were picked up, I changed into some nicer khakis. They're my only pair and don't have a single hole in them, so I think they make me look pretty respectable. I also have all of my bank statements for the past two years and proof of how much I've been paying in rent.

I'm ready. This is new to me, and I really don't know how it's going to go, but I'm prepared for anything.

On the way to the real estate office, I turn the radio as loud as it will go, pumping Dolly Parton through my poor car's speakers. I only get one strange look from someone while stopped at a red light, but if they can't appreciate the queen of country herself, that's not my problem.

I think I'm cool. Collected. I only hit the one red light on the way to the office and get a parking spot right up front.

"It's almost like the universe is conspiring for me," I mutter to myself, which is a bunch of new-age crap I don't believe in, but I'm willing to latch onto any hope I can find right now. Amber, one of the girls at the daycare, talks about manifestation all the time, like just thinking hard enough about something will make it come true.

If that were the case, I wouldn't be a single mom. And I wouldn't be living in a bedroom right next to Ricky.

Luke and I had been hanging out in the living room last night when he came in. Even without saying anything, he made me get up and take my son to our bedroom. It's not fair the two of us have to practically hide in our room to keep away from him.

But I don't like how he stares at me. How he tries to strike up conversation. How he sits down next to Luke on the sofa, how he asked him to play.

No. Absolutely not.

I slam my car door, trying to stop the thoughts swirling in my head. To be fair, it's not like I was working hard to find a new place to live. This opportunity did kinda fall into my lap.

Maybe there's something to it. I make a mental note to ask Amber, the next time I see her, what she's manifested in her life and what kind of proof she has that this really works, then smooth my khakis out one more time and walk into the real estate office.

It's like walking into another world. My workplace smells a little like diapers and chewed crayons and yogurt that's been dyed and flavored to taste like orangecicles and other unnatural things, but this smells amazing. There's a diffuser right by the front door, and I breathe in the soft scent of warm vanilla.

Classical music is piped in from somewhere, and I pause, letting my body adjust to the space. My mind races, and I need to take a deep breath, so I do, closing my eyes and counting to ten. When I open them, there's a short woman with a red pixie cut standing in front of me, a quizzical expression on her face.

"Do you need me to call a doctor?" She has a faint accent that makes her seem even more like a pixie than just her hair. Her name tag tells me her name is Denise.

"What? No." I feel a hot blush creeping up my chest. "Sorry, Denise, I was just taking a moment after a long day. I'm here to see Eloise?" Why did I ask that instead of telling her?

She blinks at me like she's wondering the same thing. Her eyes flick up and down my body; then she breaks into a smile. "Of course you are! She's upstairs on the third floor. Take the elevator," she says, jutting her thumb over her shoulder, "then go straight once you get off. You can't miss her in the corner office. I'll buzz her and let her know you're coming."

"Wonderful." I smile. "Thank you so much."

See? She's nice. She has to know that since I'm here to see Eloise, I don't have the type of money I'm sure this place usually drags in from their clients, but she didn't seem to care. She just wants me to be happy, and that's all I want, too. I don't know what I was so worried about.

The classical music is even louder in the elevator, but the ride is smooth, and I take a deep breath, suddenly feeling much more confident about what I'm doing.

I'm not just looking for a new place to live. I'm looking for a home, someplace Luke can grow up and come back to when he's older. I want somewhere safe for him, somewhere he can be happy. Home is so much more than just four walls and a roof, but when you don't even feel safe in that, then something has to give.

There's a soft ding, and the doors slide soundlessly open. Everything about this place screams money, and I hold my head up high as I walk down the hall. Plush carpet underneath muffles my footsteps. I pass a few offices, but nobody in them bothers to look up at me as I pass.

That's fine with me. I'm here to see Eloise. She's the one who told me to stop in. She's the one who can help change my life.

By the time I reach the corner office, my head is on a swivel. I don't realize she's standing in her office door waiting on me until I almost run right into her.

I suck in a breath. She's gorgeous. Tall, with impossible red heels that make her legs look fabulous in her short black skirt. Her makeup is impeccable, her lips a deep wine, her thick brunette hair held back from her face with a clip.

She's wearing a sparkling diamond necklace that catches and throws the light, and her nails match her lips. I stare at her for a moment, feeling more out of place than before, then manage to look back up at her face.

She's grinning at me.

"You must be Tina!" There's so much joy in her voice that, for a moment, I feel like we're old friends meeting up for lunch. She shakes my hand, gesturing for me to join her. "Come on in! I can't wait to hear how we're going to change your life."

See? I knew it. I might not have meant to manifest this, and maybe Amber is still full of it when she goes on and on about the universe conspiring in your favor, but this is happening.

My luck is changing.

And it's all because of Eloise.

17

ELOISE

Tina looks different up close. The first time I figured out who she was, I sat outside her daycare at closing until I saw her head out to her car, a little boy in her arms, both of their hoods pulled down low over their faces to block the wind. Part of me is surprised the police were never called on me for sitting there so long, but women have some privilege, after all.

If I had been a man sitting outside the daycare just watching and waiting, I have no doubt in my mind the police would have been called. Someone would have seen me there, seen me watching the door and the kids, and called me a pervert.

Being a woman doesn't come with a lot of benefits, but not getting called a pervert for spending time where little kids hang out is definitely one of them.

Tina looks tired, but also excited. Her bright eyes are a contrast to the dark bags under her eyes. She's thin, with the skinny look of a woman who doesn't get enough to eat. In Hollywood, and with the right clothes, she'd be chic, but here she just looks painful. All angles, elbows and knees, her cheekbones so hollowed out she looks ill.

So this woman is the one who changed the entire trajectory of my life.

I try to picture her a few years ago, full of life, not exhausted from working her fingers to the bone and parenting on her own. She was pretty in the pictures I saw.

Absolutely stunning, if I'm being honest.

But life hasn't been easy on Tina.

In all honesty, I'm a bit disappointed.

Right now Tina doesn't look like anyone would stare at her from across the bar and dream about taking her home. She's thin and tired, and her dark hair is pulled so tightly away from her face it looks painful.

But my husband found something worthwhile in her.

I'm dying to know what it was he found so alluring about the woman sitting across from me. Was there more to her than just how she looked? Or was the attraction purely physical? The latter might hurt less than the former, right? He has the money, the looks, the confidence... of course any woman with eyes would want to fall into bed with him.

But looking at her now, I can't make it make sense.

She's nothing.

I thought for sure that the first time I met her, I'd feel overwhelmed. I'd be afraid of even existing in the same space as her. Knowing my husband was with another woman, in her, kissing her... it was enough to make me doubt everything about myself.

But I don't have any doubts about myself now that I'm looking at Tina. If anything, I wonder what the hell Jared was thinking. Why her? She doesn't look like anything special. So what was it about this woman that was enough to make my husband stray?

The only way to find out is to make nice with her. I push the doubts and frustration filling my mind away and focus instead on Tina.

"I'm so glad you're here." I have to force myself to smile as I pour us two cups of coffee and set a tray down between us. "There's cream and sugar, but if you want something else, just let me know and I'll have my assistant bring it up to us."

Her eyes widen. "This is great, thank you." Two lumps of sugar disappear into her coffee; then she carefully cups the mug and takes a sip. "I had no idea what to expect coming here. I've never thought about buying a house. Are you sure you can help me?"

"I'll do anything necessary to help you." It's the truth. She doesn't know how prepared I am for long hours trying to find her the financing she needs. She has no idea that I've already picked out the perfect place for her.

And she will never know about the account I set up with ten thousand dollars in it — hopefully more than enough for a down payment if she can't come up with one. I'll call it a special type of loan, and she'll never know.

Sweet but dumb. That's the vibe I'm getting right now.

"Okay. Well, you told me to think of what I'm looking for, and I brought that list as well as all my financials. I don't make a ton at the daycare, but I've been there a couple of years, and I'm not going anywhere anytime soon, so I'm stable in that way."

I try to keep my eyes from glazing over. This woman is dull. Boring. Predictable.

All that matters is getting her to trust me.

Then I can make my husband pay for what he did to me.

18

TINA

Eloise takes a sip of her coffee and smiles at me. Even though I'm still nervous, I feel myself relax a little. This office, this view, this talk about me actually owning my own home? It's overwhelming, but Eloise seems totally confident and in control.

She's going to help me.

"Stable is great. Why don't you read me off your list of what you're looking for? Knowing, of course, that there will probably have to be some things you sacrifice to get others." She gives me a little shrug like doing so will help to lessen the blow that I probably won't get everything on my wish list.

Immediately, I like her. She's not treating me like I'm a bother or like she doesn't think I'm going to be able to afford what she helps me find. She's treating me like a friend, and I like that.

"Okay." I clear my throat and open my folder, pulling out the top sheet of paper where I've carefully written all the things I want in our new home. "Obviously, two bedrooms so Luke and I don't have to continue to share a bed."

I look at her, searching her face for pity. There isn't a sign of it, and I relax.

"Um, a yard where he can play would be great. We go to the park all the time, but it would be nice for him to have his own place to play without having to walk down the street to get there. A fenced-in yard would be preferable, but that might be out of my range. Oh, and one that isn't too far from where I work, if possible."

I stop. Put the paper down.

Eloise stares at me. She has a pen in one hand like she's about to start writing, but she doesn't move. "Is that it?"

I nod.

"There isn't anything else you really want?"

"Not really. I just want him to have a better childhood than he has right now. He's everything to me, and I just... he deserves more." Her face is unreadable, and I forge forward, wanting to make sure she understands where I'm coming from. "Do you have kids?"

"I don't."

Is that a hint of sadness in her voice? Maybe, but then it's gone before I can put my finger on even seeing it in the first place.

"Okay. I just... well, before I had Luke, I thought I had everything. It didn't matter to me where I lived or what kind of food I ate. It was all for me, and then suddenly here he was, and I needed to do better. I stopped going out, obviously, and I changed jobs so I could be around when he's around. I made a lot of changes, all of them making me a better person — a better mom — and now..." My voice trails off.

"Now you don't know who you are without considering yourself in relation to Luke?" Her voice is soft. Gentle. She reaches out and pats my hand. "You used to have things you really liked to do. Hobbies. Interests. But they fell by the wayside when you became a mom, is that right?"

I nod. My mouth is dry. Even though I want to look away from her, I can't drag my eyes from her face.

"So what is it that Tina loves? Not you as a mom, but you as a person. As a whole person. What do you love to do?"

"Read." The answer is automatic. "And cook."

"Great." She flashes me a smile and makes some notes on the pad of paper in front of her. "So maybe a porch where you can read while he plays outside? And a nice kitchen. It won't be huge, we have to remember we are working within a budget, but that doesn't mean it can't be bigger than an apartment galley kitchen."

I think about the kitchen where I live now and how we all dance around each other when we want something to eat. It's easier to just wait until everyone else is fed and then slip into the small space to make something, but Luke needs to eat regularly.

"Can you find that? Is it too much to ask?" I lean forward, for the first time, hope rising in my chest. "It sounds perfect, but it also sounds so out of reach."

"You won't believe this, but I think I have the perfect house for you." She takes a deep breath, then types on her computer before turning it around for me to get a look at the screen. "You know what?" she asks, standing and hurrying around the side of the desk to join me. "I'm going to sit with you so we can see it together. Look at this house."

One click and the little home on the computer fills the entire screen. I lean forward even though I can see perfectly well. My heart hammers out a strange staccato beat in my chest. The house is small, but that's fine. It's just Luke and me, and I don't see our family getting bigger anytime soon.

There's a yard with a big tree for climbing. And a fence. And a front porch.

I'm going to swoon.

"It's perfect," I say, reaching out to touch the screen before I remember where I am and jerk my fingers back. "Seriously, it's so perfect." I pause, almost afraid to ask my next question. I don't want to jinx this. "Will I have to wait on someone to move out if I want it?"

"Nobody lives there," she tells me, "so if you buy it, you can move right in. It's eleven hundred square feet. Great for you and Luke, but what about Luke's dad?" She glances at my hand.

"Oh," I say, holding up my hand to show her the distinct lack of a ring. "His dad isn't in the picture. It's just the two of us."

"And maybe a dog someday?" Eloise asks, moving on from the fact that I don't have a co-parent. I appreciate that, the fact that she's willing to keep the conversation going and that she isn't going to dwell on me being single.

"Oh, he'd love that. Is this home in a good neighborhood? I don't want to sound terrible, but I want to keep Luke safe."

She laughs. I turn to her, watching as she leans back, the sound bubbling out of her. Her diamond ring sparkles on her finger, huge and shiny, like a beacon to warn men off. *I'm married!* It screams.

"Trust me, this is an amazing neighborhood. I just so happen to know that firsthand."

It takes me a moment to realize what she's saying. "Do you know someone who lives there?"

"Yep." She grins at me, and it feels like we're just two friends hanging out, having a fun afternoon. At any moment I half expect her to invite me out to get a drink or some tapas. "I live there."

I can't help but laugh. Even though she looks a little surprised at the sound bubbling out of me, and even though I should stop so I'm not rude, I can't stop laughing. "I'm sorry, Eloise, but look at me." I gesture at my khakis. Yes, they're my nicest pair, but they're still not great. They're old, from goodwill, and only fit with a tight belt.

"What are you saying?" She frowns, leaning forward like she wants to get a better look at me. "Why don't you think you should have this house? What's your hang-up?"

Oof, she's good. She cut right through to the heart of it, didn't she? "I just don't think I can afford someplace like this, that's all."

Never mind the fact that I'm sitting in front of a woman who clearly has her stuff together, and I feel like I'm drowning half the time. I can't even imagine going to a neighborhood picnic. I'm sure everyone else there would be bringing freshly baked desserts and delicious casseroles, and I'd be flying by Bojangles to grab some biscuits on the way to the party.

We're just different.

"Leave your financials with me." Her voice is firm. "I have an amazing banker who's going to help me help my clients. Let me take a look at what you're working with, and I'll call you in a day or two. Trust me, Tina, I work magic."

She works magic. Looking at her and listening to her, I believe it. There's something magical about the way she seems to move in her office, like we're on two separate planes of existence. Where I'm uncomfortable, she's confident. Where I need help, she can give it.

"Okay." I nod, surprised at how quickly this all happened. "So you want to check my financials first, and then we can see the house?"

Her expression changes. "You really like it? Just from looking at it like that?"

"I do. I just don't want to get Luke's hopes up, that's all."

"Why don't we go right now while he's not here? We can both drive over there if you want, and then you'll know whether or not you want to tell Luke about the possibility of a new place." She stands up, closes her computer, grabs her purse.

My heart hammers harder. I'm standing on the edge of a precipice, well aware that whatever decision I make now will affect the rest of my life. And you know what? I'm not scared. I'm excited.

"Let's go." I stand, casting one last glance at the folder I brought with me. "I want to see this place. I want to know if I love it." A quick glance at my watch tells me I have plenty of time before I need to get Luke.

She beams. "You're going to love it. The neighbors are great." This time, when she throws her head back and laughs, I join in.

She's amazing. I trust her. Even though I haven't known her for very long, I trust her to help me, to help Luke.

It's an incredible feeling. She's like the big sister I never had, and if she can help me move into a house that looks like that, then why wouldn't I want that to happen?

19

RICKY

I don't usually make it to this end of Main Street. It's nicer here, the store windows are all clean, with flowers in the front boxes. People look nicer too, like they get out and go to the gym or tan. I know I don't fit in.

There's a green park bench on the sidewalk across from Harrison Realty, and I sit on it, scooting to the side in case anyone wants to sit next to me. I'm thoughtful. Kind. My mom always told me to think about other people and watch out for them if possible, and that's what I'm doing right now.

My eyes drift up the windows of the building across the street. It towers over this end of Main Street, built before there was a rule put into place that no building can be higher than two stories. Even just that extra third story makes it look so much bigger than anything else.

Tina is in there somewhere.

I was waiting for her here, but she didn't see me when she pulled up, all frazzled, her hair a mess as she got out of her car. She'd smoothed it down, and I reach up and smooth my own hair in memory.

There's a bruise on my forehead. I run my fingers along a scab.

Hissing in a breath, I drop my hand back to my lap.

Where did that come from?

It wasn't difficult for me to know she'd be here this afternoon. That's all she talked about with Paula over the weekend. How excited she was about this meeting. How nice Eloise was. How much she couldn't wait to meet her and hopefully get out of the apartment. They sat on the sofa talking about it, and I stood in the kitchen, unable to keep from eavesdropping.

And then her voice would drop, and I'd have difficulty understanding what she was saying, but I'd strain my ears and listen anyway. Paula would murmur and put her hand on Tina's arm, and then Luke would screech about something, and the quiet moment would be broken.

She wants out of the apartment.

My heart beats faster at the thought.

I knew she would. *That was the plan.*

Someone like her doesn't belong in a place like where we live. She's light and life and all things good, and our apartment is dark and dirty, and she and Luke want more, but I don't want her to go.

Someone walks by the bench I'm on. Pauses.

I look up.

He's older than me, with white hair and a white mustache to match. Nice pants. A button-up shirt tucked in. No tie, but he looks like he'd be at home in one.

"You need anything, fella?" His voice is kind and low enough that he's not trying to make sure everyone can hear what he's asking me. As he speaks, he dips his hand into his back pocket for his wallet.

I know what he's doing. I've seen men do that all the time.

"I'm fine," I say. My voice sounds croaky, so I clear my throat and try again, gesturing at the building across the street from the two of us. "I'm fine. Just waiting on someone."

He turns to look at the building, then back at me. His hand is still in his back pocket.

"My girlfriend," I say, liking the way the word feels in my mouth. "She's buying a house, and I'm meeting her here afterwards. Just waiting on her. Just don't want her to have to celebrate on her own."

I feel myself warming up to the lie. "We're so excited. It'll be us and our son, and we'll finally be out of the apartment we've been renting."

"Well, that's nice." His hand slithers out of his pocket. He taps his thumb against the side of his thigh. "She's buying a house, you say?"

"Yep." I feel my chest swell with pride. Look at Tina, buying a house. She's doing such a great job, and I'm right here to support her. She doesn't know it, of course, unless she were to look out the window and see me, but I can picture her now, so focused on what she's doing, so excited, that she doesn't have any idea I'm here.

"Well, good for you guys. And a son?"

"Luke." My fingers drum out a rhythm on my knee. "His name is Luke. He looks just like her."

It's a lie, it's all a lie, but I can't stop now, can't keep the lies from coming, not when saying them and thinking about them feels so good. I like the thought that Luke might be mine, that Tina is my girlfriend, and this guy doesn't know any better; he has no idea what the truth is.

That I'm supposed to —

Watch her.

Yes, watch her, and I have been doing that. I've been watching her eat and sleep and cuddle with Luke, and watching how she smiles at her phone when she thinks she's all alone, and how she laughs and her neck stretches, the little hollow there so kissable that I have to stop myself from taking her in my arms.

"Congratulations to you all. I hope everything goes well up there." He gives me a nod, obviously ready to move on, but I don't know that I want him to. I want this to continue, and if he leaves me, then it's all over, isn't it?

"She's great," I say, leaning forward a bit now.

He stutter-steps and stops, looking down at me with amusement more than anything, and I hate him for that expression, but now I can't seem to slow the thoughts in my mind, so it doesn't really matter as long as he listens for another moment.

"She's great," I repeat, and my eyes flick up to the building even though the sun is shining right on the windows, making the building glow, making it impossible for me to see anyone inside. I want to look for her, want to see her up there finding the perfect home. "She really is."

"Best of luck to you," he says, and then he's gone, and I don't care because I keep looking up at the building, imagining her right there, her hand pressed against the glass, her eyes searching for me.

She should love that I'm out here waiting on her, but I know she wants this moment for herself. I'm not going to make her feel bad about excluding me.

But I'm so proud of her. I can't wait to celebrate with her.

I liked telling this guy that she was my girlfriend.

It felt good. It made me happy.

I'm supposed to be helping Eloise, but why can't it be true?

20

ELOISE

I always listen to music when I drive, but now I have the radio off, both hands gripping the wheel at ten and two, my teeth grinding together every time I think I'm going to lose Tina at a red light. If I'd given her the address, then I wouldn't have to worry about her getting left behind, but I wanted her to rely on me.

I didn't want her to know some back road and get to the house first. I want her to see it with me for the first time.

Would it have been just as exciting to pull in behind her right as she was getting out of her car? Sure. Maybe. But I want her to fully rely on me. For this plan of mine to work, she has to think that I'm not only her Realtor, but her friend. She has to see me as someone she can trust, as someone who has her best interests at heart.

It's the only way I'm going to get what I want from her.

Traffic is light, and we zip through town. I know she wants to hurry off to get Luke, but I want to do this. There's nothing more frustrating for potential homebuyers than to have their children fall in love with the house when they can't afford it. And if she falls in love with the house first, then any complaints he might raise will fall on deaf ears.

But that's not going to be the problem here. I've sure of it. Yes, the house is in a really nice neighborhood. There wasn't any way I was going to live in a run-down neighborhood, and while the house I'm showing to Tina is the smallest on the street, there's nothing wrong with it.

It's cute. It needs work, sure, but don't all houses in this price range? And with the money I've been setting aside since I found out about Jared's affair, there's no reason why Tina won't be able to afford the place.

I just have to make sure she really wants it.

Everything depends on her moving in.

We turn into the neighborhood and I slow down, not only so I look responsible to my neighbors as I'm driving by, but so Tina can get a good look at the place she's going to live in.

Her new home was actually the guest home to our home. Originally it was half the size it is now, but past owners have built onto it, enlarging it and turning it from a little home that was barely enough space for one guest to stay in, to plenty of room for a woman and her child.

And a dog. *If they get that far.*

Finally, we reach the house. It's strange to pull into the driveway across from mine, and I look up at my house, grateful Jared isn't home yet. He has no idea I've been keeping an eye on this property and that I have plans for it. If he knew, he'd squash them before they got off the ground.

I kill the engine. Put a huge smile on my face. Get out and turn to look at Tina as she pulls in and parks next to me.

Even through her window I can see the expression on her face.

"You've got to be kidding." She's talking as she gets out of the car, not even giving me a chance to get a word in edgewise. "There's no way this is in my budget. How cute is it? And did you see the other homes here? Of course you did. It's just... wow. I never thought I could live anywhere like this." It's almost pathetic how flustered she is.

"Well, you deserve it. You and Luke."

She laughs. "I don't know if I *deserve* it, but I'm certainly not going to turn down the opportunity to buy someplace like this. Are you sure I can afford it though?" She turns to me, concern on her face. It's like the full reality of what's happening has suddenly landed on her shoulders, and it's almost too much for her to bear.

I walk over to her. Put my hands on her shoulders. Look her in the eyes. "Listen to me, Tina. My goal is to help you find a house that you and Luke can turn into a home. This place is amazing. The neighbors are great, if I do say so myself, and it's in a wonderful school district. You worry about whether or not you like it. I'll take your financials and worry with the mortgage banker about finding you a program if you need additional help to afford it."

She exhales, hard, her shoulders sinking a little bit under the pressure of my grip, but then she grins at me. "You're my hero, you know that? You're right. I'm just going to focus on the house and the life Luke and I can build here. Let's go see it, shall we?"

"Let's." I lead the way up to the house, holding the gate for her, then step to the side after I open the Realtor key box and unlock the front door.

The air inside is a little musty because of the place being

closed up for a while, but I don't think Tina will really notice. When people's emotions are running high, they tend to look past any sign that something might not be right.

She takes a deep breath on the porch, then walks in, spinning in a slow circle in the middle of the living room. "I love it."

I laugh, turning on the lights. "You haven't even seen the whole place yet. Go explore, and I'll answer any questions you have when you get back."

She does what I tell her to, leaving me alone by the front door. It takes me a moment to calm my breathing. I feel like I just surfaced after being held underwater, like I can't seem to catch my breath. Being with the woman my husband cheated on me with is more difficult than I thought it would be.

I knew it wasn't going to be a walk in the park, but I just can't seem to get my mind to slow down. I can't make sense of what happened.

But it's her. I know it's her.

Still.

It's risky and dangerous, and I could get caught and then have this entire thing fall apart at my feet, but I pull my cell from my purse and unlock it with my thumbprint. Moving quickly now, I flick over to my messages and open the one from my cousin.

It came to me months ago. Ricky isn't the type of guy to tell you something unless he thinks he's going to benefit from it.

He could have told me about Jared years ago when he snapped the pictures, but he didn't. And why? Because he didn't need money then. It's that simple.

But he does now.

My first instinct when I got the picture was to scoff and delete it. People try to discredit Jared all the time.

The old adage about women wanting to be with a rich and powerful man while men want to be him? It's bunk. Women might want to be with him, that much is true, but men don't want to be him. They want to knock his legs out from under him, watch his empire collapse. Men don't want to *be* someone they're envious of.

They want to destroy him.

So, of course, I thought this was a smear campaign at first. Who wouldn't want to think the best of their husband when an incriminating photo like this got delivered to their phone? But then I calmed down. I took a deep breath.

I drank a bottle of wine.

And I thought about it. I looked at the picture, at the way his hand was twisted in the woman's hair, at how her face was tilted expectantly up to his, at the way he was looking at her. If it weren't my husband in the shot, perfectly poised to kiss someone else, I'd think it was an ad for a perfume company.

It's gorgeous. And disgusting.

And then I looked harder at the photo. I saw my favorite button-up shirt he threw away without warning almost three years ago. I saw the hairstyle he'd cut short, saying that he thought the slightly longer hair made him look like a hippy.

I recognized the man in the photo as my husband, but he'd made a one-eighty after it was taken, obviously doing everything in his power to free himself from that image, to change enough that nobody would be able to tell who he was.

But I know. When you've been with a man, had him in

you, stood by him and stared into his eyes to say your vows, you recognize him, even when doing so drives a stake through your heart.

Then Ricky sent another. And another.

There was just no denying the truth.

"This place is amazing!" Tina's voice jerks through my thoughts. My thumb slams down on the side of my phone, turning the screen off and locking it without me really thinking about what I'm doing.

"You like it?" I slip the phone into my pocket. Focus on the woman standing in front of me. For the longest time after I got the photos, I hated her. I want to bring her to her knees and make her pay for what she did to me.

But then I thought about it more, and I realized she wasn't the one to blame. No, she didn't do anything wrong. I have a very good suspicion Jared told her he was single. Hell, in the photos on my phone, he's not wearing a ring.

So who should I be angry with? The woman who didn't know the man she was kissing was married? Or the man who vowed to love me and stand by me for the rest of my life and then fell into bed with someone else?

I want to hurt him. But I can't. I don't have the power. Jared is untouchable. He's made sure of that by keeping everything in his company in his name. If I were to walk away from him now, I wouldn't get what I want — what I need — to live the life I deserve.

But what if something else were to happen to him? What if the woman he kissed — the woman he had an affair with and knocked up — showed up? Destroyed everything? Destroyed him?

Looking at Tina, you wouldn't think she's a weapon. She

looks weak. Tired. She looks like someone anyone could easily walk all over.

But I'm not weak. And I'm going to turn Tina into a weapon, then aim her right at my cheating husband.

He has no idea what's coming.

21

TINA

Luke's already in bed, and even though I'm exhausted and should probably be curled up next to him already, I can't sleep, not with adrenaline coursing through my veins like this.

I'm just so *excited*. When was the last time something this good happened to me? Probably when I got the job at the daycare, or when Paula told me we could move in with her. I've had a few good moments in my life, but mostly it feels like bad luck strung together with more bad luck.

But maybe that's finally over.

Sighing, I tap on my phone screen to enlarge the photo of my new house as I snuggle down into the sofa. Well, it's not mine *yet*, but Eloise didn't seem at all concerned about any possibility of me not getting it. She even referred to it as *your new house* a few times, and even though I know better than to get my hopes up, I didn't stop her.

It just feels so good to have something exciting to look forward to. To have a light at the end of the tunnel, a light that tells me that the stress of my life might soon be over. Sure, owning a home will come with its own new level of stress, but it will be different than living here.

With Ricky.

Footsteps behind me make me gasp. I whip around, my heart suddenly kicking into high gear.

"You're jumpy," Paula remarks, a cup of tea in her hand. She eyeballs me, then looks at my phone. I've put my hand over the screen to prevent anyone from seeing what I'm looking at. "What's going on, Tina?"

"It's the house," I say, moving my hand and sliding the phone across the coffee table to where she can get a good look at it. "I just can't stop thinking about how great it is. It's probably not smart, getting this ahead of myself, but I keep thinking about the decoration and painting I'll do when we move in."

"So it's a done deal?" She sits down in the overstuffed chair next to the sofa, balancing her tea on her knee, then leans closer to me and takes my phone. "This is it? Your new home?"

Tears burn my eyes. "It's not a done deal yet," I say, sniffing a little bit. "But it's close, and I really think it's going to happen. We just have to make sure everything goes through with the financing."

She nods and puts my phone back down on the coffee table. Takes a sip of her tea. Looks at me.

"What?" I'm suddenly nervous.

"I just want to make sure you're not getting in over your head." She puts her tea down on the coffee table, her eyes never leaving mine.

I start shaking my head before she finishes talking. "I'm not, I promise. There's this great program they're running specifically for lower-income people like me. Single moms. Vets. People like that."

"Okay."

A tear races down my cheek, and I wipe it away. Shame burns through me that I'm crying about this, but my stress right now is off the charts, and I'm having difficulty even thinking through what's going on.

"Oh, honey. No, don't cry." Paula reaches out and takes my hand. "I don't mean to upset you, okay? I just want to make sure this isn't too good to be true. If I'm being honest, there's part of me that's sad that you're going to move out. You're a great roomie, and I'm going to miss you. I just want to make sure you're not going to get screwed over. And, selfishly, now I have to find another roomie." She grins at me to take away the guilt from her words.

I take a deep breath and picture Eloise's face. I swear, she was as excited as I was when she was showing me the house. I don't, not for one moment, think she'd lie to me about the process or how much I could afford. She's just so kind. And I read the article about her giving up her giant fees so she could sell less expensive houses to people like me.

From what I gather, people in town think she's a saint, and I'm inclined to agree.

"You're fine," I tell her, sniffling hard. "I just want so badly for this to work, and the thought that there might be anything wrong with the house is terrifying." Pausing, I look past her down the hall. Luke hasn't made a sound since I tucked him in, but he's not what I'm worried about. "I just think it's time for the two of us to be somewhere on our own, somewhere I can make sure everything is safe."

Paula blinks at me, then nods slowly as the realization of what I'm saying hits her.

"I don't want you to think I'm ungrateful," I tell her, lowering my voice to a whisper and leaning over the table so my words don't carry. "I just think it's time for me to go."

Her voice drops in response. "I understand. Trust me, I get it. And I wouldn't ever ask you to stay here if you didn't feel comfortable. But I am going to miss you."

I grin at her. I'm so focused on her face, on the love I see written there for me, that, at first, I don't realize what I'm hearing.

Footsteps coming down the hall.

"Luke?" Leaning to the side so I can see past Paula, I wait for my son to walk into view.

But it's not Luke on his way to join us.

"Mind if I sit?" Ricky moves the pillow next to me without waiting for a response and drops onto the sofa with a sigh. "What are you two doing? You look serious. And, Tina, you're usually in bed by now." He glances at Paula but locks his gaze on me.

I squeeze Paula's hand. *See what I mean?* When I look at Ricky, though, I make sure to have a smile on my face.

You never know what someone is capable of.

"Oh, just talking about our days," I say, keeping my voice light. "Did you hit your forehead the other day? You have a bit of a yellow bruise there."

He reaches up, blinking as he does, then presses hard on the center of the bruise.

I wince for him. He doesn't.

"So you're buying a house?" He blinks at me like I didn't just ask him what happened to his face, like he didn't just press down so hard in the center of the bruise that it takes a moment for the skin to stop being that sickly white.

"How did you know that?" Fear grips my heart, and I

think back through all the things I've said, all the bits of paper I might have left out around the apartment while working on my application.

A slight pause. "I heard you talking."

Oh, right. I feel so excited right now, so full of life, that it wouldn't be surprising if I was talking loud enough for Ricky to have heard what Paula and I were saying. Still, I didn't see him listening in, and that means he had to be hovering in the hall, paying attention to what we were saying.

And I didn't know he was there.

"Yes," I say, deciding to let him know the truth right now. Paula's with me, and she wouldn't let anything bad happen to me, right?

As soon as I have the thought, I shake my head to clear it. What would he do? He's not dangerous. Right?

No, Tina, think. Be honest with yourself.

He stares at me. And I hear him jiggle my locked doorknob. *He's dangerous.* I just don't want to think about it.

"When?"

I notice how quickly his chest is rising and falling, like he's sucking in tiny little snatches of air and can't get enough to really fill his lungs. It's unnerving.

"I'm just waiting to hear back from the Realtor and banker." No lies. All my cards on the table. "But I was told it would probably be pretty quick. That everything was in order and this program was designed to help people move into their new home with as little trouble as possible." I let go of Paula's hand and link my fingers together in my lap.

No comment. He just stares at me, his dark eyes locked on mine. They're red-rimmed, and I wonder if he's been drinking. I can't smell anything, but that doesn't mean he's not on something. Drugs, perhaps. You can't always easily tell when someone's high if they shoot up.

"Well, I think it's exciting." Paula claps her hands loudly, breaking the spell in the room. "And, Ricky, we're going to have to look for a third roommate. You just never know who you're going to get, do you?"

I chuckle nervously. "Sure don't. If I hear of someone looking for a place to live, I'll let you two know."

Only I won't. I hate to throw Paula under the bus like this, but I wouldn't make anyone live with Ricky if they didn't have to.

"Great." Paula takes a long sip of her tea. "Now, Tina, weren't you just saying you were heading to bed before I bothered you? Don't let us keep you up."

"You're the best." My hands shake as I plant them on the table and stand up. When I grab my phone and shove it in my pocket, Ricky stares at the lump in my jeans for a moment too long. "You two have a good night."

"You too." Paula's voice is a singsong, and she waves at me before turning to Ricky. "Now, Ricky, where are we going to find another person to live here? You have any ideas?"

I don't wait to hear what he might say in response. I hate turning my back on him. He watches me, I know he does, but I don't have a choice if I'm going to escape to my room.

I flee the living room. Pee and brush my teeth. Then, when I'm safely in the bedroom I share with Luke, I triple-check the lock before crawling into bed with my son. I hid a knife under the mattress earlier this morning, just in case.

It's still there. I make sure of it.

22

ELOISE

Hi, Eloise.

Just wanted to let you know that we need a larger down payment from Tina Miller. Her debt-to-income ratio is a little off, and I'm going to need something to keep her payments low. The 10K we thought was going to cover it isn't going to be enough since her monthly income is so low.

Give me a call when you get this and let me know your plan.

Laura

23

TINA

I feel like I'm flying. Even when something terrible happens at work, like a kid pooping on me or hitting another child, I just grin and bear it. It doesn't feel like anything can drag me down, not when I know my life — and Luke's life, for that matter — is going to change so drastically.

And for the better.

It feels like my life has been one long string of bad luck, but things are finally turning around. I keep pinching myself to make sure I'm not sleeping and dreaming and that this is really happening. And it is.

Oh, God. It is.

Luke runs to me, his arms and legs pumping, and I bend down, scooping him straight up and popping him on my hip.

"Did you have a good day with Miss Debbie?" I ask, kissing him on the forehead. He's warm, but hopefully just from running around. Today is a big day, and the last thing I need is for him to develop a fever and get sick.

"Yep. We played with Play-Doh." He giggles. "I'm hungry. Can we go to the park?"

"Not today, buddy. But I do have a snack for you." Maneuvering my free arm, I dig into my bag and brandish a granola bar. He rips into it as soon as I hand it to him, and takes a big bite before offering me one.

I shake my head.

"It's good." His mouth is full, and a bit of food flies from between his lips, but I don't fuss at him.

Not today. Not when everything is going my way.

"You look like you're in a really good mood." Bethany walks down the hall, dressed impeccably in a long skirt and flowy top. I guess when you're not down on the floor with the little kids all day, you don't have to worry about your clothes getting ruined.

I feel frumpy standing next to her in jeans and a polo. The daycare name is embroidered on one side, right under the collar. I hate it.

"We have a big errand to run," I say, adjusting Luke so I can mouth the words over his head. "Closing on the house."

"Oh, that's today?" Bethany grins at me. "You mentioned it a while back. You were able to get approved for one?"

Her question has barbs, but I manage to smile at her even though it hurts. "Yep, I sure was. I have a great Realtor, and I guess she works really closely with a wonderful mortgage banker. Sounds like there wasn't a problem at all."

"Wow. I'm impressed." Bethany's still smiling. I can see all of her teeth. She looks like a shark that has zeroed in on some prey, and I scoot back from her, trying to put enough space between us that I no longer feel crowded.

But she isn't done. "I didn't think your salary would be

able to cover a mortgage. You must have had quite the down payment."

"Everything worked out just fine." Truth be told, I still feel like I'm in a dream and when I get to Eloise's office, she's going to tell me it was all a mistake. I'm terrified she's going to laugh at me for even thinking I could buy the little house at 4 Sugarloaf Lane. Bethany has no way of knowing how hard she's pushing my buttons right now, but I feel like the walls are starting to close in on me.

"Well, that's great. I hope you don't run into any problems making the payments each month. I'm sure you know I won't be giving out any raises until next year."

"Oh, I know." We all know. All of us have discussed it before, how stingy Bethany is with raises. For not the first time, I think about the stranger I met in the bar, Luke's father, and how different our lives would have been if we had reconnected.

I wouldn't be dealing with this woman telling me she was worried I'm not going to be able to keep my house, that's for sure. I don't know how much money he had, but it has to be more than I'm making right now. He just *felt* like money.

"Well, I don't want to keep you from where you're going." She throws me a wink. Does she think we're friends? You can't sling poorly disguised insults at someone every time you see them and think that you're friends with them. "Good luck, Tina. I hope it goes the way you want it to."

"It will." I speak with confidence even though I feel a terrible ball in the pit of my stomach. "You have a good rest of your day, Bethany."

And with that, Luke and I are gone. It's a gorgeous day, which I'm sure bodes well for what we're about to do. Nobody wants rain on the day you close on a new home.

Nobody wants that dark pall on something as exciting as this.

"Where we going?" Luke's finished his granola bar and can finally speak again. He crawls into his car seat and lets me buckle him in.

"Luke, what do you think about moving somewhere with a yard where you can play all the time?" I feel butterflies dancing in my stomach.

He thinks about it. Screws up his face.

"A yard is like a private park," I offer, hoping this will help to persuade him.

"My own park?" He grips the sides of his car seat in excitement. Under his fingernails are little bits of Play-Doh, bright pink, blue, and green, looking like a funny manicure.

"Your own park!" I hop in the driver's seat, no longer able to contain my excitement. "What do you think, buddy? You and me, and maybe one day we can get a dog."

"I want a dog!" he screeches so loudly it would normally make me cringe, but nothing can bring me down now. I'm floating, high above the clouds, above the traffic as we drive, even above the insults Bethany likes to fling at me.

We pull into the parking lot, and I get Luke out, holding his little hand tightly. "I have to sign a lot of papers," I tell him. "I need you to be quiet. Be a good boy."

He puffs out his chest. "I am a good boy, Momma."

"I know." We hurry across the parking lot and through the large double doors. The last thing I want is to be late, to make Eloise think I don't really want this house. That maybe I don't *deserve* this house.

"She's expecting you," the receptionist says, wiggling her fingers at Luke as we walk by. I know it's silly, but I like that she recognized me, that she just waved us on like that. Makes me feel important.

By the time we make it up to her office, Luke has stopped to check out half the paintings on the wall. I'm going crazy trying to get him to hurry up, but when we reach Eloise's office, her door is almost completely closed.

I reach out, ready to knock, dying to throw it open and stroll in so we can get this house in my name, but then I pause.

She's talking to someone.

No, not talking. *Yelling.* And she sounds really angry.

I pause, my hand still extended, knowing full well I shouldn't be eavesdropping, that I'm being a terrible example for Luke, that this will probably come back to haunt me when he's older, but I can't seem to move.

"No, I didn't see your email. Don't you know how busy I am?"

A pause. I hate conflict. It makes me feel like I'm going to throw up.

She continues, obviously unaware that Luke and I are outside her office. "I told you this house is hers. Now, how much more money do I need to give you to make that happen?"

Her words are a little muffled, but I know I heard them correctly.

Ice shoots through my veins, and I brace myself against the doorframe, looking for some support as I feel the carpet being yanked out from under me. The house. *My* house. Is that what she's talking about?

No. Surely not.

Luke gets tired of waiting. He steps forward and plants

his hand on the door, shoving it open before dragging me in after him.

Eloise looks up. Her face is twisted in anger, her hand clenched around her phone like a claw.

"I have to go." When she speaks, her words are clipped; then she puts the phone down on her desk, face-down.

She smiles. It takes a moment for her face to form into a smile, for her lips to curl up, for her eyes to relax.

What in the world is going on?

I feel dizzy watching her, trying to figure out what just happened. It feels like I walked in on her throwing a fit, definitely getting in a fight with someone, but as soon as she saw me standing here with Luke, her expression completely changed.

Like magic.

"You're here." She's breathless, her cheeks bright pink, but I can't tell if the color is there because she's excited or upset. She stands and gestures to the chair across from her. "Come on in; sit down. There's been a small delay, but if you and Luke make yourselves comfortable, I'll handle it."

I stare at her. My feet start moving even though I'm not really thinking about walking over to her; then Luke breaks the spell and runs to the chair, getting there first. He climbs up into it, and I wince at how dirty he is.

Eloise stares at him. Her face is blank. She looks at me. Forces a smile to her face.

What the hell is going on?

24

ELOISE

Frustration burns through me when I see Tina standing at my office door, Luke already climbing into a chair on the other side of my desk. Her mouth is tight, her eyes wide, and it hits me she must have heard what I was just saying.

But that doesn't mean she knows I was talking about her.

I offer for her to sit, then pick up my phone, slipping it into my pocket. "You know, let me pop out and get you something to drink. I think there are some crayons for Luke, too. I just need to handle something for another client."

Is my voice shaking? I need to pull myself together.

Tina nods, her eyes still like saucers. Luke leans forward and grabs a pen off my desk, rips the cap off, and tosses it to the floor.

He looks so much like Jared that it's hard for me to breathe. If there was any doubt in my mind about whether or not he's my husband's son, it's gone now. I can see it written all over his face. Even though he's only been here for under a minute, he's shown me half a dozen facial expressions I've come to expect from Jared.

There had been part of me hopeful I was wrong. Part of me that thought maybe — just maybe — she got pregnant from someone else, that there wasn't a tiny piece of my husband walking around town while he and I couldn't get pregnant.

It's not fair.

"Just a minute," I say again, not sure if she's responded or if I've made myself clear. When she nods, I hurry out of my office and into the bathroom, closing the door behind me. Immediately I call the mortgage banker back.

"Eloise, I know you want to make this happen for your client, but —"

"She's in my office right now, ready to sign those papers. How much more money do you need for the down payment?" I'm desperate. Realizing someone might walk by and hear me, I turn on the overhead fan, hoping that will be enough sound to block out my words. "I thought you said ten thousand would be enough."

"She doesn't make a lot at the daycare. We need another ten."

Each of her words feels like a stab in my chest. I take a moment and let them roll around in my mind before speaking. "I wish you'd told me this before."

No response.

"Okay. Ten thousand. I'll have it transferred to the account. Is that all?"

A pause. So far, I've managed to keep Laura in the dark about where this money is coming from, but she's good at her job. Eventually, she's going to ask. But I want Tina's paperwork signed and her in the house across the road before Laura finds out the truth.

"I will need to know where she's getting these deposits. You know that, Eloise."

"Don't worry. It's part of the program we're offering," I lie. There's a black fuzzy on my white pants, and I pick it off. Flick it to the tile floor. "We're helping out with down payment for the first few clients."

Silence. It's a terrible lie. There's no way she's going to believe me. Then again, I know she works on commission, and I know Laura likes hitting big numbers. She might just bite. We've worked together for such a long time that I have to hope she'll let this one slide.

A heavy sigh. "I'll allow it this time, but next time I'm going to need paperwork proving what you're saying. Don't make it a habit."

I exhale hard and slump against the wall. "Okay, I totally agree. Thanks for making this happen. She's ready to sign and is so excited, and I don't want to have to break her heart."

"Transfer the money now, and I'll send over the documents. You can print them there." Her tone is confident. Driven. Laura always gets what she wants, which is why I wanted to work with her. If she knew the real reason why I'm desperate for Tina to move in across the street, she'd never complete the deal.

In fact, she'd probably tell Harrison. I have to cover my mouth to stop the laugh that threatens to bubble out when I think about how my boss would handle news that I'm scheming against my husband and using the woman he had an affair with to bring him down.

"You're the best, Laura." I turn off the fan and check my appearance in the mirror. "I'll send it all right now."

"Don't do it aga—" she begins, but I hang up. Turn my phone on silent. After fluffing the ends of my hair, I leave the bathroom, slapping a smile on my face when I hurry into my office.

"Hey, sorry about that," I say. "I swear, mortgage lenders are so hesitant to help people get into their homes, and all I want is to help buyers."

Tina smiles and then looks down at my hands. Her smile falters.

"Oh, the crayons," I say, smacking my forehead. "I'm so sorry. We were out, but this really won't take long. All I have to do is send Laura one bit of information, and she'll release the paperwork for you."

"Is it always like this? Kind of harried?" Luke's squirming on her lap, and she releases him. I watch as she pulls a bag of crackers from her purse and hands them to her son. "I can only imagine how stressful it is trying to get everything done if you're always dealing with last-minute things like this."

"You know, some days are easier than others." I barely glance up from my computer as I log in to my online banking and send the transfer. My heart sinks as I press the button to put ten thousand more in the escrow account for Tina's home, but at this point I'm not backing down.

What's done is done.

Besides, in the end, I'll have much more than that. This is just a minor hiccup in the grand scheme of things.

"Alright. Now we wait just a few minutes. Have you told your son?" I click over to my email and keep an eye on the screen while I wait for Tina to answer. Luke is currently stuffing crackers in his mouth and dropping crumbs all over the floor.

I do my best to ignore how filthy my office will be when he leaves. All I can think about when I look at him is that he's Jared's son.

My husband's son. My husband's son. My husband's son. My husband's —

It's like a heartbeat, thrumming through me, making it difficult for me to focus on anything at all.

Tina's talking, and I rip my thoughts away from how happy Jared would be to find out he's a dad so I can focus on the woman sitting across from me.

"He's so excited," she says. "And to think — we'll each have our own bed! It will be really nice not to be kicked awake in the middle of the night, I've got to tell you."

"You two really share a bed? You said that, but I wasn't sure if you were serious." I shouldn't keep talking, but I can't help myself. And besides, won't me asking her questions make her more likely to trust me in the end? I have to get close to her, and this is how to do it.

She doesn't have to know that I already know the truth. I know everything about how she and Luke share a bed. How she tries to wait until the kitchen is free of other roommates before cooking for him.

I know it all.

She blushes. "Yeah, like I said, our place isn't that great. But we're almost out of there. I'm hoping we can get the keys and move right away."

"We can help." The words tumble free from my lips before I have a chance to consider what I'm saying. "Move, I mean. I don't want you to feel like you're all alone, and my husband is pretty strong."

She laughs. "Thanks, but I don't want to take away from your family time this weekend. Luke and I can manage. Besides any boxes of stuff, there's just a bed and bedside table. We didn't have much to begin with."

I eyeball her skinny little arms and try to picture her moving furniture by herself. Out of the corner of my eye, an email from Laura pops into view, and I click on it before answering.

Print.

Behind me, the printer whirs to life. I'd originally planned to have Tina and Luke over for dinner one night just to see the expression on Jared's face when they finally meet, but why put it off? Why not let them meet sooner?

I just can't wait to see my husband squirm.

"Oh, you're not taking time away from anything. Let us come over and help you. I know where to come." I grin at her, then reach behind me to pull the stack of warm papers from my printer. "Now, let's not argue. Let's get these signed and get you in your new house!" I press a button on my phone.

"Eloise, are you ready for me?" A man's voice fills my office.

"Ready. Come on down." When I release the button, I look at Tina, who has a questioning expression on her face. "The lawyer. Harrison runs a tight ship around here so we can complete all our work in-house. We have to have one around when you sign; then he'll get the papers off to the courthouse and get them filed. You'll be on your way to your new home by then."

My voice is tight with excitement. Can she tell? If she can, will she just think I'm excited because I'm looking forward to helping her out? I'm not sure, and she's difficult to read.

She smiles and grabs the pen Luke was playing with from my desk.

"Let's do this. I'm ready for the first day of the rest of my life. Luke and I need this."

Yes, they do. They need this, and I need them to move in across the street. It's the best way for me to get what I want.

And for Jared to get what he deserves.

25

RICKY

Eloise's house is too clean. The air feels stiff, which sounds crazy, but there is no breeze in here, not when the windows are always kept closed. There are timed fragrance releases in a few places around the house, and they keep puffing out plumes of lavender.

It's enough to give me a headache.

I'd open the door and get a fresh breeze in here, but I want to stay hidden. Even my junker is back around the house. I took the mostly unused service driveway that exits out behind the neighborhood so no nosy neighbors would be able to say they saw me here. It's just better that way.

Walking from the living room to the kitchen, I hop up on the counter and lift the blinds so I can peek out. Down the large front yard, past the huge garden Eloise hires gardeners to fill with annuals every year so she can dig in the dirt and feel like she has a green thumb, and over the road is the house.

Tina's house.

Tina's house without me.

I did what Eloise asked. I kept an eye on Tina and let Eloise know what she was doing. I watched Tina and listened to her and waited until she went to bed before I went to bed just so I could know she was okay, but there was one thing that happened that I don't think either of us expected.

I want her. And I don't want her to move out of the apartment.

Add to that Eloise's plan and —

"No, no, no." I drop the blinds and hop down from the counter, hurrying back to the living room. "Don't think about that, Ricky, just think about how sweet and innocent and perfect Tina is."

Movement catches my eye, and I watch as Eloise's car pulls up into the driveway. She waits for the garage door to open, then slides inside. I hear the rumble from the garage door as it drops back into place.

A moment later, the door at the other end of the living room opens. Eloise walks in, a heavy bag on her arm, a travel mug in her hand, flowers tucked against her body. She turns to key off the alarm, but I've done it for her.

"Hi, Eloise," I say, walking over to her. I feel like I'm vibrating with energy, like it's flowing through me, and even though I know I need to take a deep breath and let her answer, need to give her space, I feel the words in my mouth, and then suddenly they're free. "How's Tina? Is she okay? Is Tina really moving out of the apartment?"

Eloise sighs. Drops the bag to the floor. Closes and locks the door behind her. "How did you get in here, Ricky?"

I have a key. I stole one the last time I was here and she was drunk, talking about her plan, and I made a copy. I've seen her turn off her alarm before, and I memorized the code.

"Where is Tina?"

"She'll probably be across the road at any time, but you can't be here." One accusing finger stabs the air in front of my face. "You'll ruin everything. You know you're not allowed to just stop by. How are you even in here right now?"

I ignore her words and how wrong she is. Eloise is my cousin, and I love her, or I'm supposed to love her, but I don't like how she just assumes that I'm the problem and that everything is going wrong because of me.

"Tina won't see me," I tell her. "I parked around back."

She rolls her eyes and brushes past me into the kitchen. "What's your plan, then? You did what I wanted you to. Now you just have to wait until the second phase of our plan."

The second phase. Just those three words give me a sick feeling of dread. I swallow hard and follow her.

There's a soft puff of lavender right as I'm about to walk through the door into the kitchen. Turning my head, I see the thing, a white little orb with a soft blue light.

Without thinking about what I'm doing, I stop, turn. Unplug it.

"— I just want you to be careful. I'll let you know when I need you again, but until then, go home, Ricky. Stay away. Hell, give me the key, wherever you got it from."

Not a chance.

Instead of responding, I head into the kitchen. Eloise pulls a bottle of wine from the refrigerator. Pops the cork. Pours a full glass and leaves the open bottle on the counter. She reaches back in and pulls out a pan covered in tinfoil. I don't move as she rips off the cover and puts the entire thing in the microwave.

Spaghetti.

My stomach rumbles.

"I just want to make sure she's okay. That she moves in okay." I'm by the window, and I tug at the blind again to look for Tina. *Where is she?*

"She's fine." Eloise's words are sharp. "I didn't ask you to stalk her."

"I'm not stalking her." How dare she insinuate something like that? "I'd never stalk her."

"Right." She takes a sip, but her eyes never leave my face. "What would you call what you're doing, then?"

"Protecting her. Watching her. Like you asked."

She laughs, and I feel my hands clench into fists. Eloise is supposed to be on my side, but then why is she acting like this? Why is she acting like I'm stupid or don't know what I'm talking about? I'm the one who lived with Tina and saw how much help she needs.

"Okay, Romeo. Why don't you go on back to the apartment? You don't need to be here. I'll call you when it's time."

Her words echo in my head, and I close my eyes. "Fine." The word is bitter in my mouth. "Fine, I'll go home."

"Good. That's smart, Ricky."

"Tina will be home soon."

She pauses. "She probably will."

"I'll see her there."

Eloise nods. "I'll be in touch."

I spin away from her, no longer able to spend another second in this lavender house, with my cousin staring at me like I'm the bad person here, like I'm the issue, when I'm the reason Tina is nice and safe, and protected. My heartbeat thuds in my ears as I hurry through Eloise's home, out the back door, not even bothering to close it behind me, then to my car.

It fires up with a roar.

Throwing it into reverse, I don't look over my shoulder as I whip it around and angle it back down the driveway. Eloise doesn't know how much I've done for her. She wanted me to keep an eye on Tina, and I did that, and I'd do it again.

She might not want me to now, but how can she stop me?

Tina needs me. She's moving out and thinks she's going to be fine on her own, but she needs me.

Eloise wants me to just go home and wait for the next stage of the plan.

But Eloise is wrong. She's wrong, she's wrong, she's wrong, she's wrong.

26

TINA

The key is heavy in my hand, which is silly, because it probably weighs less than a few quarters, but I still heft it, enjoying how serious this moment is.

It's really happening. Luke and I are going to have our own place. I won't have to worry about making rent, or Ricky, or whether or not someone is going to be too loud and wake up my son. Yes, there will be other worries, like paying the mortgage and keeping the yard free of weeds.

I'll have to keep an eye on the roof and hope it doesn't leak like I've had happen in other places I've lived. If there are any repairs to be made, then those will be on me. But I'm ready.

"You ready, buddy?" I hold the key up to show Luke, but he's plopped down in the front yard and is digging in the dirt. So much for any fanfare. Turning back to the door, I insert the key. Turn it.

Open the door.

Home. I'm home. Yes, it smells a little funny, and I definitely will want to finish ripping off the wallpaper that remains in some of the rooms, but it's home, and it's mine, and I couldn't be happier. After casting one glance over my shoulder at Luke to ensure he's not going to wander off, I walk into the kitchen and put my purse down on the counter.

Here's where I'll put a little table for the two of us to eat breakfast. Over there, under the windows, I'll tuck the sofa. It'll be perfect for catching light from the setting sun so we can snuggle up together and read before bed.

That's one thing we'll need to get — another bed. I'll let Luke sleep on the one we have now and see about getting a sofa from Habitat for Humanity for myself. I can sleep on that until we get a second bed. It's not ideal, but sometimes, as a parent, you have to do what you have to do.

It's a shame we can't sleep here tonight, that we have to spend another night under the same roof as Ricky, but the countdown has started, and that's more than enough to keep me going. I reach the front door and am about to call to Luke.

But he's not there.

"Luke?" His name comes out as a question, and I clear my throat. "Luke! Where are you?"

No answer. No giggle to clue me in to the fact that he's hiding and thinks he's being funny. No flash of color as he runs away from me on his chubby little legs.

"Luke!" Fear washes over me, and I hurry to the edge of the porch, my eyes searching the dark spot under the bushes by the front gate. He was *right here*. Where could he have gone? I turned my back on him for just a moment, just five seconds, if that, and he disappeared.

Guilt fills my lungs, making it difficult for me to breathe.

One moment of happiness, that's all I wanted, all I had, and then I messed it all up.

The thought that I'm the reason my son is missing, that I looked away and lost him, makes me choke. I take a wobbly step down the stairs, then another, then hit the ground at a dead run, tearing around the side of the house.

This is where I want to put a swing set for him. I know how expensive they are, but my monthly mortgage payments are even less than I thought they would be.

She works magic.

There's no reason why I can't save up for one, no reason why he can't have his very own private park here — except for the fact that he's gone.

"Luke!" I race around the back of the house, looping around it until I'm in the front yard. Bracing my hand on the thick bark of the tree in the front yard, I try to slow my breathing.

And then I hear it. *Him.* Luke. I hear his little voice, and I think for a second he's crying, but then I listen harder.

Laughing. He's laughing.

"Luke?" My voice is too loud, but still he doesn't answer. "Luke, where are you? Come out now!"

"Tina?"

I recognize that voice, I swear I do, but right now I'm too stressed out, and I can't put my finger on where I've heard it before. My heart is thudding hard in my throat as I run to the front gate. Luke has to be here, he has to. I can't live my life without my son, he's everything, and even though this house is going to be amazing, nothing will be worth living for if I don't have my boy.

"Momma?" Now it's Luke's turn to call my name, and I slow a moment, trying to wrap my mind around what I just heard. Is he upset? Is he scared? I can't tell if he's in pain or worried or happy, sometimes his voice is just so *flat*, so unreadable, even though I think there should be much more emotion packed into it so I can tell what my son is thinking.

My feet slam against the scrubby grass growing in the yard, and it's like the blinders I had on when we first looked at this place and then when I signed the papers just a short time ago fall away, and I see it for what it really is, and I see all the hard work it needs. It's not beautiful and perfect or home, but it can be, but only when Luke is okay.

"Luke!" I step through the open gate and grab him, sweeping him into my arms. Can he feel how hard my heart is beating? Does he even care? "Are you okay? Why did you go through the gate? What did you think you were doing?"

He squirms against me, and I let him go, finally looking at the owner of the voice that called out my name.

Eloise.

I knew I recognized it. I just couldn't put my finger on who was calling me, who might be standing here at my house when the only thing that mattered was making sure Luke was okay.

"Tina, I'm so sorry." Eloise practically trips over herself in her apology. "I was bringing something by, and Luke came to get the gate for me. We were talking for just a moment, but I never meant to scare you! I thought he could help me with the gate, and then we'd walk right up to your house."

I see her now, really see what she's carrying, and my heart drops. All of the adrenaline that had been coursing through my body, powering my muscles to do insane things like lift cars off my son if that's what it came to, disappears, and I suddenly feel weak.

I grab the fence for support. "You brought flowers." My voice is weak. Shamed. "And food?"

She finally smiles. The tension between the two of us is still there. I swear, I could touch it, could twist it into a rope and use it to strangle myself, but when she nods, I feel it start to break into smaller pieces.

"I had a feeling you wouldn't have everything you needed for your kitchen to be able to cook dinner, but I thought you'd want to have something to eat. So I made a big thing of spaghetti and meatballs and brought it with some garlic bread."

"Oh, gosh." I'm embarrassed now. My face burns, and the sweat that had broken out on my forehead feels like it's boiling on my skin. "I'm so sorry, I never would have freaked out if I'd known he was talking to you. I thought... well, it doesn't matter what I thought, I just —"

"You're in a new home and a new environment and you thought something happened to Luke." Her words are firm, and her eyes never leave mine. "If you hadn't freaked out a little bit, I would have wondered what was wrong with you. I should have thought about what I was doing. I'm so sorry."

I take the dish of spaghetti from her. It's still warm, and my mouth waters when I think about how good it's going to taste. Now that my body understands I don't need to worry about Luke, I'm suddenly ravenous.

"No, you did nothing wrong." I look down at my son. "Hey, Luke, will you please take the garlic bread from Mrs. Eloise?"

"Yes!" He takes it, then sniffs the foil-wrapped package. "Yum!"

I laugh. So does Eloise. The fact that she doesn't seem angry at me makes me relax a bit more.

"Oh, and one more thing." She turns and points across the street to a large house that seems to tower over mine.

I glance up at it, surprised at how big it really is compared to mine, surprised at how I didn't notice how it seems to block out the sky, a monolith. I was just so wrapped up in my own little house.

"Jared is bringing over a card table and two folding chairs for you. You and Luke shouldn't have to eat on the floor your first meal here." She points, and I squint, trying to make out the figure walking down the driveway. "There he is. Oh, this is great, you can meet my husband."

Her husband. Right. This is good, because I have a feeling if I run into any problems around the house, Eloise will be more than happy to send him over. She seems like that kind of person.

A friend, maybe?

Is that too much for me to think?

"So if I run into problems with the new house..." I say, knowing I'm being forward, but not really caring. Women get it, and Eloise is the type of woman to lift others up. I know she's going to see me being forward as just trying to take care of myself and Luke.

Besides, she already offered to help me move.

"Oh, you just give him a call. Jared. He'll be more than happy to pop over and help you out, although I don't know how handy he really is. He spends a lot of his time locked up at work or in his home office. But yeah, I'll make sure you get his cell in case there's an emergency. In fact, here." She digs in her pocket and pulls out a business card, leaning over and tucking it in my front pocket.

The moment feels intimate.

I knew we were friends.

I grin at her. "Thanks. Seriously. It sounds like he's a lot more trustworthy than my roommate."

Eloise laughs. Does she seem nervous? Whatever expression was on her face is there and gone as she adjusts the bouquet of daisies. "Yeah, I think you could say that. He's a good guy. I can't wait for you to meet him."

The figure draws closer. It looks like he's struggling a little bit with the chairs, but then he stops in the middle of the street and adjusts his grip, taking his time to ensure he has everything held close to his body so he doesn't drop it.

I stare at him, a little voice in the back of my mind working overtime as I try to figure out where I've seen him before.

Maybe he came into the bar where I worked before I started at the daycare.

Maybe I've seen him out grocery shopping. It's hard to tell, not until he gets a little closer.

Finally he does, stopping right in front of me and leaning the chairs on the fence so he can shake my hand.

"I'm Jared, your new neighbor," he says, his wide smile disarming, his dark eyes locked on mine. I take in his broad shoulders, his tousled dark hair, the bit of stubble growing in after he shaved this morning.

I'm going to throw up.

I have to force myself to reach out and take his hand. Shake it. Try to smile at him.

My heart beats out a fast rhythm. Sweat breaks out along the back of my neck. When I look at Eloise, she's grinning at me, a huge smile that reaches her eyes, one that's probably supposed to put me at ease.

He stares at me. There's a flicker of something behind his eyes, then it's gone, but I know what it was.

Don't say a thing, please, for the love of God, don't say a thing; just pretend we've never met, that this is the first time, that you and I weren't —

"I'm Tina," I say, finally pulling my hand back so I can gesture at Luke. "And this is Luke."

I manage to say all of this with a lump in my throat. I manage to say it all while studiously avoiding the way Eloise is standing there, a grin on her face, looking between the two of us like she can't be happier about how this is going.

Somehow, I manage to say all of this to Luke's father.

27

ELOISE

Jared and I are getting ready for bed, the two of us at our matching bathroom sinks. He's washing his face, the sound of his hands rasping across his stubble making my heart flutter.

So many years I've known the man and slept next to him, and still it's little things like this that make me want to wrap my arms around him and lead him to bed. He doesn't even know he's so sexy, or at least I didn't think he did.

Until I found out the truth.

I bend over the sink, holding my hair back, and spit out my toothpaste. Has Jared been different since we went across the street for him to welcome Tina? I don't know if he has, but he's always been really good at holding his cards close to his chest. He's a tricky one to figure out, that much is for sure.

But he remembers her. There's no way he doesn't.

I rinse, then spit again, finally turning and staring at my husband while he pats his face dry with a towel. They're new, fluffy and white, and I bought them in a desperate attempt to turn at least some part of our home into a relaxing spa, but right now they seem laughable.

How in the world am I supposed to relax when my husband cheated on me?

I clear my throat. "What did you think of the new neighbor? Tina?"

"What do I think of her?" He wads the towel up and tosses it by the sink even though I'm standing right here, even though I've asked him half a dozen times to hang it back up where he found it so it doesn't get all gross.

"Yeah, like, I don't know. What do you think?"

He pauses for a moment. The silence is thick, but I'm not about to be the one to break it.

"I think she looks like a single mom who's on her last leg, if you want my honest opinion. And you said she works at a daycare? How in the world did she afford that place? I just hope she doesn't lower the value of the other homes here. Especially ours." He doesn't look at me while he speaks, he's too busy putting lotion on his face, carefully rubbing it on his skin, making sure to pat around his eyes.

"I told you, it's a good program we're running." No way in hell I'll ever fess up to footing her entire down payment. Jared doesn't know, and he doesn't need to know. In his mind, we have so much money that we don't even need a budget, and while that's definitely true, it's that same lackadaisical attitude that allowed me to move so much into a private account for this very purpose.

"Well, I hope she can make her payments." Satisfied with the way he looks, he turns to me, but his eyes don't meet mine. "You ready for bed?"

I am, and I'm actually exhausted to the point that just

standing here talking to him is enough to make me want to cry, but I'm not finished with this conversation.

He remembers her. It had been there when he saw her — when he really saw her. I know it was. Just a flicker of emotion behind his eyes, there and gone before anyone could point it out.

"Hey, are you okay?" Jared's voice pulls me out of the chasm of my thoughts. He links his fingers through mine and steps closer to me, kissing me on the forehead.

I have to fight to keep from pulling away from him. Ever since I found out his secret, I don't want his hands on me.

But ever since I found out the truth, it's been more and more important that he not know something is up. That I know what he did.

"You're deep in your thoughts, Eloise. I know the look you get when something is going on. Talk to me."

How good a liar is my husband?

"I'm just really tired," I finally say. "It's one thing to sell a house to someone with a lot of assets and income, but another entirely to get someone like Tina into a home. But she deserves it, don't you think? Raising that little boy by herself?"

He pauses. I'm reading into the silence growing between us, trying to tell if it's sweet and innocent, or dangerous and thorny, when he speaks.

"What's his name again? The boy?"

Oh, God, I have to tell my husband the name of his bastard son. I have to whisper it into his chest and let it take root in his heart. Even though this was the plan the entire time, to make them meet, to force him into realizing what he did, I wanted him to learn more about Luke on his own.

"It's Luke."

"Luke. Good name. I think that one was on our short list for a while, wasn't it?"

Yes, it was. It was on the list, for more than a while, for the entire time we thought we might be able to get pregnant — thought *I* might be able to get pregnant, but then that ship sailed and the list got shoved to the back of the junk drawer with all the rubber bands and half-used pads of sticky notes.

"Yeah, I think it was." I force myself to pull away from him. Look him in the eyes. I'm looking for deceit, but I don't see any there. *God, he's good.* "I think I'm ready for bed now. I'll probably sleep like the dead."

"You want some sleeping pills just in case?" He picks up the little orange bottle he keeps by the sink and rattles it at me like I'm a stray cat he's trying to entice with some kibble. "There's nothing wrong with using science to help take the edge off."

"No, I'm good. I have a pretty good feeling I'm going to pass out right now, but thanks. Feel free to take one if you need to."

"Oh, I only need these when I'm really stressed." He puts the bottle back. "And I have nothing to be stressed out about right now. I have this incredible house and an amazing wife. I love my job. I love our little family. What more could I want?"

"I can't think of a single thing."

We walk to bed, him pulling the crisp white sheets back and helping me in before he walks around the other side.

He clears his throat. "Alexa, turn off the lights."

There's a soft *boop,* and we're cast into darkness. I roll over to face the window. From here I can see the little house across the street, the little guest house where my husband's son and the woman he had an affair with live. I want to roll over and look at Jared, want to see if there's worry etched in his face, but there's no reason to.

My husband is a very good liar. He's great at composing his face and making sure nobody knows what he's thinking, but only when he's had time to think things over. When life comes at him fast, out of left field, that's when it all falls apart for him.

I may not have known he had an affair for a long time after it happened, but that's because he had time to figure out how to keep his face calm. How to keep his lies hidden.

That's why I wanted him to see Tina without any preamble. He didn't have time to compose his face, to work up a lie, to convince himself he could hide his secret from me.

I saw it there, just for a moment.

He remembers.

And that means it's time for the next step in my plan.

I have to make my husband want to rekindle his affair. I have to get the neighbor to fall for him.

It's insane, but I need to drive him from my bed to hers.

And I have the perfect idea of how I'm going to do just that.

28

TINA

I go through the motions of getting Luke ready for bed in our apartment. As much as I'd like to be in our new home tonight, there wasn't any way could stay there tonight, not without our bed moved.

We ate dinner at the new house, and I'm just grateful Luke was so excited about our new home and the spaghetti that he didn't notice I was quiet.

The food tasted like paste. The air was stale, hard to breathe. And even my son's relentless chatter about how exciting everything was wasn't enough to pull me from my funk.

Eloise, the woman who helped me buy this home, the woman I trust and think I could really enjoy spending time with, the woman who went out on a limb for me and saved me from Ricky and this terrible apartment I have to sleep in until we finish moving out... she's married to Luke's father.

And she has no idea.

There's no way she knows, not with the smile she was giving us both, not with how eager she was to give me Jared's business card so I could reach out to him if I needed anything. Right now the card is on my bedside table, an accusation of what the two of us did, a sick reminder of how hard I looked for him after he ended things.

After I found out I was pregnant.

I was so stupid.

Tears burn my eyes, and I wipe them away before kissing Luke on his forehead and closing the bedroom door. I need to get some rest too, but right now I'm too wound up to relax enough to fall asleep. I can't seem to focus on anything, and I know I'll just toss and turn for hours, keeping Luke awake, if I go to bed with him.

So I wander back into the living room. Ricky's out with friends, which probably means he's at a bar and won't be home for hours. Paula is in the kitchen, washing her dishes. She's humming to herself. I collapse on the sofa, press my face into a pillow.

Let out a sob.

Ever since I had my affair with Jared, I thought he was the one. Now I see how foolish I was to think a man like him could ever want a woman like me. He didn't even tell me his real name, let alone the fact that he was married.

Although... I sit up and grab my phone from next to me, eager for answers. Maybe they weren't married then. Maybe they hadn't met. It's possible he knew Eloise already, which is still really crappy of him, but he didn't have a ring on his finger. I know men do take them off, hide them in the pocket of their jeans, but still.

He didn't seem like the kind of guy to do something like that.

And when he broke it off with me, he didn't mention anyone else. He mentioned wanting to focus on his company. That he didn't want to ruin his company's reputation.

That I wasn't good enough for him.

"Yeah, cause you really know anything about what kind of guy he really is." I mutter the words to myself angrily, then sink my fist into the cushion, dropping my phone back on the sofa.

"What are you going on about?" Paula appears next to me, a beer in her hand. She tips the bottle towards me, but I shake my head. "You're muttering. That's not an attractive quality."

"Ugh." I drop my head into my hands. Maybe I should have just gone to bed even if I might have woken up Luke. I wouldn't be sleeping but at least I wouldn't have to try to explain what's going on to my roommate. Pretty Paula, with raccoon eye makeup who waits tables at the grill down the road, doesn't have problems with men.

Because she doesn't date them.

"Men." I drop the one word I know will cause her to roll her eyes.

She does. "Ugh. Men. Right? You don't have to tell me twice. It's why I only date women. There's still drama, but it's of a different caliber. What's really going on?"

I could tell her. I could come totally clean with Paula. Even though we're not best friends by any means, she's never given me any reason not to trust her. She tells me secrets all the time, in fact, and always gets in Ricky's way when he comes home after a late night of drinking with a glint in his eye.

"What if I told you I met Luke's dad?" Each word is heavy, but I manage to get them out.

"Get out. Really?" She has a death grip on her beer and

takes a swig. Her eyes never leave mine. "Where? How do you know it's him? Are you sure, or are you projecting?"

"That was one time." I take a deep breath and press down hard on the pillow on my lap. I'm not going to punch it again with her sitting right here, but I still need to do something with my hands. "It's him. I just know it. I remember his face and his hands and, well, he looks just like Luke."

She cocks an eyebrow at me but doesn't say anything.

"Okay, fine." Anger rushes through me. Even though I know it's misplaced for me to be mad at her, I can't help it. I want her to believe me, and for that to happen, she has to see proof. Leaning forward, I snatch my phone from the coffee table. "Let me show you."

Now that I know who he is, he's easy to find. I know Eloise's last name and his first name, and a quick Google search takes me right to the company he owns. JJones PR and Marketing. It's in the most luxurious building downtown, and I have a very good feeling his office will be on the top floor, overlooking everyone, allowing him to live out his perfect life.

How did I not know he was right here in town? I have to blame my laser focus on Luke and work, and the fact that I hardly get out anywhere that isn't the park or the library.

"Here." I type in his name and click on a recent photo. He's at a gala of some sorts, dressed in a tux, Eloise looking stunning on his arm. She's staring at him while he laughs, his grin an exact replica of Luke's when he really gets going.

Paula holds her beer between her legs and takes the phone from me. "Whoa," she breathes, using two fingers to enlarge the photo for a better look. "He does look like Luke, but how can you be sure? Did he say anything?"

"No." I have to fight the urge to take my phone back from

her. "No, he just brought over a table and some chairs for the two of us tonight, but he didn't linger." I hate the way my eyes burn again when I think about how his gaze slipped over me.

Like I wasn't there. Like I didn't matter.

Except for just a moment when I saw something behind his eyes.

"Wait, he what? Where did you see this guy?" Now I have her full attention. Her beer is forgotten, and she leans forward to get a better look at me.

"He's my new neighbor." I almost choke on the words, but there's more for me to say, more that I'm sure will cause her to gasp in shock. "He's married to my Realtor."

"Get. Out." Her mouth drops open, and she finally leans back, resting against the arm of the sofa. It squeaks when she does, and I'm suddenly, irrationally angry.

I'm angry at this terrible little apartment with furniture that needs to be replaced. I'm angry at her for looking at me like I just grew another head and she doesn't know what to do with me. I'm angry at Jared and at the little house I just bought, and I'm angry at Eloise for being married to the man who lied to me about his name and then gave me a son.

"What the hell am I supposed to do now?" I'm fighting to keep my voice low. The last thing I want is to wake Luke up and have him see me this upset.

"You're sure it's him? Do you have any proof?"

"Like what?"

"DNA. Or him admitting it."

I shake my head. "There's no way he's going to suddenly admit he's Luke's father."

"Is that what you want?"

I don't have an answer for that.

"He's rich, right?"

I nod.

"Can you imagine the child support?" Her eyes are wide, and she stares at me like I just won the jackpot. "Seriously, Tina, think about it. You wouldn't have to worry about a thing. Your bills would be taken care of. You'd have an actual savings account."

I would. I can't imagine what it would be like to check my balance without crossing my fingers that it won't be in the negative. I could fix my car. I could buy the furniture we're going to need for the new house. I could have a life. Luke could —

But then I come to my senses, and I shake my head. "No, I can't do that. You don't know Eloise. She's amazing and kind and —"

"Married to a cheater." Paula leans forward and snaps her fingers in my face to get my attention. "Think this through, Tina."

"I don't know if they were married when he and I... were together. They might not have been."

"I guess you need to find out, don't you?" She looks satisfied and finally takes another pull from her beer. "Besides, he told you he was single. You did nothing wrong."

"But how would I even know for sure? It's not like he's going to just tell me the truth. There's no way."

"DNA test." Her words are snappy, like they've been locked and loaded and she's just been waiting for me to ask the question.

I blink at her. "What?"

"A DNA test. He's your neighbor, right? Get yourself invited over there and steal something with his DNA. Bada-bing, bada-boom, you'll know if he's Luke's dad."

"It would destroy Eloise." I'm hung up on that, and I know it's silly, but I really like her. "You don't know what she's like, Paula. There's no way anyone else would have worked this hard to help me get a home. She gave up her commission." I say it like it's a big deal. It is, to me.

But not to Paula. "Don't care. It's nothing personal against her. You need money to raise Luke and give him what he deserves, right? So get it from his biological dad. At least do a DNA test, and then you'll know for sure. If this guy isn't Luke's dad, you can move on."

"But if he is, I can get some money from him." My voice is flat, but there's a bubble of something growing in my chest.

Excitement, I think. But it's mixed with something.

Worry, over hurting Eloise. I don't want to hurt her, but I have to be a good mother, and that means putting Luke first.

"Think of the money." Paula prods me in the arm.

I am thinking of the money. But I'm also thinking about the nights Jared — *Jared, not Damon* — and I spent in bed together. Jared, the man I fell for, who broke my heart and watched me cry while he did it.

But how can I do that to Eloise?

She'll hate me. She'll turn her back on me, and I want her to be my friend. I would get money, but lose Eloise.

Drag Luke through the mud.

"I don't think I can do it." I shake my head, my jaw tight. Paula looks as surprised at my admission as I feel, but what choice do I have?

I'm going to pretend I don't know who Jared is. I'll pretend I've never seen the man before in my life. I'll distance myself, make sure he can't put two and two together.

I have a job I love. A house. A son I'd do anything for.

What if Jared tried to take him from me?

The thought fills me with fear.

"Luke is all that matters. I won't do this to him. To Eloise."

Would it make my life easier? Sure, it would. Money makes everything easier.

Unless it hurts Luke.

I'll do anything for Luke.

That's why I have to keep him as far away from his father as possible.

29

ELOISE

I've always loved taking a day off work when I've sold a house. Getting to lounge in bed and enjoy my morning without a rush to the office with everyone else heading to Main Street has always been appealing. And now's my time.

Even though I was fully expecting the floodgates to open now that I've helped a single mom buy a home, nobody else has reached out to me yet. That's fine, because Tina was the one I really wanted to help. Of course, I'll work hard with anyone else who walks into my office.

I have to keep up appearances, after all.

I've done everything I can to set myself up as the loving Realtor, the woman who wanted a child and loves her husband, and when everything falls apart here soon, I fully expect to have the entire town on my side. So if that means I need to keep working with people who can't actually afford a home just so I can keep up appearances, I'll do it.

And I'll do it with a smile on my face.

But this morning is all for me.

Jared's already in the shower when I flip back the covers and roll out, fully intending to wander downstairs, make some coffee, then bring it back to bed with me. Maybe I'll even spill it. He'll have a fit when he sees coffee all over his expensive sheets, but that's the point.

His getting angry at me will just force him across the street even faster.

Leaning against the counter while I wait for the coffee to brew, I check my email. No new messages that need an immediate response. There's always work to do, but it can wait for a few hours. I just want some time to myself this morning.

To celebrate.

"So why not celebrate?" I murmur, grabbing the bottle of Kahlua from above the refrigerator and tipping some into my mug. I fill it the rest of the way with fresh coffee and store the bottle back where it goes so Jared doesn't see it and get on my case.

It's delicious. It's so good, in fact, that when my phone buzzes, I almost don't check it. I want so badly to enjoy this moment without any interruptions, but it buzzes again, then rings.

What the hell?

"Why are you calling me?" My voice is low as I answer. Bending a little, I use my shoulder to shield the phone. Even though I can still hear Jared thumping around upstairs, I don't want to clue him in to the fact that I have a call. Not on the phone he doesn't know about.

"I don't want to do this." Ricky sounds panicked. That's never a good sign with him. He needs to be kept even-keeled so I don't have to worry about him doing something stupid. His voice is high and tight.

First he sneaks into my house. Now he's backing out? This can't happen.

I have to get my key back from him. I should have demanded it when I first realized he had one, but I just wanted him calm.

Now, though, I have to talk him down off the ledge.

"Have you slept?" It's the first thought to cross my mind. Even without seeing my cousin, I know what he looks like right now. Worried. Exhausted. His eyes rimmed with red, his hand shaking as he tries to light his cigarette.

"Of course not. I've been awake. Making sure she's okay."

I knew it. Even though I know I should be worried about him doing something stupid right now, I knew moving him in with Tina would push her out of the apartment. It was my best option. My only option, really.

My cousin is frightening. He latches onto people. It was a gamble, that he would be the catalyst for her finally deciding to look for a new place to live, but a risk I was willing to take, because I didn't see how it couldn't work.

Creepy.

"So you, what? Sat up in the hall all night long to keep an eye on her?" When Ricky doesn't answer, I know I'm correct. "Where are you now? I can come get you."

"No, I'm fine. I'm in my room. She's been packing, Eloise. I don't want her to pack."

"Don't say my name," I hiss. Heat rushes to my cheeks. *What if Tina hears him?* "This is the plan, Ricky. Remember the plan. Remember the money."

He's a loose cannon. I thought I could control him, but maybe that was stupid of me. While I wait for him to answer, I take a sip of my coffee. It's just what I need, the Kahlua smooth on my tongue.

"The money, right." Ricky exhales hard.

"Hey, do you have any sleeping pills?" It's a long shot because I know my cousin has trouble hanging on to anything he can sell. Sleeping pills might not fetch a high price on the street, but I wouldn't be surprised if he'd traded them for something a little stronger. Everything on the street has value, and Ricky lets it all slip right through his fingers when he's jonesing.

"Yes." He answers too quickly for his response to be honest.

I sigh. "Okay, how about this? I'll head out of here in a little bit and bring you something. You need to get some sleep, or you're going to crack up. Can you stay in your room and not leave the apartment until I get there?"

Silence.

"Ricky, can you stay there until I bring you something?"

"Yes." He sounds like a little kid, petulant and caught with his hand in the cookie jar. "Yes, I can stay here. But you don't understand, you don't know what it's like to know she's leaving."

So much for lounging around the house.

I hang up. Tuck my phone into my pocket. When I turn around, I slam right into Jared.

"Good morning, wife," he says, lightly grabbing my right wrist and holding it in place as he looks me in the eyes. "Where are you off to so early this morning?" He sounds like he always does in the morning, a little sleepy, very interested in what I'm going to be doing that day.

I swallow hard and slap a smile on my face. Does it reach the corners of my eyes? I can't tell, not without taking too long to try to figure it out.

"I have another client waiting on me," I lie, looking him

right in the eyes. "And Denise needs me to bring by some more flyers about the program I'm running. It probably isn't an emergency, but when people are trying to move so they can get out of a bad situation, then I want to hurry and not leave them waiting."

"You're so kind." He hasn't let go of my wrist. "Did you leave me any coffee?"

"Sure did." Can he smell the alcohol in my mug? I don't want him to ask to take a sip, so I lift it to my lips and drink the rest before he can say anything. Tugging lightly on my wrist, I try to step away from him.

He doesn't let me go.

I feel my heart rate kick into high gear. Swallowing hard, I chuckle. "You're going to have to let me go, Mr. Jones, if I'm going to be able to take care of people who need it."

His eyes are dark. They're locked on me. Finally, with a nod, he steps back, dropping his hand down to his side. "You'd better run off, then, Eloise. Sounds like you have a busy morning already lined up."

"I do." Grateful now, I rinse my mug in the sink, then put it in the top rack of the dishwasher. "What about you? Busy morning?"

"Always." His back is to me now as he busies himself pouring a travel cup of coffee. I watch him, how his button-up shirt pulls across his wide shoulders, how he moves fluidly, like he's so comfortable in his skin that nothing fazes him. It's easy to see why someone like Tina — or anyone, if I'm being honest — would fall into bed with my husband.

My question is why he kept going back to her. How could he keep their affair going for months before ending it? I want to ask him these things, but there's no way to do it right now, and get what I want.

Maybe at the end. Maybe when he's already lost.

"Tell me what you know about our new neighbor." His voice is strong.

Jared's back is still to me, which means he can't see the look of surprise that crosses my face.

"What about her?" I'm casual. Unbothered. On the inside though, I'm screaming. I need to get to Ricky. I need to prevent him from doing something stupid.

And then it hits me. Right now, while I'm having this conversation with my husband, it hits me that I might ruin everything. If I show up to Tina's place and give Ricky sleeping pills, then she'll know I know him. Everything will fall apart.

I close my eyes. Pain shoots through my head, the beginning of a migraine, but I have to ignore it. I have to figure out how to get Ricky off the ledge without Tina knowing our relationship.

And I have to finish this conversation with my husband.

"I don't know," he says, turning and leaning against the counter to get a better look at me. "She just doesn't seem like she belongs here, does she? In the neighborhood?"

"I think she'll be great." *I have to get out of this conversation. Call Ricky back. Get him out of the apartment so I can meet him.* "She seems nice, and it'll be kinda fun to have a kid running around for once."

His eyes never leave mine. He nods; then it's like a switch flips in him. I swear, if I weren't looking right at him, I wouldn't believe he could do it. He changes from staring at me like he's trying to read my mind, to completely relaxed. Comfortable.

"Shame it couldn't be our kid running around, right?" He's in front of me now and wraps his arms around me, pulling me to him for a hug. I feel stiff, but I force myself to relax into him. "I know you always wanted that. Kids."

"We did," I say, but that's the only thing I can say because my brain is screaming at me to get out of here. "We did, Jared. But things don't always work out the way we want them to."

He kisses me. His lips are demanding on mine, and I have to kiss him back, have to keep him thinking everything is fine, even though I want to scream at the sensation of his tongue dancing against mine. The urge to bite down on it is almost overwhelming, but I manage not to. I put my hands on his chest, to let him kiss me deeply before stepping back from him.

"I love you, Eloise. You're my person."

"And you're mine." I hold his gaze. If he knows something is going on, then he's good. Better than I thought, better than I am. "I'll see you after work?"

"I look forward to it." He throws me a wink. "Don't get too busy at work that you show up late, darling. I'll be waiting."

With that, he turns and leaves the kitchen. It feels like he's taken all of the air in the house with him, and I exhale hard, bending over and grabbing my thighs as I inhale again.

I know he recognizes Tina. There's just no way in hell he doesn't.

Now I have to push them together. Make sure everyone in town knows about them.

But first I have to take care of Ricky. He can't be a loose end.

30

RICKY

I'm exhausted, but pacing is keeping me awake. Back and forth, back and forth, each step making the floor squeak as I pass that one place in the hall where there's a board so loose I can actually feel it bounce a little under my weight.

Back and forth.

Back and forth.

I wrote down everything I was thinking; then I ripped it out of my diary and tore it up, just like I was taught, just so nobody could ever really know what I'm thinking.

But still I can't settle my thoughts.

There's a sheen of sweat on my forehead, and I wipe it away before checking my phone. Eloise should be here by now, shouldn't she? She's not going to leave me hanging, I don't think, but she's not here, and I feel like I'm coming out of my skin.

"Excuse us." It's Tina, her voice just loud enough to break through my thoughts, and I gasp and turn, locking eyes with her. Then look down at Luke. He's gripping her hand, his eyes wide, his thumb inching slowly to his mouth. I've heard Tina telling him over and over to stop sucking his thumb, that she'll take him out for ice cream when he does, but he does it when he's nervous.

Then I remember she said something to me.

"Sorry." I step out of the way. "I'm waiting for someone."

"Great." She gives me a nod, pulls Luke closer. They start to inch around me, her hand reaching out for the front door, but I'm not ready to let her go.

"It's a friend," I tell her. I want her to stay and talk to me. If I can't have the pills I need to sleep, then I might as well talk to her. She's better than sleeping, anyway. She's more fun and interesting.

And pretty.

"That's great, Ricky." Her hand is on the door, but it's locked, and she sighs, flicking the lock to the side with a loud *click.*

"A girl. She's a friend who's a girl." Why won't she look at me and stop and talk to me? I want her to stay here with me or at least ask questions about what friend is coming over, but she doesn't seem to care. She gives another nod, her hair falling down around the side of her face so I can't read her expression, then the door is open, and she shuttles Luke through it.

It slams shut.

Cold air wraps around me.

I wince.

"A friend who's a girl," I mutter, yanking my phone from my pocket. It's not the Eloise-issued phone, not the one I'm supposed to use when reaching out to her, but that one's in my room, and I'm in a hurry. She's saved in this one, though, and I tap her name, then the green button that pops up.

It rings once. Twice. Then the third ring cuts off halfway through, but I don't give her a chance to say anything before I'm speaking.

"Where are you? I need you here, and you said you were coming, and you're not here."

"Why are you calling me on this phone?" There's venom in her voice, and I recoil, leaning against the wall. I look at my phone, pulling it away from my ear for just a moment so I can make sure I'm really connected to Eloise, that I'm talking to her, not to someone else.

"I just need to sleep." The words sound whiny even as I say them, but there's no taking them back now. She knows I need to sleep, she knows how hard this is on me, yet she's taking her time.

A sigh. "Meet me in the parking lot."

There's a beep, and she's gone.

"Dammit." It's chilly out, I know that from when Tina opened the door and left me, but I don't want to go back to my room for a coat. My T-shirt is thin, with holes. It's for sleeping, not for going outside, but I need the pills.

I walk outside and stand on the small balcony outside our door. It has a metal grate, and the metal is cold on my bare feet. Shivering, I pull the door closed behind me as a car turns into the parking lot.

Eloise.

I'm moving faster now, practically running to talk to her. Before she can kill the engine and get out, I'm at her door, waiting.

When she opens it, I'll have to step back out of her way, and I do, a rock digging into the bottom of my foot.

"Dammit." Bracing myself on the side of her car, I lift my

foot and flick it off. When I put it back down on the ground, I finally look at my cousin.

Her mouth is small. Tight. Even her perfectly plucked eyebrows look thinner than normal. Her cheeks are bright red, her eyes squinting.

I take a step back.

"Did you bring the sleeping pills?" I hold out my hand. Wind tears through the parking lot, making my shirt whip against my torso, and I shiver.

Eloise is in a bright red jacket. If the wind bothers her, she doesn't show it. Her hair doesn't even move with the breeze; she must have so much hairspray in it.

"I have them." She pulls a bottle from her jacket pocket and rattles it at me. I'm so tired I want to yank it from her and down a few of them right now, but she pulls it back, tucking it closer to her body like she can read my mind. "But you can't call me on your phone. And you have to leave Tina alone."

I scowl. How dare she say Tina's name?

She raises an eyebrow. "You want the money, don't you?"

I have to answer her. "Yes."

"Good. And that means you need to let me take control from here. I'll let you know when you're needed again. Ricky, you can't keep sticking your neck in places where it doesn't belong. You need to listen to me. Follow directions. You could ruin this."

She holds the bottle out, and I snatch them. God, I'm so tired. This might even be a hallucination from lack of sleep. It's just so hard to sleep when I know Tina is on the other side of the wall, curled up in her bed, just some drywall separating us.

"... you slept?"

"What?" I blink at her. The picture of Tina curled up in her bed disappears.

"When's the last time you slept?"

"I don't know."

But I think I do know. I've caught little catnaps here and there, but I don't think I really slept hard since the night I passed out on the sofa. And before that? Probably around the time I moved in.

"Get some rest. Stay away, Ricky. No coming to my house, no following Tina around. You keep your distance until I'm ready for you, got it?"

I nod. It's the right thing to do when she brought me the pills I need, but I don't agree with what she's saying.

She wants me to stay away from Tina, but how am I supposed to do that when she's so amazing? Maybe this all started out as Eloise's plan to get rich, but there are more things to life than money, right?

I think about Tina. Her gentle smile. The way she twists her hair around her finger when she's nervous. Her singing to Luke in the bathtub. The smell of her shampoo as she walks by me.

I have to see her again. She's been moving out, but I'll go visit her.

I know where she lives.

Eloise's eyes narrow as she looks at me. "Do you have my house key with you? I want it back, Ricky."

"I don't." My fists pulse.

She sighs. "Ricky, stay away. The money will be worth it in the end." Eloise nods at me, then gets back in her car. She pauses before closing the door. "Just sit tight."

The door slams.

The money will be worth the wait.

Her words echo in my head.

The money will be worth the wait.

The money will be worth the wait.

The Tina will be worth the wait.

Tina will be worth the wait.

31

TINA

With all the windows open in our new home, the cross breeze is amazing. I have everything we need for sandwiches in the refrigerator, and Luke and I just returned from another trip to our apartment with more of our things. We really need help this weekend getting our few pieces of furniture moved over, but it's been wonderful moving our clothes and books and toys into the house.

Doing it after I get off work is exhausting, but what choice do I have? I want nothing more than to get out of the apartment as soon as possible.

And this place is starting to feel like a real home.

Of course, it will feel more like a home when there aren't a few boxes in every room, but that doesn't really matter for one reason. Those boxes are ours. They're stacked along *our* walls. They're in *our* home. It fills me with more joy than I thought possible when I think about the fact that this is our home and nobody can take it from us.

Well, I guess the bank could if we missed payments, but that's not going to happen.

I'm even going to put a little extra on each monthly payment to try to get this place paid off sooner rather than later. It's going to feel amazing to make my final mortgage payment, and I'm already looking forward to that day even though it won't be for years.

Decades, even.

"Luke, come on out of your room!" I call, grabbing some plates from boxes and making sandwiches. Really, I just want to use those words, *your room*, because he's never had his own space like this. It's always been *our room*, and now he finally has somewhere he can go and hide and curl up without worrying about getting in my way.

It's amazing.

There's a momentary pause, and I stop, the knife slick with jelly above a slice of cheap white bread, but then there are his feet, pitter-pattering towards me, running across the empty house.

I smile.

He wasn't allowed to run in the apartment because there was always the chance we'd wake up our downstairs neighbor. Mr. Fred hated little kids and made that clear every single time we saw him out and about. Luke had to pretend like he didn't exist, which is really hard when you're a toddler.

So, should he be running in the house? Probably not, but I'm not going to stop him. I want him to enjoy himself and to feel at home here.

"What is it?" He tugs at my jeans, and I scoop him up and plop him on the counter to see what I'm making.

"PB and J with some chips. There's cookies too, for any

little good boys who eat their crusts." I poke him in the stomach with the handle of the knife, and he giggles. "Do you want to eat inside at our little table or have a picnic in the yard?"

"Picnic!" He throws his arms into the air, and I pick him up and deposit him back on the floor.

"Grab the blanket from my bed, okay? Then wait for me to go outside, and I'll join you at the front door in a minute. Lemonade or water?" It's a silly question, one I already know the answer to, but I still smile when he shouts back for lemonade.

Just a few finishing touches on our plates and I'll be ready to join him. I break open the store-bought cookies and put two on each plate, then dump some chips in between the cookies and sandwiches. It's a simple meal, and I really can't wait to start doing more actual cooking here, but I keep telling myself it's okay to wait until we're moved all the way in.

Right now, I just need to get some calories in both of us.

The front screen door opens and slams, and I stiffen, turning to look out the window above the sink. "Luke, wait for me!"

Ever since he opened the gate to let Eloise in the yard after we first moved in, I've been paranoid about letting him outside without me. I know there are gate locks I can buy to ensure he can't just open it on his own again, but that's just one more expense on the list of things we need.

He knows not to go outside without me. He's just excited. That doesn't mean anything bad is going to happen.

I move faster now, putting the plates and glasses of lemonade on a tray. I take time to rip two paper towels from the roll by the sink to use for napkins and stuff them under a plate before grabbing the whole thing and carefully carrying it to the front door. Thank goodness I used to wait tables as a teenager, or I might have dropped the tray maneuvering it to get outside.

"Luke?" I call as soon as I'm on the porch even though I see him in the yard, right by the front gate, carefully spreading the blanket out. He's standing in the middle of it while trying to get it to smooth out, and in just a moment he's going to get frustrated that it's not working the way he wants it to. "Just a minute, buddy, I'm coming."

I look down for a moment to navigate the stairs.

I swear, that's all I look away.

Just a moment.

And the sound of the gate swinging open makes my heart stop.

Not again.

"Luke!" I'm almost to the bottom of the stairs now, and I have to keep going, or I'm going to risk dropping the tray I put together for lunch. I'm hurrying, barely noticing when I hear voices.

But I do hear them.

It's a man, his voice low and deep, talking to my son, and at first I can't place who would be here, at my new home, talking to Luke like they're old friends.

I look up and freeze. Moving carefully, like an injured animal terrified of drawing attention from a hunter, I turn and put the tray down on the ground. The ice rattles in the glasses of lemonade, and the man standing in our yard talking to my son looks up.

Ricky.

"Tina, did you really think you could move away and not

say goodbye?" He smiles, baring his teeth more than anything.

I'm tense. Every cell in my body screams for me to run at Luke, to scoop him up, to carry him back inside the house and lock the doors. But I know there's no way I'm faster than Ricky. There's no way I could get Luke in the house where he'd be safe without Ricky beating me to the punch.

"Oh, I was going to say goodbye." My voice sounds breezy, and I hope Ricky can't hear the note of terror under my words. "Luke and I were just moving smaller boxes today. Tomorrow we were going to come get everything else, and I was going to say goodbye then."

He eyeballs me. Of course he doesn't believe me. The man is dangerous, but he's not stupid, and I have no reason to think he's not well aware of the fact that I'm terrified of him.

I walk up to the two of them and loop my arm around Luke's shoulder, pulling him to my side. He's silent, staring up at Ricky like he's unsure of what he's supposed to do.

"Well, why don't you invite me, and I can give you a proper goodbye?" Ricky reaches out like he's going to grab my arm, but I take a step back, and his hand falls down by his side. His eyes are dark and never leave mine.

He looks rough. There are huge dark circles under his eyes, and his hair is messed up like he just rolled out of bed. I saw him this morning when Luke and I were leaving, but maybe he slept again since then.

Whatever he's been up to, he looks dead on his feet.

"We're having a picnic." Luke takes this moment, when it feels like time is stopping and Ricky's eyes are going to bore straight through me, to speak up. "You can sit with us."

"Yes," I say, clearing my throat. Any time with Ricky is ill-advised, but better to have him outside, where he can't sequester me in a room by myself. At least out here, maybe a neighbor will be able to see us, keep an eye on us, tell if something is going on.

"I'm hungry though." Ricky takes a step towards the house. "Come with me and make me something to eat."

I tighten my grip on Luke's shoulders. "No, you can have mine though. I made a sandwich, but I'm not really hungry. Why don't you grab the tray and then join us on the picnic blanket?" I gesture behind me where I left the tray on the ground, but he's already moving towards it, knocking against my shoulder as we pass.

I exhale. Surely there are going to be neighbors out and about today, right? I know it's Friday afternoon, but recently in town there's been a big push for a four-day workweek. The garage where I take my car doesn't open on Fridays. There have to be other places where the staff will be off, wandering around.

But I highly doubt people who work with my mechanic are able to live in a neighborhood like this one.

"Just be nice," I whisper to Luke, guiding him to the picnic blanket. "Don't make him mad."

He nods but is clearly more focused on getting something to eat. I want to keep him right next to me, using me as a buffer between him and Ricky, but Luke sprawls on the blanket, making it impossible for me to protect him.

"This is nice." Ricky joins us, putting the tray down in the middle of the blanket and snatching a plate like he thought I wasn't really going to let him eat it. He yawns, stretches. Rubs his eyes like he's trying to wake up. "It's like we're a little family or something. What do you think, kid?" He directs the question at Luke but starts talking again without giving my son a chance to answer. "I'm just happy to be here. I don't know when you were going to invite me."

My stomach drops. "How did you find my address?"

He pauses. I swear, I can almost see the gears working as he thinks up an answer.

"I followed you." He takes a big bite of my sandwich and drains half a glass of lemonade. Luke is too busy munching to pay attention to the tension growing between us. "What, you think I was going to just let you leave? You and I have something, Tina."

I'm screaming on the inside but doing everything I can to keep my face calm. He can't know how terrified I am. I'm about to come out of my skin. I feel my stomach doing flips, and I want to scream.

A car drives down the road but doesn't stop. Why would it? We look like the perfect family celebrating the purchase of a new home. I wouldn't look twice.

"I think you should go." My fingers dig into my thigh as I speak. It's taking all my self-control to talk to him right now and not scream in his face. "Luke and I have errands to run."

"Leave him here with me." He finishes my sandwich and burps before eating a chip. "I'll hang out with the kid."

No.

I can't. I *won't*.

32

ELOISE

I'm in my office, looking over the paperwork for another applicant who wants to buy a house, and trying to ignore the dull ache in my chest.

My head is light. Swimmy. My stomach cramps.

I've finally set everything in motion. There's no turning back now. I moved her in across the street. Introduced her to Jared. He knows exactly who she is, I know he does.

I saw it on his face the other night and confirmed it yesterday morning. If I hadn't been looking for it, I might have missed it, but I'm onto Jared now. He can't keep lying to me and think he'll be able to get away with it any longer.

Slamming the folder shut, I stand and walk over to the window. This job is a farce. I wonder how much Harrison will rub it in my face when I tell him there's very little chance of most of the people looking for a home actually finding one. He'll love knowing he was right, that even though Jared threw his money at the real estate company for this position to be created, no amount of money can keep it afloat.

It's not like I'm going to pay the down payment for every person who walks into my office. Tina was a special case.

Is a special case.

And now word has gotten out I helped a single mom working at a daycare, of all places, get a lovely little starter home in Sugarloaf Estates, my phone is ringing off the hook. The follow-up article about me in the paper sold a lot of copies, I'm sure. I can tell by how many people it's bringing out of the woodwork.

And I can't help them all.

"Dammit." I make a fist and press it up against the glass, feeling the warmth from the outside air. I'm going to get what I want at home, but I have to figure out a way to walk away from this job without Harrison blaming it all on me.

Then I remind myself this is all part of the plan. Jared has what I want, and I'm going to take it as punishment for what he's done to me. Nobody will blame me from walking away from this job when my life is falling apart. Nobody will blame me for wanting to curl up in my house and mourn my husband.

But I won't really be mourning him, will I? And as long as I have people's sympathy, nobody will ever know.

If I divorce him, I lose it all thanks to a prenup so good even Johnnie Cochran himself couldn't help me. But if Jared dies, I get everything.

And I have it all planned out.

That's the thing about men that they don't realize. They all think they're so smart, that they control everything and make all the decisions, but women are the ones in control. I just have to make him think he's choosing his son and mistress over me.

Then the money is all mine.

"You gotta get your head in the game." I whisper the words to myself, trying to pump myself back up. It all seemed so simple, seemed like the right thing to do. But just look at the two of them.

How could anyone think the two of them belonged together?

Yet I have to make sure people think they're a couple. That way, when it all falls apart, she'll be easy to blame.

I don't want a cheater. I deserve more.

I make a fist and slam it into the top of my thigh. The result is a dull ache, and I do it again. Again.

Again.

I have to remember the facts.

Jared had an affair. He had a child with another woman. I might love him, might have stood there in white and told everyone watching that I would be married to him for the rest of my life, but they weren't the ones he ran around on. They weren't the ones he made into a fool.

So he got the baby we wanted. Too bad he won't be able to enjoy being a father. He's going to think he has it all; then I'm going to make sure he loses everything.

It's that simple.

"It's that simple," I repeat. I need to get my head back in the game and stop feeling bad for myself. This is the plan. It was well within my rights to live out the rest of my marriage knowing about Tina and Luke and not doing anything about it. I could easily stay married to Jared and never have pushed the two of them together, never forced their meeting.

Because, to be honest, what was the likelihood of them meeting again without me there to orchestrate it?

Slim to none, that's what.

But I did orchestrate it, and I've put things in motion now. There's no stopping it, and even if I could, I won't.

I have to see this through. Jared made his choice about what kind of life he wanted to have when he slept around, and now I get to take control and have the type of life I want.

One where I'm rich.

I'm almost ready to sit back down at my desk and make some calls to try to help the next woman I have waiting for me to help her buy a home when there's a knock on the door and it swings open.

It's Harrison. Even without seeing him standing in my door, I know it's him, because he's the only one cocky enough to just push through a door without waiting to be invited. It must be nice to have the confidence of a middle-aged man who has never been refused anything in his life.

I'm working on it. I'm just not there yet.

"Harrison." I turn and smile, gesturing for him to have a seat at my desk. "What can I do for you?"

He doesn't sit, so I don't either. Instead, I face him, crossing my arms and waiting for him to explain why he stopped in without any warning.

"This new program," he begins, and I feel my heart sink. "I don't know how sustainable it is. Not if you're going to give away your commission each time."

Even though I was just thinking the same thing, I'm not willing to go down without a fight. Not right now. Not until I have everyone in town on my side. Not until my husband is dead, Tina has taken the fall, and I'm rich.

"You agreed that we needed something like this in town to help first-time homebuyers who would otherwise fall through the cracks." I point at him, making sure he knows I'm well aware of his role in the creation of my new position.

I'm also well aware of the role Jared's money played, but we're not going to discuss that. Not right now.

"Right, but it's a losing proposition."

"So is being poor. These people are going to be punished even more than they already are if you don't let me help them." Even as I speak, though, I know there's a lie there. The only way I can help everyone who comes into my office wanting great terms on a loan, wanting to get away without a down payment, is to offer them the same deal I offered Tina.

And I can't keep skimming money from my personal accounts to pay for other people to have a home.

I'm not that generous.

"I'm not the one who made them poor." He sighs and runs his hand back through his hair, a sure sign he's more frustrated than he's letting on. I can't help but wonder what would have made him change his mind so quickly about this position.

Did Jared figure out what I'm up to and call Harrison to squash the program? He knows how everyone in town is rooting for me to succeed right now. Is he punishing me?

I don't think so. If he were onto me, he'd approach me. He wouldn't avoid the confrontation. So what is this all about?

Money. I bet it's all about Harrison wanting as much money as possible.

I clear my throat. "No, but you're part of a system that oppresses them and keeps them poor." I've found my soapbox, and I'm ready to get up on it. If I hadn't married Jared, I might very well be one of the people walking through this door, looking for help buying a home. I'm not turning my back on them. "Think about Airbnb. Think about rising home costs. Most people can't afford a home, and your offering this service through Harrison Realty will help them. People will love you."

"I won't love the hit to our bottom line."

I frown at him, trying to figure out exactly where he's coming from. His face is difficult to read, so I play my ace. "Jared funded this."

"He did. But he's not going to be happy to fund it forever, and neither of us took into consideration the fact that you would work for free. When you passed on your commission for that first home you helped someone buy, the company didn't get paid, either. It's not just you taking money out of your pocket, Eloise. I still have to pay everyone else who works here and keep the lights on. This," he says, waving his hand around to encompass my office, "is going to end up costing me a fortune if you keep passing on your commission. Tell me that's not going to continue, Eloise."

There are warning bells going off in my head, but I keep my tone steady when I respond. "So what would you have me do?" I point at my desk and am gratified he looks at the stack of folders sitting there waiting on me to work on. "Those are all clients looking for homes. Single moms. Men out of jail and trying to get back on their feet. What do you want me to tell them, or were you going to be willing to call them all and explain why I'm not going to help them?"

There's a pause. It's longer than normal, which is saying something. Harrison always chooses his words carefully, but the fact that he's still staring at me like I've grown another head makes me a little nervous.

"You can help them." He jabs a finger at the folders, then points it at me. "Just them. But that's it. Then we need to sit down and see how much of a hit this is going to be to the company's bottom line. I'm willing to help you, Eloise, but not if it hurts what I've built. Jared paid for your new office. Business cards. Advertising. He didn't pay for you to take money from our bottom line."

When he spins and stalks out of the room, it suddenly feels empty in here. I exhale hard and stumble to my desk, sitting down heavily in my seat.

I think the timeline just got moved up.

33

RICKY

This is the way it was always supposed to be.

Tina and Luke and me. Sitting on a picnic blanket. The three of us having a delicious meal Tina made for us, although I'm not entirely sure why she isn't eating. I'm sure she's hungry. Maybe there just isn't enough food in the house, or she doesn't have enough money to pay for more groceries.

For a moment I feel bad about eating her food, but she offered it and didn't seem to mind when I said I was hungry, and I am, I really am. I haven't had anything to drink since yesterday, and now my hands feel a little shaky and my vision is blurry, but I want to remember this time with Tina, and when I drink a lot, I tend to forget things.

I don't want to forget our first picnic together. I don't want to forget how happy she and Luke look, how willing he was to open the gate for me and let me in even though he doesn't really know me. That's Tina's fault because she was always so careful keeping him to herself and making sure he didn't talk to strangers, but we were roommates, right, not strangers, and even though I feel a little angry at her for keeping him from me, I don't blame her, not really. She's a mom and had to do what she thought was best.

"This place is great." I make a point of looking around the yard to show her that I'm really paying attention. That's the first step in showing someone you like them, right? Paying attention to their interests even if they don't interest you? I remember that from counseling in high school.

"Thank you." Her words seem robotic, and she keeps looking down the street like she expects someone to come along.

I hope they don't. I want this time alone with her where I can show her just how much I like her and her son.

It's difficult to think of what to say next. Just one drink would really take the edge off and make it easier for me to talk to her, but I don't have anything, and I'm not going to ask her if she has a drink.

"Do you like it here?" There. That's safe.

She eyeballs me, then looks at Luke. I'm sat between the two of them and look at him while he eats. He's oblivious to our conversation as he turns and digs one grubby finger into the dirt right off the picnic blanket or stares up at the sky, watching the clouds slowly go by.

"Yes, we do. Thanks for asking."

Silence again. I want to tell her how excited I am to be here with her, how scary it was following her here, how I had to pay someone in an Uber almost the last bit of money I had to drive me because I was so tired that the road swam in front of me when I got behind the wheel of my car, and then I was low on gas anyway. How weird it was to lean forward and say *follow that car!* like I was in a movie, how I made them park down the street so I could walk up to the house like I lived here and not scare her when an unknown vehicle pulled up, but I don't say any of that.

"Yes. You're welcome." God, have I always been this bad at this? I pull my phone from my pocket, fully expecting there to be a text from Eloise. She always seems to know when I'm talking to Tina and when I'm going to say something stupid, but there's nothing.

Because I have the wrong phone. *My cousin will kill me if she ever finds out, but I just have to keep her from finding out, that's the best way to deal with all of this, and then she'll never know I came by.*

I don't know what to say to Tina, but I want her to know how happy I am to be here with her. Just telling her that though seems silly; do people really do that, just be honest with how they feel about someone? It feels dangerous.

I clear my throat.

Luke wiggles, stuffing his mouth. Tina stares at me like she can't wait to hear what I'm going to say next. She needs me to talk so we can enjoy our time together. The knowledge that she's just as nervous about this time alone with me as I am makes me happy.

That makes two of us, Tina.

I know. I'll ask to see the house. She'll show me the house, and that will give us plenty of things to talk about. Maybe I can tell her how much I'm going to miss her at the apartment. She'll see that I care, that it's nothing bad for me to come by and sit out on her picnic blanket with her and Luke, that the nervousness she's feeling is perfectly normal, and that I feel it as well.

Closing my eyes, I take a deep breath. So far, our conversation has been stilted. I can do better.

Eloise will want me to do better so she knows exactly

what's going on with Tina. And Luke. What she said earlier, about sitting tight and waiting? No, she couldn't have meant that.

Maybe I dreamed it. Maybe I was so tired that it was all a dream, maybe she did bring me sleeping pills, but everything else I think happened didn't really happen, and I'm supposed to be watching Tina, if not for Eloise, then for me.

I have to do my job.

I clear my throat.

34

TINA

My phone is charging in the kitchen, well out of reach. Any neighbors who might be around sure aren't making themselves known. It's supposed to be a perfect day, with a cool breeze and plenty of sun, but even though I'm sitting in a patch of bright sun, I'm chilled.

Goosebumps break out all over my skin as I look at Ricky. He has a dark expression on his face, his eyebrows knit together, his mouth tight as he watches me. I know what he wants — it's the one thing he's wanted from me from the moment he moved into the apartment. The one thing I've so far managed not to give him.

And I'm not about to give in to him now.

He clears his throat and tilts his head towards the house. "Why don't you give me a tour, Tina? Luke can sit outside."

He's awkward, his tone stilted, like he's not sure exactly how to speak to another person. I get the feeling he has to dig deep for every single word, like just talking to me is painful.

Not something he's used to.

Still, every word has an undercurrent of malice.

I bite my tongue. There's screaming in the back of my head, and I know if I were to open my mouth, I'd be making that same noise. Maybe *that* would be enough to get some attention from the neighbors.

Luke looks at me, his face bright. He wants so badly to be grown up, to be a big kid. I know the thought of getting to stay outside while I go inside has to be killing him. He bounces a little up and down on the picnic blanket.

"I think Luke has to pee," I say, immediately recognizing the beginning of a pee dance. "Why don't I take him inside to use the bathroom, and then I'll give you that tour?" I stand, yanking Luke by the hand to join me before either of them has a chance to respond.

"Momma, I'm fine," Luke argues when he's on his feet and realizes what's going on. "I don't hafta pee bad."

"Okay, but if Ricky and I are going to have some time without you interrupting, then you need to take a little pee break, okay, buddy?" I smile at Ricky. My lips feel tight and my face like plastic, but I'm pretty sure my smile says *you can trust me. I'm on your side. Just give me a minute to get rid of his pesky kid, okay?*

"That sounds nice. Do what your mom says, Luke." Ricky grins, then uses his pinky nail to pick at something stuck between his teeth.

My stomach turns.

His acting like Luke's father, like he could be half the man Jared is, it's enough to make me sick. That thought hits me before I have a chance to guard against it, and I have to correct it.

Jared didn't want to be a father.

He wouldn't have lied to me about everything if he had.

I pick Luke up and hurry away to the house before Ricky can say anything else.

"But, Momma, I don't have to pee," Luke complains, but I shush him.

"I need to call someone," I say, leaning into the kitchen and grabbing my phone. "You try to pee, and you can have another cookie, okay?"

That does it. Luke grins at me and races down the hall to the bathroom. I'm going to join him to make my call, but he slams the door, the lock clicking into place.

"I'm a big boy!" he shouts.

I groan, but tap on my phone. A quick glance at the front door reassures me that Ricky hasn't followed me inside.

I hurry to it and lock it, then turn and lean against it.

My fingers tremble as I go to my contacts. I don't have a lot of people I can rely on, and certainly very few people Ricky would actually listen to, but there's one person who might help.

I tap his name.

Crossing my fingers, I hold the phone to my ear. It rings once. Twice. Then it clicks to voicemail.

My stomach sinks as I listen to the mailbox message. I was screened, and that means I'm more on my own than I thought I was.

"Hey, Jared, this is Tina. Uh, listen, I know this is strange, but I have something I need help with at the house if you're around. I know Eloise said you two would be able to help me this weekend, and I don't want to be a bother, but if you're free, will you please give me a call? Thanks." I rattle off my number, then mentally kick myself.

He'll see it on his missed calls list. Stupid.

I'm just really shaken and don't know what to do with Ricky right outside. If I had any other friends I could rely on to hurry here, I would do that just so I could get their help, but Paula's working, and I'm not about to call Bethany or Debbie.

Ricky terrifies me. He's the reason, more than the single bed, more than the cockroaches in the kitchen from time to time, that I knew Luke and I had to move. Living in that apartment, with that man, wasn't going to end up well.

And now he's followed me here. Goosebumps break out all over my arms, and I rub them, then lightly rap on the bathroom door. "You okay in there, buddy?"

"Coming, Momma!" There's the sound of the sink being turned on, allowed to run for a moment, then cut back off.

I take a deep breath and slap a smile on my face when the door opens.

"Ricky's here. Come on."

"Yes, Ricky's here." I consider sending Luke to his room so he can at least close the door. I don't know that Ricky would hurt him, would even really pay attention to my son, but what do I know?

Tears spring to my eyes. I wipe them away with the back of my hand.

I refuse to cry in front of this man.

"Let's go." Luke pulls on my hand, trying unsuccessfully to get me to follow him down the hall.

I plant my feet, my mind racing as I think through what might happen.

Then I hear something.

A car.

Hope rises in me, hot and bright, but it's immediately tempered by the thought of whatever Ricky might say to whoever stopped by. He might tell them to leave, tell them I don't want visitors.

He could lie and pretend the two of us are in a relationship, and if I'm not there to stop him from saying that, there's no reason why the person wouldn't believe him.

I want it to be Jared out there. Maybe he'll have heard my voicemail and decided to swing by. It's entirely plausible, right? He's a good man.

Yeah, a good man who lied to me about his name and then disappeared, leaving me to raise our child myself. A good man who might have been married when we slept together. A good man willing to lie to me, to his wife, to everyone to get what he wants.

Still. He's my only hope.

"Let's go, Luke," I say, squeezing his hand tighter. "I want you to stay with me, okay? No talking to Ricky on your own. Keep your hand in mine and we can get ice cream later."

"Ice cream!" He jumps, still holding my hand with his, and then wiggles when he lands. For being an uncoordinated little kid, he sure knows how to express just how happy he is about getting what he wants.

We hurry towards the door. Ricky has walked to the gate and is leaning on it, his body language casual, like he doesn't have a care in the world. I feel my fear rise again, that someone will have stopped by to talk to me, but he's going to send them away.

The screen door slams shut behind us, and Ricky turns to look. As he does, his face slowly changes, from one with a soft smile on it, to a grimace. I see the dark expression on his face, see his little rodent teeth, and resolve solidifies in me.

"Faster, Luke." I'm practically dragging him down the stairs to the sidewalk, but now we're on it, on flat ground, running to the fence.

Ricky steps to the side, but the movement is slow, like he's not happy about doing it, like he'd much rather block my view.

There's a black Escalade parked right on the other side of Ricky. My heart is in my throat as the driver's door opens; then Jared leans out. His back is to us as he talks on the phone, looking up at his house, but I recognize him.

His broad shoulders. Thick dark hair. The way he rolls his head from side to side to crack his neck. I swear, it's stupid, but it feels like time stops, like everything slows down, and all the fears I had over what Ricky was going to do to me disappear.

"Who the hell is this?" Ricky grumbles the words at me as I push through the gate, still holding tightly to Luke's hand.

I glance at Jared. He's still far enough away that he can't hear me, but I need to act quickly. In just a moment he'll turn around and walk over to us, and then I won't be able to lower my voice enough to keep what I want to say private.

"That's my boyfriend," I say, staring Ricky right in the eyes. They're beady. Bloodshot. He doesn't blink. "You need to leave before I tell him you were bothering me."

"Boyfriend?" He reaches out, his hand a claw on my forearm. Worry crosses his face, but it's gone in an instant, doubt taking its place. He scoffs. Shakes his head. "Boyfriend, right. You don't have one of those, isn't that right, Tina?" Another scoff. He uses his free hand to pick at the skin on his cheek, then exhales hard.

He's confused. That's good. Hopefully that means he'll listen to me.

"I'll leave, but I know where you live, and I have no doubt you'll open your door to your old friend Ricky."

I yank my arm away from his grasp, but my skin still crawls.

What is Jared doing? I glance back at him, willing him to walk over here, but he still hasn't looked back at us. Whoever he's talking to must really have something to say for him to be so involved in the conversation.

"Leave. Now." I glare at Ricky, then, feeling brave, point down the road. "You need to go."

He pauses, running his tongue over his lower lip. I'm suddenly terrified he isn't going to leave like I want him to and I'll have to explain to Jared the lie I just told.

I can't imagine that would go over well.

"Fine. I'm leaving." Ricky scowls at me. He slinks away from the gate and down the sidewalk. I catch the backwards glance he throws me and ignore it, bending down to talk to Luke.

"Go to your room," I tell him. "But grab two cookies on the way." I'm suddenly terrified of Jared getting a good look at Luke and figuring out who he is. My heart pounds as my son runs to the house, and I wait until he's inside before turning to look at Jared.

He's still on the phone, but then he hangs up, slipping it into his pocket and turning to face me. I swear, my heart does a little dance at the sight of him.

"Tina, I got your message. What's going on?" Jared stops a few feet away and crosses his arms on his chest.

"Someone was here," I say, but my words sound flat. Without Ricky here to be proof of there being a problem, I feel silly. "I was worried he wasn't going to leave, but he left just when you pulled up."

Jared frowns and peers past me to the house. My heart thuds as I wait for him to say something. "Who was it?"

"Just some guy." I shrug, run my hands up and down my arms. Now would be the time to say something to him, to ask him if he remembers me, to figure out what he thinks about me moving across the street.

But the last thing I want is for him to know how he broke my heart.

Or that we have a son.

"Well, I'm glad he's gone." His voice is stilted, but he reaches out, lightly touches my cheek. I don't mean to, but I lean into his touch. It feels electric.

Before I can respond, another car drives by. It slows and turns up into his driveway. I watch it go, a feeling of dread growing in my stomach.

Eloise is home.

35

ELOISE

The garage door slowly trundles closed behind me, the squeaking of the wheels on the tracks so loud I clap my hands over my ears. Then it settles with a dull thud, one I feel in my bones more than I hear, and I blink in the darkness.

Our garage light went out a few months ago, and I keep asking Jared to replace the bulb, but he's so busy. It's on me, too. I could easily call someone and have them come replace it for us. I don't need to wait on my husband to take care of problems around the house, but sometimes I just want him to handle everything for me.

Is that too much to ask? Is it too much to wish he would see what was wrong, see what needed to be taken care of, and do it? My mother always told me never to expect men to see issues around the house, that they're all wrapped up in their own lives.

She certainly never paid attention to the multiple affairs my father had.

But I'm not her.

Taking a shuddering breath, I open the door and get out, only leaning back into the car long enough to grab my purse and some folders I brought from the office. Even though this was the plan, even though I wanted to drive Tina and Jared together, seeing him lightly cupping her cheek was a shock.

It certainly happened a lot faster than I thought it would, that's for sure.

I take a deep breath. Open the door to the house. Key off the alarm.

Now I just have to make sure everyone in town knows they're together.

I stumble into the kitchen, tossing my belongings on the counter, and pour myself a glass of Merlot. It goes down easily, and I chase it with a few crackers from the cupboard before pouring another one. Surely Jared will have seen my car. It's not like I was invisible driving down the road and pulling into our garage.

Yet he hasn't followed me home.

A laugh bubbles out of me, and I allow it, throwing my head back and letting it pour from my lips. Men are so stupid. Jared thinks he's in control, but he has no idea what I'm capable of.

I could call him. *That* would get his attention.

Even though the thought is tempting, I only entertain it for a moment before pushing it aside. Sure, I could reach out to him and ask him what he's doing, but why would I stop him from spending quality time with Tina when that's exactly what I want?

Still, it's one thing to learn your husband had an affair with someone and another entirely to push him back into her arms. Energy flows through me, and I pace the kitchen floor, not able to stop pacing while I think.

I should be using this time to prepare, that's what I should be doing. Rather than worrying about Jared over there and what he and Tina are doing together, I should be preparing.

So that's what I do.

Still gripping my wine like it's a lifeline, I hurry upstairs to the bathroom. He could be home at any moment, but even if he were to catch me here, there wouldn't be any reason for him to wonder what I'm doing. I'm just getting ready for my shower, just slowing down for the rest of the day. So I'm showering a little earlier than usual. So what?

I put the glass of wine on the bathroom counter and drop to my knees, open the under-the-sink cupboards, and pull out a stack of fluffy white towels. These I set on the floor without a second thought.

What I need is behind them.

My fingers brush the brown box, and I grab it, yanking it out and sitting back on the floor. I place it on my lap before opening the lid and letting out a soft sigh.

It's still here. Although, to be fair, if Jared had found it, I highly doubt things would be nearly as pleasant around here as they have been. He'd be so angry if he knew what I had hiding here under the sink, but what man digs around behind the towels?

None of them. They just like having everything catered for them. I've never met a man willing to actually do house-work without being pushed into it by his wife.

Slipping my fingers under the lid, I open the box and pull out one of the two small boxes tucked inside. I'll leave one here for Jared and take one downstairs with me to use on Luke. That's going to be the tricky part, getting the boy on his own.

Jared's going to be much easier, especially when I make sure he sleeps like a baby tonight.

"You have no idea what's coming," I say, then close the bigger box and tuck it back under the sink. Once I'm sure it's hidden, I tuck the smaller box under my arm, and I head downstairs, carefully holding my wine. 123DNA promises speedy results without requiring someone to spit a ton in a tube.

I knew there was no way I'd get a teaspoon or whatever of Jared's spit without him wondering what the hell was going on. But this is going to be easy.

Reaching up, I put the small box I brought with me in a cabinet over the refrigerator, then pour a second glass of wine. He's still not home, and my heart starts to thud hard in my chest as I consider what I'm about to do.

Back up the stairs. I'm practically running now, my heels kicked to the side, my breath coming in little gasps. He could walk in at any moment, but now I wouldn't be able to explain what I'm doing.

I have to try to finish this before he gets home. It's partly the thrill of being caught, I think, that makes my heart skip like it is. Partly the excitement of knowing that I'm putting an end to all his lies.

Yet as I turn in the bathroom, slowly taking in the marble countertops, the gorgeous Italian tile, the custom-built shower with six shower heads for maximum comfort, I know it's more than just that. It's the thrill of having all of this to myself.

My hands tremble as I shake out three sleeping pills, then walk them back to the kitchen, drop them in his glass of wine.

Give them a stir. They dissolve so much faster than I ever thought they would.

The first time I did this, as a trial run to ensure I'd be able to get Jared's DNA, I was terrified, but that fear is gone now.

I know exactly what to do to get what I want, and I'm not afraid of anyone getting in my way to stop me.

I'll continue to play the role of a loving wife. I'll let him think everything is fine.

Then, when he's fallen in love with the idea of being with Tina, I'll rip the rug out from under him.

I'm going to get the last laugh.

36

TINA

He's dropped his hand from my cheek, which, *thank goodness*, means I can breathe again. I've stepped back from him, needing to put some space between the two of us. When I was looking for him, so desperately needing him back, I would have done anything to have him here with me.

But now I know he's married. To Eloise. And I'm just not that person. I'm *not*. Guilt over the fact that he was probably married when we were together in the first place threatens to choke me, but instead I manage to put a smile on my face.

"I missed you," he tells me. He's breathing quickly, each breath shallow. Clearly he's not getting enough oxygen to his brain if that's how he thinks this conversation is going to go.

Nope. Not today. Not when I know whom he's married to. Not when his son is hiding in the house and he has no idea that he's a dad. *He doesn't know, right?* What man would have that information, would know he had a child, and not want to be a part of that child's life? I need to change the course of this conversation.

"Thanks for that," I say, flapping my hand in the direction Ricky went. "He won't take no for an answer."

Jared takes the hint. "Yeah, anytime." He scrubs his hand down his jaw. "Old friend of yours?"

"Old roommate," I correct. It doesn't matter if Jared thinks I hang out with people like Ricky, but I don't want him to get that impression of me. I want him to think I'm better than that. "He's actually the main reason I knew we needed to move out."

"I don't blame you. I was headed home early for the night and got your message, so I decided to swing by and make sure you were okay. You sounded a little stressed out."

"You could say that again."

The sound of the front screen door slamming shut behind me makes me wince. I close my eyes for a moment, willing Luke to go back inside, but of course he won't. He's three, and three-year-olds want to be included in everything, even if that thing is me talking to his biological father in the front yard.

"Momma, I want ice cream."

He's confident. When I turn to look at him, I'm not surprised to see him standing in a superhero pose, his little fists pressed hard against his hips. That's the pose we make every morning before going to daycare so he feels as confident as possible.

Superhero pose. What I wouldn't give to have some of his confidence right now.

When I don't answer, he runs over to me and presses his little body up against mine. Reflexively, my arm loops around him, and I snug him close.

Jared barely glances at him before looking back at me.

I chuckle, then realize I'm holding Luke in a death grip.

"Hey, Luke, why don't you go play in your room? You can head inside, and I'll be there in a moment to get you some ice cream."

It's working. He tugs away from me, and I feel like celebrating. I just want the two of them to be as far away from each other as possible. Although, to be honest, with the way Jared won't look away from me right now, I don't think he'd be able to tell Luke is his.

Luke starts down the sidewalk to the house but then stops. He turns, staring at me. "I want it now."

"In a minute. Let me talk to my friend."

"You said." His bottom lip wiggles, and his eyes suddenly flood with tears. "You *said*, Momma."

I sigh. "I'm so sorry," I say, turning to Jared. "He's turning into a little lawyer."

"Then let's get the boy ice cream." He looks over his shoulder at his house, but the garage door is down. Eloise's car is gone. If I hadn't seen her pull in, I never would have known for sure if she was there.

Is he checking for his wife? Or maybe wishing he hadn't stopped? He could very well rather be in his house, away from this drama, away from Luke. I have no idea if he even likes kids. He sure isn't looking at Luke very much.

And that's a good thing.

"Okay, if you're sure," I concede, following Luke to the house. Still, it isn't until we're all in my tiny kitchen that I allow myself to believe Jared isn't going to turn tail and run at the first opportunity.

He's here. In my house. It makes me want to throw up.

Do I want Jared? Yes, I did in the past. Both for me and for Luke.

But Eloise is my friend. She took care of me, made sure I was able to buy this house. And Jared is a cheater.

"Okay, ice cream for Luke for being such a good listener." I chirp the words, trying to sound happier and less stressed than I feel right now. "Chocolate or moose tracks?" The cold air from the freezer helps to cool my burning cheeks, so I stand with the door open while I wait for a response.

"Chocolate!" Luke practically sings the word.

"I'd like moose tracks."

Jared wants to eat ice cream in my house. With our son. Keeping my face neutral, I pull the two cartons from the freezer and scoop out three bowls. I have to fight to keep myself from looking at him because I'm afraid of what I'll see on his face.

Desire. The one thing I've seen on his face since he cupped my cheek and I leaned into his touch.

"Okay, you're all set," I say, handing Luke his bowl and putting the cartons back in the freezer. "Why don't we go to the table to eat?"

"I'm going to my room!" Luke announces his plan of action and disappears as I'm leading Jared to the card table he brought over.

"Sorry about that," I say as we both sit on rickety folding chairs. "He has a lot of energy."

"I did too when I was little." Jared takes a bite, and I stare at him.

Does he know?

I suddenly lose my ability to make conversation. All I can do is stare at Jared while he eats. It's almost laughable how out of place he is here in my house. The walls all need a fresh coat of paint. There isn't any art hanging up except for a few drawings Luke did that are taped to the fridge.

It feels like a prison cell or dorm room.

"I like what you've done with the place." Jared grins at me over a bite of ice cream. "Very modern."

I laugh. I can't help it. "Yeah, just wait until I save up a little money and can fix this place up. It's got great bones, or so Eloise said, but it needs my touch."

I say her name on purpose, wanting to remind him he's married, as if the thick gold band on his finger isn't enough. He needs to know where I draw the line.

I study his face, looking for any sign he's upset with me mentioning Eloise, but there's nothing. He still looks just as relaxed as he did when he arrived.

"So you and Eloise don't have kids?" The question is out of my mouth before I can stop it. I already know the answer, but I want to hear it from him. "I was hoping there would be some friends for Luke in the neighborhood, but I'm not sure that's going to happen."

"No kids." He shakes his head as if to drive home the point. "We were never that lucky. I would have loved some, of course. I can only imagine how incredible it would be to look at my son and see myself reflected back."

I freeze. A chill runs down my spine as I think about what he just said.

He has to know.

"I always wanted Luke to have his father in his life, but that didn't happen. Still, I think I'm doing an okay job." I stab at my ice cream and lick some off the tip of the spoon.

He nods. "He seems like a good kid. Why anyone wouldn't want to be in his life, I don't know. I wanted kids so badly that I can't imagine having them and not being around for them."

I want to scream. This is a sick dance the two of us are

doing, especially when I know his wife is right across the street. And he never really looked at Luke. His eyes haven't left my face.

Turning a little in my chair, I look across the street at his house. It's huge. Gorgeous. The front lawn makes mine look laughable. I can imagine Luke running around in the grass, a puppy nipping at his heels, pure joy on his face.

Then I realize Jared said something, and I totally missed it.

"I'm sorry, what?" I scoop more ice cream into my mouth and do my best to focus on what he's saying, not on the thoughts racing through my head.

"I asked if Luke's dad was in his life at all. I'm sorry if that's too personal, I just know what it's like to be raised by a single parent, and it's hard."

"Oh, no." I give a little shrug. "He wasn't interested at the time, I guess."

"That's a shame." Jared smiles at me and then stands up. He's towering over me, and I shiver, amazed at how much he fills the room. Not only does he have that type of personality, but he's tall, with broad shoulders. I stand too, my ice cream melting in my bowl.

"Thanks for the treat. I'd better get home." He pauses, looking down the hall.

Is he looking for Luke?

"But tomorrow is the big day, right?"

"Big day?" I blink at him, trying to sort through what's coming up so I can understand what he's asking me.

"Moving day." He laughs and scrubs his hand down his chin again.

I watch, mesmerized.

"Oh, yes." Giving my head a little shake, I grin at him. "You and Eloise are so kind to offer to help me move, especially on the weekend. I'm sure you have much better things you'd like to do than truck furniture across town."

"It's what neighbors do. Besides, I'm sure Luke has some stuff back at your apartment he'd prefer to have here."

I laugh. "You'd better believe it. The thing I think he's most excited about is when I buy a second bed and we don't have to share."

He's not laughing now. "You sleep in the same bed? Why didn't you tell me when I brought the table and chairs over? Tina, I want to help you. Let me."

Oh, that's embarrassing. How can he even stand being here and talking to me when we're obviously so different? I hate the thought that he might be here out of pity, and if there's anything that will make someone pity you, it's telling them you share a bed with your toddler.

"It's not a big deal." I take his bowl to avoid looking at him. "Anyway, I'll see you and Eloise tomorrow, okay?"

Remember your wife, Eloise?

"Tomorrow." He nods, a mask falling into place, then he walks through the living room, his strides long, and he's gone.

I stand, watching the door as it slams back into place. My heart races, and my mind is going a million miles an hour as I try to figure out what just happened.

What I'm going to do.

I found Luke's father. It's my friend's husband.

There are probably women all over the world who would turn on their friend to have a man in their life. But I'm not like that.

Jared had every chance to be with me, and he walked away. Yes, I looked for him, desperately.

But now that he's back, I'm not going to ruin the good thing I have going here. I just have to make sure he never finds out Luke is his son.

37

ELOISE

I'm just about to come out of my skin waiting on Jared to come home from visiting with Tina when I hear the garage door go up and then close. I freeze, leaning against the kitchen counter. My head pounds, not just from the wine, but from the reality of what I'm doing.

How many women actively shove their husbands into the arms of someone else? It's not like he abuses me; he never raises his voice, has never hit me. But he cheated on me, and even though I love him, that's one thing I can't forgive.

If he's done it once, he will likely do it again. As much as I hate to admit my mother could be right about anything, I've read enough books and seen enough movies to know this is the truth.

The only way to ensure he doesn't cheat on me again — doesn't father another child with someone else — is to get rid of him. Take his money and run. And, yes, Tina will be collateral damage, but there's always going to be some, right? There's no way all of us can come out of this with our hands clean.

When the door to the house swings open, I put a brave smile on my face. Jared's whistling as he enters, something he does only when he's really happy.

Was he whistling when he left the seedy hotel room where he took Tina to sleep with her? Does he whistle when he thinks about their time together?

"Hey there." He walks over, presses his lips against mine.

I freeze, then kiss him back, my body going through the motions even though my head is screaming for me to push him away.

"When did you get home?"

"Oh, just a bit ago." I lift up my wine. "Just long enough."

"That looks good." He kisses me again, then turns, picking up the glass I poured for him and gently tapping it against the side of mine. When he takes a sip, his eyes never leave my face. "How was work?"

I eyeball his glass. Did the pills all dissolve? I think they did. I *hope* they did. If he finds pills in his wine, then he's going to know I put them there; he isn't stupid. I just need him to finish the wine so I can take the next step.

"Great." Lying to my husband has gotten easier than I ever thought it would be. "You? Did you have a good day?"

"I had something to take care of, but nothing major." He yawns and stretches. Drains half of his glass. Now I can see a bit of white residue at the bottom of his glass, and I shiver, taking it from him before he can notice it.

He stares at the glass in my hand, then gives a small shrug as I top it up, swirling the glass round and round to try to finish dissolving the pills. "What time are we helping Tina move tomorrow?"

I don't answer. Instead, I press the glass into his hand and watch as he takes a sip.

"Eloise." Jared reaches out and lightly takes me by the chin, turning my head so I'm looking at him. Just having his fingers on my skin like that makes me shiver. "Are you okay? Do you feel okay? You look pale."

"I don't feel great." He's just given me the perfect excuse not only for my strange behavior right now, but also a great excuse to hopefully get out of helping with the heavy lifting tomorrow, which means it will just be the two of them doing most of the work. Alone. I give my head a little shake. "I'm sorry, I feel really weak and tired."

"Why don't you go to bed?" He puts the back of his hand against my forehead. "No fever. I'll bring you up a throw-up bowl and help you get changed into your pjs, if you'd like to go to bed early."

I nod. "That's probably smart. Thanks." I move slowly, making each step as deliberate as possible. The last thing I want is for Jared to suspect that I'm lying about not feeling good.

Tonight's the night for getting his DNA. And the best part? He'll be passed out and won't ever suspect a thing.

"Is this really going to work?" I mutter the words, leaning against the wall at the top of the stairs. There's a gallery wall surrounding me, all photos of our wedding, of us dating, of us traveling the world. Jared and I used to travel a lot, back before the stress of not being able to have children got to us.

I stumble away from the wall and make it the rest of the way down the hall.

My movements are jerky as I tug off my clothes and pull on my pajamas. Just as I get the covers yanked back and I'm climbing into bed, Jared enters the room.

"Whoa, let me help you." His hands are warm on my hips as he lifts me up onto the bed. I turn and curl into a little ball, allowing him to tuck me in. "Hey, this is going to sound crazy, especially since you were drinking."

He pauses. I wait.

"What, Jared?"

"Do you think there's a chance you might be pregnant?" The question would be innocent if it weren't for our history. He must see the way my face changes, because he forges ahead. "I know, it's wild to ask that of you, but is there a chance? You don't look good, kinda like you might throw up, and I know that can be a sign someone might be pregnant."

"I'm not pregnant." The words are heavy. Final.

"Oh. That's fine, then. I just thought I'd ask." He leans over me and presses his lips to my forehead.

I close my eyes.

"It's just that seeing the new neighbor — your client? — and her son running around makes me want one. I know it's not in the cards for us, but —"

"Then let's not talk about it." I roll away from him and fluff my pillow, closing my eyes to try to keep the room from spinning. "It's not in the cards, Jared. We tried. We always talked about adopting, though. You were just never on board."

"I wanted our own." He sounds like a child, and I inhale sharply.

The mattress next to me depresses, and he stretches out, still wearing his suit from work as well as his shoes. Normally I would tell him to change, or at least to take off his shoes so he doesn't get the coverlet dirty, but the sleeping pills must have hit him hard.

His breathing slows.

I wait. Count to fifty, then to one hundred for good measure, before rolling over.

"Jared." I'm not whispering his name, not exactly, but I'm still quiet enough that I'm not surprised when he doesn't move. Louder this time. "Jared." I poke his chest.

Nothing. He's out like a light, and I exhale hard, sitting up and walking around the side of the bed to get a better look at him. He's breathing slowly, and for just a moment, I have a stab of fear that I gave him too much. I lean over him and press my ear against his chest.

Like I'm going to be able to tell if there's a problem. I'm a Realtor, not a doctor, but his heart thuds steadily and reassuringly in my ear.

God, what if I kill him now? Before I'm ready?

The thought makes me laugh, and I turn away from the bed. Hurrying now, I crouch in front of the bathroom sink and get the small DNA test kit box out. There's a swab for me to run along the inside of his cheek as well as a little bag for collecting a few hairs.

"Open your mouth, darling," I say, pressing down on his chin so his mouth falls slack. He snorts a little but doesn't move as I run the cotton swab along the inside of his cheek. Once it's sealed in its bag and tucked in the box, I pluck a few hairs from his head.

It has to hurt, but I don't care. I sit on the edge of the bed while I pack everything back up, then return to the bathroom, where I tuck the small box in the main box and put the towels back in place.

There. He'll never even know it's there. I'll use the other box to collect DNA from Luke and then send it all off. It's not necessary to know that Luke's his son. Really, I'm going to continue with my plan no matter what I learn, but I still want to know. I want to have all the facts.

There's just one more thing to do tonight, and I fire off a quick text to Ricky.

> Be out of the house early tomorrow. If you are, I'll put an extra two thousand in your account.

I don't have to wait long for a response.

> ok

This time, when I curl up in bed, I'm ready to sleep.

I've put a lot of things in motion, and now all I have to do is sit back and watch how it all plays out. Everyone in town loves me, I've made sure of that. And Tina will look like a gold digger who took advantage of me. And of Jared.

She has no idea what's coming.

And her being nice isn't going to get her out of it.

38

TINA

I'm bouncing on the balls of my feet as I look out the window of my apartment, hoping Jared and Eloise will show up soon to help me move.

If I'm being honest, I hope it's just Eloise who shows up. I don't want to be alone with Jared right now because maybe he knows. He might have taken one look at Luke and figured out that he's the dad.

I don't know, and I don't want to.

Hey, remember how we slept together? And I'm pretty sure you were married at the time. And I was in love with you, but you broke my heart? Oh, and this is your son. We're your neighbors.

Nope, definitely not something I want to bring up, and not something I want him to realize.

I chuckle at the thought.

"You want to share what's so funny?" Paula walks into the bedroom and leans against the doorframe. "You're moving out, leaving me here with Ricky and the need to find someone else to help share the apartment, and you're giggling. It's not kind."

"I know." Begrudgingly, I walk away from the window to talk to her. "And you know that I love you and have loved living with you. It's just that Luke deserves more."

There's a crash from the closet, where Luke is currently playing with a few cars we'd held back in the move to give him something to do while the adults carried the furniture outside. Not that there's a lot.

My bed. The mattress. A dresser. A small bedside table Paula is giving us as a going-away gift.

Really, I only need one person to help me out, but Paula told me she won't carry furniture because she doesn't want to break a nail. And there wasn't any way in hell I was going to ask Ricky.

But then Eloise offered like the friend she is. I have no doubt she'll bring Jared for the muscle. The thought makes my stomach twist.

I'm nervous about being around them both.

A door slams outside, and I rush back to look out the window. Jared's there, dressed casually in a pullover and jeans, and I stare at him while he stretches. He's alone, all alone, and the thought gives me chills.

Did Eloise not come?

But just then the passenger door flies open, and Eloise bounces out. Her hair is pulled back in a ponytail, and she looks right up at the window where I'm standing to wave. *Thank God.*

I step back.

"You okay? You jumped back like you saw a ghost." Paula comes to stand next to me at the window, then lets out a low whistle. "Okay, if I saw that man get out of a car to come help me, I don't think I'd have control over my body, either. Is that his wife?"

"Sure is. My Realtor." I keep my voice light. Airy. "We're friends."

I'm going to keep telling myself that as often as I need to hear it. Eloise and I are friends. We're friends.

She not only helped me buy my new home, but now she's helping me move into it. She never has to know what happened with Jared.

Still.

Still, there's a voice in the back of my head. *What if he figures it all out? And worse, what if she does?*

I push it away.

"Luke, stay in the closet. I'm going to let Eloise and Jared in." I shoot a look at Paula, hopefully one she'll understand means to not mention anything about Jared being Luke's dad; then I step to the front door.

When I swing it open, I step back. Jared fills up a space. I noticed it yesterday in my home, and now he's here in my apartment, making it hard for me to breathe.

"Good morning." His voice is chipper, and if he notices how I choke when I'm around him, he doesn't give any indication. Instead, he steps past me, his head on a swivel, taking in all the little details of our apartment I wish he wouldn't notice.

I suddenly realize what a terrible idea this was. I don't want Eloise or Jared to pity me, but how will they do anything else once they've been here? How will either of them be able to look me in the eye and not judge me once they've seen the water stain on the ceiling, the dirty carpet, the way Ricky leaves his plates out on the coffee table until Paula or I have *had enough* and finally pick them up for him?

"Hi," I say, turning from him to look at Eloise.

She grins at me, then throws her arms around me.

Oh, we're hugging. That's a surprise.

It makes me feel even more guilty about the way Jared was cupping my cheek yesterday. And then I leaned into his touch like an idiot.

"Today is the big day! Well, the big day after the other big day." She squeezes me hard, then steps back. "Jared brought the muscle. I brought something for Luke to help keep him entertained. Where is he?"

"Playing in the closet." I feel like I'm in a dream, like it's impossible for me to think straight. I watch as Paula gestures for the two of them to follow her to my room; then I close the front door.

When I reach our bedroom, Eloise is in the closet with Luke, sitting on the floor with him to show him what she brought. Paula is off to the side, watching, and Jared already has my mattress slipped from the bed frame.

"You and me," he says, pointing at the mattress.

My face flames.

"We're going to move this outside." His words are innocent, but his eyes don't leave mine.

I'm dying inside.

"Let me get the front door." Paula moves quickly, obviously pleased to have a job she can do without risking her nails. She hurries to the front door as I grab one side of the mattress. It sags in the middle when we lift it, and I grunt, pulling it closer to my body as I back out the bedroom door.

In the closet, Luke laughs.

My head swims as I try to keep from cracking up. Luckily, the mattress is too heavy for me to think about Eloise playing with her husband's son. She doesn't know the truth.

She can't know the truth.

"Around the corner," Jared says, yanking me back to

the present. "Go slowly down the hall, and then we'll switch so I can go backwards through the front door and down the stairs. The last thing I want is for you to trip and fall."

"Great." I take little baby steps, shuffling more than anything, until we're by the front door. When Jared puts his end of the mattress down, I exhale explosively, then lean forward, one hand on the mattress to keep it from falling, the other on my thigh.

Paula walks by me, patting me on the shoulder. "I'm going to grab my coffee. You two got this?"

I nod. This is more difficult than I thought it would be, and I'm grateful I have some help.

"You're doing great." He's suddenly next to me. When he speaks again, his voice is lower. His hand rests on my back. "Did that guy reach back out to you? Did he give you more trouble?"

Ricky. I shake my head and force myself to stand up. His hand falls from my back.

"No, he's at work. Or drinking, I'm not sure. I haven't heard from him. Thanks so much for that, I know I put you in an awkward position, and it wasn't fair of me."

"It's fine. You needed help, and I was there for you. It's what neighbors do."

Neighbors. Right.

He's too close to me. He's so close I can smell his after-shave. I could reach out just a few inches and plant both of my hands on his chest. Instead, I focus on keeping the mattress from tipping over.

But I still need him to put some space between us.

Jared pauses, and I think he's going to say something else. Without thinking about what I'm doing, I tilt my head up to look at him. I'm waiting. Curious, even though I know I need to move away from him.

"You two look cozy." It's Eloise. Her words are friendly, and guilt stabs through me.

I gasp. Step back from Jared.

Instantly, I can breathe better. I just need to make sure to keep some space between us. *Leave room for Jesus*, as the middle-school teachers would always say at dances when kids were pressed too closely to each other.

Jared doesn't respond to his wife. He just gives his head a little shake and takes my place at the mattress, moving so he can grab it and maneuver it out the door and down the stairs. I take a deep breath, fully prepared to apologize to Eloise for being that close to her husband, to come up with *something* to say to undo whatever terrible thoughts she's having, but then I look up at her.

And the words die in my mouth.

She has Luke on her hip, a contented smile on her face. His arms are wrapped around her neck, and his head rests on her shoulder. My son doesn't cuddle with people. He doesn't like people enough to let them get close, to allow them to touch him like this.

But he's snuggled up so close to Eloise you might think the two of them are good friends. Or that she's family.

She sees me looking at her, then at my son. She smiles. "I guess he just feels really comfortable with me. I did always want to be a mother, so it just fit."

Panic eats at the back of my mind, and I whip back around to make sure Jared isn't looking.

He can't see Luke. He can't know the truth.

39

ELOISE

The look on Tina's face when I came out of her bedroom snuggling her son made me want to laugh. She's so clueless, completely and utterly unaware of anything going on around her, and I can't help but be amused by that.

And it's obvious, to me at least, that she wants to keep Jared as far away from Luke as possible. So when I offered to bring him here so she and Jared could get her bed and other furniture moved into her new house without him underfoot, she wasn't suspicious.

She was just falling over herself with gratitude.

It's perfect for me, because it means I get some one-on-one time with Luke, and it also means she and Jared get to be alone together. He has to be going crazy knowing who she is and not having her.

The one he dumped to keep optics as good as possible for his company.

And now the two of them are alone together, moving her bed.

I laugh. I can't help it.

Luke laughs too.

"Life is so funny, isn't it?" I ask, lightly brushing his hair out of his eyes.

He nods but doesn't stop shoveling ice cream into his mouth.

He's sitting on my kitchen counter, swinging his legs while he eats a bowl of ice cream. Across the road, Tina and Jared are getting her crappy furniture moved into her home, so I need to work quickly. They'll be back before long, especially because I'm sure Tina doesn't want to be away from her son.

Or maybe it's because she doesn't want me to be suspicious of her and my husband.

"You have something in your hair." I make sure to sound a little worried, like whatever is in Luke's hair is really cause for concern.

His eyes widen. He reaches up with one hand like he's going to try to bat at it, but I grab his wrist. "No, don't touch it. I think it's a spider. It might bite you."

Real terror fills his face. Part of me feels a little bad about scaring him, but I'm still going to go through with it. I reach up, pinching a bunch of strands of hair behind his ear.

"Oh, Luke, I think it's going to bite you; let me try to stop it." My heart beats hard as I yank my hand back, pulling the hair out at the roots.

"Ouch!" Now his hand does fly up to where I pulled the strands out. "Ouchie." His eyes fill with tears, and I turn away, dropping the strands into an open and waiting ziplock bag. I zip it quickly, then stuff it in the waiting box on the counter.

Those strands should be more than enough for me to

prove Luke is Jared's son, but I'm not finished. I want more DNA. I want this to be irrefutable. 123DNA doesn't need both the hair and the cheek swab, but I was thorough with Jared, and I want to be thorough with his son.

"Oh, honey, are you okay?" When I turn back to Luke, I pull him to me, rubbing his back and lightly kissing the top of his head. "You're okay. You got bit, but the pain is over, right? It won't hurt you again." I stamp my foot on the floor. "There. Got it."

He sniffles and looks up at me. "You killed it?"

I nod, then look out the window. Still no movement from across the road. I'm fine on time.

"I killed it. Hey, let me see something in your mouth, okay? I think I saw a wiggly tooth."

"Really?" His eyes light up, and he opens his mouth obediently.

This kid is so easy. Tina has done a really good job raising him so far. Whoever takes over after this will have an easy time. Hopefully he'll get some good adoptive parents when Tina goes to jail for killing my husband.

"Ooh, look at those chompers." I pull two Q-Tips from a bag and rub them across the inside of his cheek. "You think the Tooth Fairy will bring you something really good when you lose your first one?"

He nods, pulling back from the Q-tips, and I drop them in another waiting bag. Zip it up. Tuck it away.

"I think so." He spoons a bite of ice cream in his mouth. "Where's Momma?"

"Across the street. She's getting your bed moved into your new home, and then she'll be back." I hesitate, wondering how I'm going to continue keeping him occupied while Jared and Tina enjoy some alone time.

Toys. I have toys, and little kids love them. If he goes and plays for a bit, then that will give me plenty of time to get this all boxed up and in my car. I'll drop it off at the post office this afternoon, and it'll be ready to test on Monday.

One of the reasons I chose 123DNA was that they offer faster results if you're willing to pay a bit more. Sure, it was an additional thousand dollars for each set of DNA on top of their usual fee, but when I'm going to be as rich as I will in the future, what does that matter?

I just want those results back ASAP.

"Hey, I have some toys in the living room that you're welcome to play with."

"Toys?" He sits up straight.

"Yep. For friends when they come over with their kids." I lift him down and put him on the floor, pointing in the direction to send him out of the kitchen. It's a lie, of course. I picked up the toys when I thought Jared and I were going to be able to have kids of our own, but nobody needs to know that.

Luke will just be happy to have something to play with. And the happier he is here, the less likely he'll want me to go find his mom. I honestly don't care if my husband is over there for most of the day.

In fact, I'd love it. I'll keep Luke here, out of the way. The two of them can reconnect. And then, when Jared ends up dead, it'll be easy for the police to believe it was she who killed him.

40

RICKY

My cousin has always thought she's better than me. Living in this neighborhood, married to Jared. She doesn't have to work, but she wants to, that's what she's said before, which is so stupid. She's just used to everyone doing whatever she wants, and now that's exactly what I'm doing.

I squeeze the steering wheel as tightly as possible, making my hands ache. Pain shoots up through my arms, and I grit my teeth, but I don't make a sound. And I don't move. I'm parked halfway off the road, my headlights killed, my car a silent sentry, and even though this neighborhood claims their *neighborhood watch* is the best in the area, that they'll be able to keep an eye out for anything bad going on, nobody's noticed me.

Or, at least, nobody's come out here to ask me what I'm doing. To tell me to move.

But I'm not doing anything, am I? I'm just sitting, just watching, just keeping an eye on Tina. That's what Eloise wanted me to do in the first place. She wanted me to keep an eye on her and make sure she didn't do anything stupid. She just wanted me to watch her, watch her, watch her, and I'm doing it for Eloise.

She's been gone almost a week, almost a whole week, a week without Tina and without her laugh, and I think I'm coming out of my skin. Eloise can't know I'm here, that I'm watching. She wants me out of here so Tina won't see me and know something's going on, but she told me to watch Tina, and now that I've started, I can't seem to stop.

"Where are you going, Tina?"

My breath catches in my throat when I see her walking across the road with Jared. She's holding a big dish, like a casserole, and they must be going to his house for dinner, but that doesn't make it any better that she's walking with him. With Jared, the man who started all of this in the first place, the man I saw kissing Tina at the bar. And I took their pictures, and I'm glad I did, because if I hadn't sent them to Eloise and told her what her husband was doing, where would I be?

Not living right by Tina.

But that's all coming to an end now, and I don't want her to have moved. I've liked watching her and even Luke. I've liked keeping an eye on them for Eloise.

And then, when I stopped by her house to say hello, what did she do?

She lied to me.

It took me by surprise, that's what it did. I had no idea Tina could lie, that she'd be that type of person, but of course I know who Jared is, even though Eloise doesn't have me over for dinner. Even though the wedding was so long ago and Jared had been drinking so much that he apparently doesn't remember me, I remember him.

So I know Tina lied to me about having a boyfriend.

But the man she pretended was her boyfriend is Luke's dad.

And Eloise's husband.

I would have said something then, but she took me by surprise; it took me by surprise that someone as good as Tina could lie to me, and maybe she's not as good as I thought, maybe —

"Stop it, stop it, stop it." I let go of the steering wheel and grab the sides of my head, squeezing hard to try to keep the thoughts from ricocheting around in my brain. They get started, bouncing around, making it hard for me to think about anything else, and I can't stop them. They take on a life of their own, and I don't need that right now, don't need the pressure of not being able to think things through.

I have a job to do. No matter what Jared is doing, I'm just supposed to watch Tina.

The two of them work their way up the driveway. They're walking far enough apart from each other that he would have to step closer to put his hand on her back, to guide her up to the house, and I stiffen, waiting for him to do just that.

What if he reaches out and touches the small of her back? Eloise will be so upset, right?

No, that's the plan, you idiot, that's the plan; pay attention.

No, I'm the one who will be upset. Eloise wants this. She wants to punish Jared. She told me that's the next step of her plan, and I have to help her with it, but maybe we need to talk about it.

I fumble my phone from my pocket. Eloise bought it for me and told me to only call her. Only text her. Don't ever let anyone else have the number.

Tina and Jared are almost to the house, but they stop and turn to look at the stars.

I shrink down in my seat.

Fire off a text.

> what happens after he falls in love with her

Suddenly it feels like there's no air in my car. I take a deep breath and try to fill my lungs, but it's like breathing water, and I can't seem to clear the dizziness in my head. This is the first time I've wondered what will happen when Eloise gets what she wants. I feel like I'm coming out of my skin as I wait for her to respond.

And wait.

And wait.

Tina and Jared are still outside, still looking at the stars like they've never seen anything more beautiful in their entire lives. I shoot a glance at them to make sure he hasn't put his arm around her. It looks romantic, the two of them standing out there, but that should be me. I'm the one who's been watching her and making sure she's in bed at a decent hour. I'm not the one who cheated on my wife with her and knocked her up and left her.

I'm the one who cares about her.

I'm about to grab the door handle, about to throw myself out of the car so I can go up to the two of them and tell Tina she needs to stand and look at the stars with me when my phone beeps.

Eloise.

A text from her burner, from the phone she told me to call, the one she said nobody knows she has.

You know the plan. Think it through, Ricky.
Then get some rest if you need to.

Get some rest, like I'll be able to do that now that I'm worried about Tina and Jared, yeah, right, but I put my hand back in my lap and try to slow my breathing as I try to remember the plan since apparently I know what it is.

And then it hits me.

Jared will be dead. He deserves it. He deserves to die, to never get to see Tina again.

That makes sense.

But then what happens to Tina?

41

TINA

Spending time with Luke in our new home honestly feels like heaven. To know we're the only people in the house, that nobody is slinking around, listening to what we're saying, to know that we can do whatever we want and nobody can stop us?

It's nothing I ever thought I'd feel before.

Sure, I'm worried about Luke slipping out the front door and making a break for it.

And I'm worried about Ricky.

But right now I push all of those thoughts from my mind. Right now there's just one thing I want to concentrate on. And that's going to dinner across the road, with Eloise.

And with Jared.

It's the first time I've been invited over, and even though I'm excited to see Eloise and spend some time with her, I'm nervous. Jared came over to help me carry the casserole I made as well as the bottle of wine I picked up, even though I told him a few times that I had it all under control. We're working our way across the street to his house, and I just have to ignore the fact that the man next to me is Luke's dad.

Not tonight, he's not. Right now he's just my friend's husband.

No, not just tonight. That's all he'll ever be. That's all he *can* be.

It's a little strange, him coming over to help me carry things across the street. Still, I have to admit, it would be a slower trek if I were carrying everything on my own. I'm wearing heels for the first time in recent memory, and Luke is with Debbie so I can have a lovely dinner with the neighbors. But as nice as this evening will be, I was a little worried about accepting their invite at first.

I mean, who really wants to go to dinner with your baby's dad and his wife? Not anyone I know, that's for sure, but Eloise practically begged me, telling me I'm her best friend, and that she really wants me over.

So I'm doing it. I can't exactly avoid them forever, can I? And even though I'm nervous right now, I'm going to have a wonderful dinner with them, then I'll pick up Luke, and this night will be a memory.

"The stars outside are gorgeous, Eloise," Jared says, throwing open the kitchen door and gesturing for me to walk through before him. "You really need to step outside and see them, darling."

Silence. I'm quiet, holding my breath for a moment as I listen for Eloise to respond.

"Darling?" Jared puts the food down on the stove.

"Something's burning," I tell him, putting the wine down on the counter. There's a pair of hotpads by the stove, and I grab them, then open the door. A plume of black smoke billows out, and I cough, waving it away. In a moment, I see a burned roast, and I grab it, almost dropping it on the floor before I manage to get it on the stove. "Why would she leave this in the oven to burn?"

The question is stupid, and we both know it.

Jared stares at me for a moment before pointing upstairs. "I'm going to go check upstairs to make sure she's okay. Will you check down here?"

"Of course," I say, but he's already gone. I listen for a moment as he pounds up the stairs; then I leave the kitchen, trailing through the dining room. The table is already set, crystal wine glasses and gorgeous china making it look like something out of a fancy restaurant.

"Eloise?" I call her quietly, almost like I'm afraid of someone hearing me. It's a strange feeling, being in someone else's house, and even though I know I haven't done anything wrong, I still feel nervous. "Eloise, are you here? Are you okay?"

Nothing. Leaving the dining room, I cut down a hall, then hesitate. She told me one time that Jared's office is down this way. I can't think of a single reason why she'd be in there, letting dinner burn, but there's also a bathroom.

And the door is closed.

"Knock, knock," I say, rapping my knuckles lightly on the door. "You in there, Eloise?"

"Tina." Her voice is garbled, and I hiss in a breath, then jerk my hand away from the door before I can stop myself.

She surprised me, that's all.

"Hey, I'm coming in, okay?" Without waiting for her to respond, I twist the knob and push the door open. The bathroom is larger than any I've ever had, and my eyes flit around the space for a moment before landing on Eloise. She's sitting on the toilet with the lid closed, her head in her hands.

I kneel by her. In the back of my mind I'm well aware I should let Jared know I found her, but I really just want to make sure she's okay.

"Hey," I say, lightly touching her shoulder. "Are you okay? You feeling alright?"

She exhales hard before lifting her face up to mine. For just a moment, we stare at each other; then she gives her head a slow shake. "I just don't feel good."

"Oh, I'm so sorry." My knees hurt from crouching here, but I don't want to leave her. "I'll get Jared, and then I'll go, okay? I don't want to hover if you don't feel good."

She grabs my hand. The movement is so fast and unexpected that I gasp.

"No, don't go home," she says, her voice a moan. "Tonight was supposed to be really special."

"We can do it another time," I tell her, squeezing her hand. "I promise, okay? I know you were really hoping for us to share a meal tonight, but we'll just plan it for next week."

"No." She shakes her head. "Jared wanted to do something nice for you for dinner. This was supposed to be your big welcome to the neighborhood, and I ruined it." Fat tears roll down her cheeks. "I've ruined it."

"No, no, no, you haven't." I press my hand to her forehead. She's warm, sure, but not nearly as hot as I'd expect her to be when she didn't feel this good. "Seriously, this is not a big deal. You guys have done so much for me. I can't imagine being upset about this."

"You're so sweet," she says. "But Jared will have to eat something, and I think I burned dinner." She hiccups and sobs, closing her eyes and taking a deep breath. "He has to eat something."

"I brought a side dish," I offer, hoping to smooth this over. I feel terrible that she's so sick. Nobody deserves to feel this bad, especially when they're so kind. And it's obvious she feels real guilt over dinner getting cancelled and Jared wanting something to eat.

"No, Jared will want more." She shakes her head and sucks in a shaky breath. "Maybe... and this might be too much to ask, but would you go out to dinner with him?"

"Just the two of us?" I have to fight to keep the surprise out of my voice.

"If you don't mind. He likes a big dinner, and there's no way I can make anything. He won't be happy ordering in, and you planned to eat with us. It's not fair to either of you." Another sob. Her cheeks are bright red, and I feel a wave of guilt wash over me.

"If you really think —"

"I do." She sniffs. Tries to smile at me. "I really do think so, Tina. He needs something to eat, and you two might as well go out and enjoy the evening. You look so nice. He looks nice. Please, let me be sick at home by myself without people hovering."

This is the last thing I want to do, but how am I supposed to argue with her? I want to make Eloise happy, but going out to dinner with Jared, with the man I thought I could love, isn't something I want to do.

But how do I say no?

"Okay." I nod and force a smile to my face. "Let me help get you to bed or the sofa, at least. You're all dressed up, and we'll get you out of your heels before we leave, okay?"

"You're the best." She lets me help her stand. "Seriously, Tina, what would I do without you?"

I don't answer. I have my arm looped around her waist to help her down the hall to the living room, and even though she looks like she really doesn't feel good, she's not leaning on me that much. She must be using a last burst of energy to make it down the hall without making me do most of the work.

When she's settled on the sofa, I kneel next to her and slip off her shoes, putting them out of the way so she won't trip over them. I'm just in the middle of tucking her in with a blanket I found on a leather recliner when Jared walks in.

"What's going on?" He stops in front of Eloise and glances at her but then stares at me, obviously expecting me to answer his question.

"She's sick," I begin, but Eloise cuts me off.

"I feel terrible. I told Tina to go out to dinner with you so you could salvage the evening. Just leave me here. I don't think I could make it through appetizers."

Jared frowns. Scrubs his hand down his cheeks. When he turns to look at me, I swallow hard and look away from him.

I don't know that going out to eat with him is the best idea. Not that I'm going to do anything stupid, I wouldn't. But he broke my heart and somehow doesn't realize Luke is his son, and I don't know that I want to go down that path at all.

"Great." Jared nods, the decision made. "I'll take Tina to Postero. Want us to bring you anything?" He bends and brushes his lips across Eloise's forehead.

Was that a smile on his face?

She shakes her head. "Just have a good time. I'll probably be in bed when you get back."

And that's that. The next few minutes are a blur as Jared grabs his jacket and wallet and keys. I want to stay with Eloise or go get Luke and go home for a quiet night, but how am I supposed to do that without it seeming like I really just don't want to be around Jared?

"Are you ready?" He's standing by the garage door, his eyes locked on me.

I'm at the island, my hands planted on its cool surface, trying to think through my options. Not that I really have any. I can leave here and be rude, or go with him and pretend like nothing's going on.

"Have fun!" Eloise's voice is weak as she calls from the living room. "Thank you for doing this, Tina, it makes me feel a lot less guilty."

It's like she knows what I was just thinking. "Be safe and feel better," I call back. Then I look at Jared, who has his keys hanging from his finger, his eyebrow cocked as he waits on me. "Let's go," I murmur, brushing past him and opening the door to the garage myself.

I'll go with him, but it's for Eloise. Never mind this was what I wanted for so long. Never mind I thought he and I could be a couple. That was in the past. This isn't for him. And it isn't for me.

It's for Eloise.

That's all. And then I'm picking up Luke and going to bed, and I'm not going to think about my past with Jared.

42

ELOISE

From my vantage point on the sofa, I can see Jared's headlights as he backs down the driveway. They sweep across the front of the house, and even though I know there isn't a chance he could see me, I keep still on the sofa until they've driven away. Then I count to thirty and finally flip back the blanket I was curled up under.

That, if I say so myself, was some of my best acting. There's no way either of them suspected anything. Even if Jared did, if there was some little part of his brain that thought I might be lying to him, he was so eager to get out the door with Tina for some one-on-one time that he wasn't going to pay attention to what the voice in the back of his head was telling him.

For just a moment, though, I thought Tina might be onto me. She'd let her hand linger on my forehead just a little too long, and I probably should have played up just how weak I was feeling when she helped me down the hall to the sofa, but what's done is done, and she's gone, swept up and away by my husband.

This night couldn't possibly get any better.

Leaving my painful high heels on the floor, I stroll into the kitchen and open the fridge. Tina's casserole is still on the stove, and I ignore it, digging around instead for some leftovers I can heat up. I made chicken cordon bleu last night, and I pile some on a plate with green beans and mashed potatoes.

If, on the off chance Jared smells that I had something to eat while they were gone, I'll just tell him that I tried to eat dinner but had to throw it away. Keeping that in mind, I scrape some of the extra food into the trash before grabbing my hot plate and sitting at the counter.

Things really couldn't be going any better than they are right now. Sure, Ricky has been a bit of a wild card, but I think there was a part of me that always knew that was a possibility when I roped him into my plan. The problem with wild cards is that they tend to act out in a way you don't expect, but they're great because they'll get their hands dirty.

Grabbing my phone, I start scrolling through social media, checking out a travel influencer I love to follow. She has the dream life. Not only is she young and pretty, but she's independently wealthy and gets to travel whenever and wherever she wants.

That's what I want. I'm going to have that as my life, and there isn't anything anyone will be able to do to stop me. Judging by the money in the bank and how hard Jared saves for the future, I won't have to lift a finger.

I'll just get to enjoy all of his hard work, which is what I deserve after being married to the man for so long. One quick phone call to make sure Jared and Tina have a wonderful night, and I can rest easy they'll be gone for a while.

My dinner is delicious, and I take another bite right as headlights illuminate the front windows.

I freeze. My fork is halfway to my mouth, and I put it down carefully, slipping from my chair and hurrying to the light switch. When I flick it, the kitchen is thrown into darkness. If that was Jared then he'll already know I was up in the kitchen, but this will at least give me the opportunity to see out without someone seeing in.

"Why are you back so soon, husband?" I ask, walking to the front windows. Bracing myself for the sound of the garage door rising, I lift a slat of the blinds and peek out.

The vehicle is big, but it's not Jared. Whoever it is is parked in the driveway and hasn't pulled into the garage. I calm down for a moment before I realize who it probably is.

Ricky.

"No, you bastard, you'll ruin everything." Dropping the blind, I rush to the front door. My hands shake as I try to turn the lock, and it takes me three times to throw the bolt. I lied earlier about being sick, but now I really do feel like I might throw up, and I fling the door open, stepping out onto the deck.

The cold wood underfoot makes me shiver as I hurry across it. My bare feet slap against the deck, and I rush down the stairs that lead to the walk, my eyes slowly adjusting to the dark.

Someone's coming. The man is big, bigger than Ricky, bigger than Jared, and for just a moment I pause, completely terrified that someone might have been able to read my mind, that they know what I'm doing, and I freeze.

"Mrs. Jones?" A softer voice than what I would have expected from a man of this size, and I nod, my words trapped in my throat. "Great. I just need you to sign for this delivery."

He has a package under his arm but thrusts an iPad in my face. My finger trembles as I scrawl my name across the screen. The wavy line appears, looking nothing like what I tried to write.

"Okay, you have a good night." The iPad disappears, and the package is right in my face. I take it without thinking and tuck it under my arm like he did.

"Thank you," I manage, then turn and hurry back up to the house. It's only when I get inside and have the door closed and locked behind me that I look at the shipping envelope.

123DNA. Right there on the return address. Right there on the front of the envelope. It's like they wanted to advertise it to everyone that I just ordered a DNA test.

What would I have done if Jared and Tina were here when this arrived?

Jared always likes to get any deliveries. If I allow myself to imagine it, I can easily see his face darkening, his grip tight on the envelope, his mouth small as he looked up at me —

"Stop it," I say, taking the envelope with me into the kitchen. I flick the light back on and sit down at the counter. All of a sudden my appetite is gone, and my legs feel weak. "He's not here, and he won't find out about this. I just have to know."

That's it. I just have to know. Luke being Jared's son — *or not* — isn't going to change my plan. It's just me; I need to know; I have to have all of the information. That's how I've always operated.

My fingers tremble as I grip the pull tab on the envelope.

I yank it hard, and for just a moment, it doesn't pull, but then there's a ripping sound, and it's open. I drop the strip of paper to the counter and reach inside. Inside the envelope is a sheet of paper as well as a few pamphlets. Dropping the pamphlets to the counter, I smooth the paper out on the counter.

Across the top is:

DNA Test Results

My heart beats faster.

There are two columns with information. Different alleles are discussed, and even though that word brings up some hazy memory from being in high school biology, I keep scanning, desperate for the one bit of information that will prove everything to me.

There it is.

At the bottom.

"Probability of parentage," I whisper, running my finger over the percentage that follows. "That's a lot of nines."

So it's true. Jared is Luke's dad, and even though I knew it in my heart just from looking at the two of them, I still needed it spelled out for me. Gripping my hands into tight fists, I take a deep breath, then another.

This was always part of the plan. And, honestly, things are ticking along at a pace I didn't quite expect. I just have to keep this hidden from Jared.

That thought lights a fire under me, and I grab the envelope and pamphlets. The paper with the DNA results gets folded and shoved into my purse. Yanking my keys from the hook by the garage door, I look back into the kitchen.

Did I forget any part of it?

No. I have it all. I have no idea how long Jared and Tina will be out to eat, so I'm going to have to hurry, but there can't be any sign of this test in my house when they get back. I'll drive across town and dump the pamphlets and mailer envelope in a gas station trash can.

It'll never come back to me.

I need this information, but Jared would be a loose cannon with it. He'll never find out.

Nobody will ever find out.

43

TINA

Postero is one of those places I always wanted to go to eat but never actually thought I'd be able to afford.

And to be fair, I still can't afford this place. But Jared can, and he's obviously really well known. We walk in the front door, and immediately the maître d' falls all over himself to help us.

"Mr. Jones!" The little man is short and has a bent back, but he twists a little to look up at Jared while he shakes his hand. "And..." When he turns to me, his words falter.

"This is my neighbor, Tina." Jared puts his hand on the small of my back to push me forward a bit to meet the man.

I smile at him, well aware he was about to call me *Mrs. Jones.* Well aware that I'm not Jared's wife, and everyone in this restaurant probably knows that.

"It's a pleasure to have you dining with us tonight." The man has discretion, I'll give him that. He obviously knows Eloise but doesn't comment on the fact that she's not here and I am. "Your usual table is booked, though, so I'm going to have to put you by the window, but Mrs. Jones was able to get you a table, which is pretty lucky considering how full we are."

"That sounds fine." Jared's hand is still on my back, and he gently guides me after the maître d'. I feel conspicuous, and I'm just grateful I'm in heels and a dress.

"Eloise called after we left to get us a table?" It's shocking to me that she'd do that when she felt so bad, but she really is that nice.

Jared just shrugs and guides me along.

He doesn't seem bothered by that, but it's weird. She acted really sick, so why would she call ahead like that?

But, at the same time, I don't know how sick she really was.

As I walk, I'm aware of just how much I stand out. No, I don't fit in here, but at least I'm not wearing jeans. On the way to the table, Jared stops and talks to a few people. He introduces me each time, and even though I shouldn't enjoy the attention, I can't help it.

My entire life I've been invisible. For the first time, I feel like I'm really being seen, and it's nice. I do exist.

"Here you are." The maître d' sweeps his arm at the table, and Jared immediately pulls out my chair. "I'll have the waitress come by with a menu in just a moment. First you two can get settled." He pauses, then forges ahead. "The Antinori Tignanello is delicious, Mr. Jones."

"Please." Jared answers the man but doesn't look away from me. We're both seated now, across from each other, at a table that's so small our knees keep brushing.

This is not how I thought the night would go.

The maître d' leaves, and this suddenly feels like a terrible decision on my part. I shift uncomfortably and look around the restaurant. Everyone else seems to be enjoying themselves, but I highly doubt anyone else is in my position.

"You look lovely." Jared reaches across the table for my hand.

I'm faster, though, and I tuck it into my lap. "Thank you," I say, doing my best to look him in the eyes. "That's very kind."

Silence. The maître d' is back, and he pops the wine, pouring us each a glass and leaving the bottle. As he turns away, he leans down to Jared, but I still hear what he says. "Just let us know when you want to order. We don't want to rush you."

Jared nods.

My heart sinks. This was a stupid idea. Coming here with my friend's husband would be bad enough, but there's too much history between the two of us for me to think we could sit here across from each other and not feel uncomfortable.

Or, rather, I feel uncomfortable. Jared seems to be having a great time.

"It's just surprising to see you after so many years."

Oh, God. Are we doing this?

He takes a sip of his wine, then gestures for me to do the same.

My hand trembles as I pick up my glass. It's probably not smart to drink this entire thing, so I let just a little bit onto my tongue.

"It's good to see you," I say. "I'm just so grateful for Eloise coming into my life."

I'll bring up his wife. Over and over if I have to.

"She doesn't know, you know." He leans forward, and even though I know his voice is quiet enough that his words are for me only, I still shiver. "About us. I wouldn't tell her, but now..." He lets his voice trail off.

Grabbing the edge of the table, I stand. My chair scrapes loudly against the floor, and some other diners turn to look at me.

I don't care. Let them look.

"I have to use the restroom," I say. When I speak to him, I make sure to look at a spot right above his eyebrows. Hopefully he won't realize I'm not really looking him in the eyes.

I just can't.

Jared stands too, ever the gentleman, and I scurry through the restaurant, hurrying around tables and making sure I don't trip as I make my way to the bathroom. The door swings open at my touch, and I rush to a sink, grabbing both sides of it and taking deep breaths before I look in the mirror.

"You okay, darling?" There's an older woman next to me, and I gasp, jumping a little at her voice. "I'm sorry," she says, holding up her hands. "But you look a little too stressed out to be eating dinner with such a handsome man."

"He's just a friend." The words are automatic, but the woman obviously doesn't believe me.

She winks at me. "Sure he is, honey. I saw the way he was looking at you before I came in here. Like he wants to eat you up. I swear I've seen that man before." She runs water over her fingers without using soap, then flicks them dry.

I wince.

"I know." When she snaps her fingers, a bit of water flies and hits me in the face. "Jared Jones. I was in his office just the other week for work. Handsome man you have there."

"Just a friend. He's my best friend's husband." Sweat trickles down my back.

She laughs, throwing her head back as she does. "Honey, I've had a lot of friends but never kept one when her husband looked at me like that. *You* might be just friends with him, but that man has it bad for you." She's still laughing as she leaves the bathroom.

My heart sinks. When I look in the mirror, I try to see what Jared might see. But does it even matter? I don't care what Jared sees; what matters is that nothing can happen between us.

After splashing some water on my face, I head back out into the restaurant. Jared is still there, sitting patiently, like I didn't just disappear and have an existential crisis in the bathroom. When I sit back down, he smiles at me, and my stomach flips.

"I went ahead and ordered for us both. I remember what you liked to eat."

What I liked to eat when I was head over heels for the man, when I didn't know he was married, when I didn't know he was the type of guy to knock someone up and then never pick up their calls.

I smile back. "Thank you. This place is pretty amazing."

"It's my favorite. They all know me here, and that means I get the best treatment." He grins at me like I should be impressed with that. "But I'm just glad I get some time alone with you. To talk."

"Right." I take a sip of wine. Even though Eloise really pushed me to come here with Jared, I should have turned her down. I should have just gone to get Luke and gone to bed. That would have been the smart thing to do.

"I know I ended things pretty abruptly. I know I told you I loved you. It's just —"

"That you were cheating on your wife?" I finish his sentence for him, unable to help myself.

His eyes widen, and he sucks in a breath like I just slapped him.

"Things were hard at home; you have no idea what we were going through." Jared's leaning forward like proximity will be enough to get me on his side. "We'd just lost another baby, and things weren't good between the two of us."

I take a deep breath.

Then another.

Anything to keep from saying what I want, which is that *I* had his baby, that he had a son with me, not with his wife. As tempting as it is to spit those words at him, he doesn't know about Luke, and I don't want him to.

Funny how, for the longest time, I would have done almost anything to find Luke's father. Now I've found him, and he's not mine to have.

"Your meals." The waitress appears, putting two plates down in front of us. I smile up at her, grateful for the distraction and the fact that her presence means Jared won't keep talking. I want him to be quiet because the more he talks, the more he digs himself into a hole. "Let me know if you need anything."

"We're fine," I tell her, picking up my fork. Normally I'd be pinching myself over the fact that I'm sitting at Postero with a handsome man and a steak that looks grilled to perfection, but right now I just want to go home. Instead of saying that, I smile at Jared.

"This looks amazing. Thank you again for dinner."

He stares at me. It feels like he's looking into my soul, his eye contact is so steady. "Thank you for coming with me even after everything." A pause as he swallows. "And thank you for not telling my wife."

It's the first time he's brought up Eloise, and that emboldens me. Still holding my fork, I stab it towards him. "What we did was a mistake," I say. "More yours than mine since you lied to me about it and broke it off *for your company*." I make air quotes around the words, which is difficult while holding a knife, but not impossible. "But I refuse to hurt Eloise. And I refuse to let you do that, either."

He nods, and my heart breaks.

Not for him, God, no. He messed everything up. But my heart breaks for younger me, who thought this man in shining armor was real, who believed his lies and let him love me in the way no man ever had. My heart breaks for her and for the lessons she had to learn the hard way.

Jared is nothing to me anymore. Let him parade me here at his favorite restaurant. I see the way everyone looks at us, like they're envious of me for being across the table from him. I see the men who nod at him, who obviously know him from work. They're all thinking something terrible, I'm sure of it.

Let them think it. What Jared and I did is unforgivable, but it won't happen again. No matter what he thinks.

I can be an adult and live across the street from him without anything stupid happening. And, as blind as he seems to be towards Luke, he never has to know the truth.

If he asks, I'll lie.

It's that simple.

44

ELOISE

I'm on my second cup of coffee when Jared finally makes his way down the stairs. He's moving slowly, heavily, and I know exactly why.

He wouldn't ever drink too much at dinner and put anyone else in the car with him in danger of an accident, but he sure dipped into the whiskey when he got home last night. I found the dirty glass in the kitchen sink and the half-empty bottle sitting on the floor.

No lid. I'm just glad I didn't kick the stupid thing over when I came in here this morning to start my coffee and make breakfast.

"Hey, honey," I say, plastering a huge smile on my face as he walks into the kitchen. When I catch full sight of him, though, my smile falters.

He looks, sorry to say it, like shit. He hasn't shaved this morning, and the bit of scruff combined with dark circles under his eyes and messed-up hair makes him look more like Ricky than my handsome husband. Still, I force myself to walk over to him.

I wrap my arms around him and give him a hug before stepping back.

"I need water," he says. His voice sounds painful, like his tongue is sandpaper rubbing against the roof of his mouth. "And a painkiller."

"Sorry you don't feel good," I say, walking to the cupboard to grab a glass. "I feel fine this morning, so it must have just been a little bug I caught. You'll probably feel better in no time."

He slumps into a chair at the counter and only looks at me when I slide the glass of cold water to him. I fumble out two painkillers from the bottle in the drawer, then glance at him before shaking out two more.

Four should do it.

"It's not a bug," he says, like I don't know he's got the worst possible hangover.

"Well, these will help no matter what it is." I hand him his pills and watch while he takes them. The man probably doesn't even remember leaving the whiskey and dirty glass out last night. I'd wager he doesn't remember much after dropping Tina off, if anything.

"Thank you." He groans and rubs his temples before finally looking at me. "So you're feeling better?"

"All the way," I say. "Like if I ran, I could run a marathon. But instead I'll probably work in the gardens. What's your plan for the day?"

"Not dying." He closes his eyes for a moment.

"Was dinner good? Or did something happen?" I'm insanely curious about what sort of thing Jared and Tina would talk about without me there. Would they discuss their affair? Or is that off-limits? Do they talk about how stupid I am for not knowing that they were together?

"Oh, it was fine. It was fine. Postero was packed. Everyone who was anyone was there." He flaps his hand.

Good. I hope everyone saw you with your mistress.

"Tina had fun? You didn't bore her talking shop with everyone else, did you?"

"No." He takes a deep breath. "I introduced her around. We had fun. She's nice."

"She is, isn't she?" I'm humming now, pleased at how well this is all going. Of course, I knew Postero would be slammed last night. It is every Friday night, and when I'd made the reservation for the two of them last week, I'm pretty sure I was lucky enough to snag one of the last tables.

We're silent, me working at the stove, him sitting at the eat-in bar, probably wishing he were dead.

No worries, Jared. Just wait a little bit longer.

"Is there anything I can make for you for breakfast?" I do my best to sound honestly worried about him. When I turn to look at him, he's wincing and shaking his head.

"I think I'll be sick if I eat," he says in a strangled voice.

"Well, don't mind me, then. I'll go eat outside so I don't bother you." My plate is loaded with bacon and scrambled eggs. There are three pancakes, and I pour a river of maple syrup on the plate to top it off. "It's really nice outside, and I wouldn't mind the fresh air." I pause, waiting for him to take the bait.

He doesn't, so I continue.

"You know, a fresh breeze in your face will really help you feel better. I bet you won't feel nearly as queasy if you come outside, even if you don't eat anything."

"You're probably right." Jared stands. He lumbers, each step purposeful and heavy as he makes his way to the deck door.

I follow him, slipping my phone in my pocket just in case.

The sun is still creeping over the treeline, but the day is going to be warm. I'd be willing to bet the house itself that Tina and Luke will be outside playing this morning in the gorgeous weather. Settling myself in a chair at a high-top table, I gesture to the one next to me.

"Come on, Jared. If you sit here, then you'll get the breeze that blows up the front lawn. Trust me on this one." From here we have a perfect vantage of Tina's new house. That wasn't the goal when we built the deck. I wanted someplace huge to entertain, and Jared was more than happy to bring my plans to life.

The fact that we get a front-row seat to her and Luke is just icing on the cake.

My husband sits next to me, sighing heavily as he does.

When the breeze hits us, I can't help but wrinkle my nose. I hadn't been sure if he showered last night, but the answer is pretty clear now. He smells like he woke up on a bar floor.

I pop a bite of bacon. Even though I know Jared would love nothing more right now than for me to be quiet so his head can feel better, I feel fine, and I'm not going to let him sour my mood. "I was thinking," I say, around a bite of my breakfast, "about hiring someone to replace most of the rosebushes with peonies. They'll love the sun there, and I just love how they smell when in full bloom. What do you think?"

He nods but doesn't speak.

Laughter threatens to bubble out of me. "There are so many things I want to do to kinda spruce this place up this summer. I think a little elbow grease will really bring my vision to life."

Not that you'll be here to see it when it's all completed, honey.

"Whatever you want to do." Jared sounds like he's dying.

If he only knew.

Tina's house is too far away for us to hear anything over there, but I'm keeping my eye on the front door. Surely the two of them will come outside and play. The weather is gorgeous this morning and is only going to get nicer.

We'll just have to wait them out.

While the two of us sit, I keep up a constant stream of chatter. Without Ricky around to keep an eye on Tina, I want to do it myself. I wish there were a way to get into her head and know what she's thinking, but even though she thinks we're really good friends, I doubt she'd open up to me about what's really going on.

What woman, in her right mind, would want to tell her friend about an affair with her husband?

No, that won't happen. I'll just keep watching her to see what she's going to do. And with Jared right next to me, I can keep an eye on them both.

"I really want to go to bed," he finally says, interrupting my stream of consciousness about Tina. I know I should stop thinking about her, but she's wormed her way into my mind. I keep looking at her, then at Jared, imagining the two of them together.

Although, thanks to the pictures Ricky sent me, I don't have to do much imagining.

"Okay, yeah, I know you really don't feel good." I eat the last bite of egg and swallow down my coffee, then turn to look at him. "Are you sure you don't want anything to eat? I can make you whatever you want for breakfast and bring it

up to you so you don't have to worry about coming downstairs when you're hungry."

He doesn't answer. His face is pale and drawn, but he's
looked like that since he got up. I watch as he slowly stands,
carefully tapping his toe on the deck before putting all his
weight on his legs.

He thinks he's going to fall over.

"Jared?" Worry shoots through me. No, it wouldn't
be the worst thing in the world for him to drop dead of
a heart attack right here on our porch, and that's
honestly what it looks like. There's no color in his
cheeks, and his eyes are wide as he stares across the
road.

If he were to die here, of a heart attack, I wouldn't be able
to finish my plan. I wouldn't be able to punish Tina.

"Tina's out." His voice is strangled, and I turn from him,
shielding my eyes against the bright sun that's finally
starting to crest the trees. "Look."

He points, like I don't see her walking down the sidewalk
with Luke. He's skipping at her side while she blows bubbles
from a bottle. Every few feet she pauses and blows, sending a
stream of shiny bubbles into the air before they float off
and pop.

Luke keeps laughing, we can both see that, and his little
voice floats to us on a breeze.

"Jared, are you okay?" I look back at my husband, lightly
touch his arm. When he doesn't respond, I turn my attention
back to Tina.

And to Luke.

Who just so happens to be standing completely in
profile, his hands on his hips, his little chest jutted out. How
many times have I seen Jared stand just like that when he

was trying to make a point or get something through to someone?

How many times have I seen Jared frown just like that, his nose wrinkling up as he tries to think through a problem?

I look up at Jared, and it hits me. *He knows.*

Immediately, my heart beats faster as I try to think through what to do next. Tina has done such a great job keeping Luke from Jared, and I really didn't think he'd be able to tell at this distance, but it was the distance that made it so much more obvious.

"I need to go to bed." Jared sounds like he's drowning. The words gurgle a little bit in his throat.

"Do you feel okay?" I'm everything a wife should be. Loving, worried, willing to do whatever it takes to make her husband feel better. Leaving my plate on the table and keeping my eyes turned away from Tina and Luke, I loop my arm through his and help him to the house.

"I don't feel good."

He allows me to walk with him up the stairs. I get him tucked into bed and kiss him on the forehead before leaving the bedroom. Once in the hall, I sag against the door, unable to stop myself from grinning like a fool.

Jared just figured it out. He knows the truth about Luke.

But he still has no idea I'm one step ahead of him.

45

RICKY

I'm not supposed to text or call Eloise on the weekends. That was part of the plan, part of the deal I agreed to, even though I knew the weekends were going to be hard for me, that they would be frustrating because I have to sit around and wait for her to finally reach out to me on Monday, but I did it, and I was good, and now I'm pacing the floor, waiting on a call.

She always gets in touch with me on Monday because she knows I can't handle not checking in with her. I stayed away from Tina this weekend even though it was hard and even though that means I don't have any money left because I drank it all away at the bar, buying rounds and rounds for everyone so we would be friends, and now I need to talk to Eloise for two reasons.

I need to know about Tina. And I need more money.

Again.

I'm pacing, each time I take a step the feeling of being ungrounded shoots through me until I put my foot back on the floor, but even then I feel like I'm not really here, like I'm floating, and I won't stop until I know about Tina.

"You're driving me nuts. Go outside." Paula appears in front of me, her arms crossed, her brow furrowed. "You're going to wear a hole in the floor if you keep walking like this, and my patience is already thin."

I stare at her. She points at the door.

"Seriously, Ricky. You've been off since Tina moved out, and there's no way anyone will want to move in with us if you're walking around like this all hours of the day. Get outside. Get some fresh air. I promise you, you'll feel better, and we won't have to worry about a noise complaint from Mr. Fred."

I doubt it, but I give her a stiff nod and go outside. On the landing outside our front door there's a stiff breeze, and I shiver into it before heading down the three flights of stairs. Once on solid ground, I turn and look up at our apartment building.

It really is a dump. But Tina's new place is so nice. Sure, it needs work, but I can do work. I'll do whatever it takes to get the house up to her standards. Mine are pretty low, but Tina is classy. She deserves more, and I'll make sure she gets it.

But first I have to talk to Eloise.

My phone still hasn't rung, and I frown at it as I pull it from my pocket.

Two phones. One to use with Eloise, one to use with everyone else.

One is upstairs.

One right here.

Maybe she's calling the other one. Maybe she forgot. Whatever it is, I don't want to wait any longer. Taking a deep breath, I tap on the phone, then hold it up to my ear as it rings.

And rings.

And rings.

"Hi, you've reached Eloise Jones, at Harrison Realty — "

Wrong phone. I used the wrong phone.

I hang up. The way my head pounds makes it really hard for me to think. That might also be the alcohol I had last night, but it doesn't matter what the problem is, I just need to talk to Eloise. I need to know how Tina is. If she were at the apartment, I could just swing by there and check on her, but she's not.

She works.

I could go to her work.

I don't even let the thought fully form before I'm digging in my pocket for my keys. They're not there, which means they're in my room on my bedside table, and I rush back up the rickety outdoor staircase, bursting into the apartment without preamble.

"Holy hell, Ricky, you're running like the devil himself is after you!" Paula calls to me from the living room, but I don't stop to talk to her. I can't. I have to check on Tina.

My second phone is right next to my keys, and I hesitate a moment before scooping it up. There aren't any missed calls, but that doesn't mean Eloise isn't going to call me soon. She'll probably be mad at me for calling her from my main phone, but I don't care about that right now. The only thing that matters is making sure Tina is okay.

I'm halfway across town to the daycare where Tina works when my phone rings. It's in my cupholder, and I fumble it, my finger almost tapping the green button to answer, but then it slips from my hand.

Lands by my feet. Slides under my seat.

"Dammit!" My palms sting from me smacking the steering wheel. Without signaling, I pull over and park in a gas station parking lot. It's busy, with lots of people getting gas, so I drive up on the grass and get out of my car.

The phone is still ringing.

I have to push aside fast-food wrappers to dig it out, but I finally do, and I answer, pressing it to my face as I get back in the car.

"Eloise."

"Ricky!" She hisses my name, and I wince even though she can't hurt me. "I told you I'd call you, so what are you doing calling me? And on the wrong phone! Only use this one; don't you remember that?"

"I remember." I'm flushed, hot. And I do. What I don't tell her is that sometimes it's just too hard for me to do the right thing because all I can think about is Tina. Eloise doesn't understand. She just wants things done her way, and I have to play by her rules.

But if I had, I wouldn't have gotten this close to Tina in the first place.

"Good. Don't make that mistake again." She pauses, and I have the sudden mental image of her holding a stick with a carrot dangling from the end, waving it in my face, her lips curled up in a cruel smile as she watches me watch the carrot, watches me try to grab it and pull it down so I can get it, but she keeps twitching the stick, and the carrot dances in front of me, and I just can't reach it, can't —

"What did you say?" She's speaking, but I forgot to listen.

A heavy sigh. "She's fine. Tina. She's fine. I know you're worried, but you just need to relax. Now, I want to talk to you about the timing because I think we're getting close. It's important for her and Jared to be seen out and about a little bit more, and then it will be time to move forward with the plan."

The plan.

Just thinking about it makes me choke a little. I swallow hard, trying to get rid of the lump in my throat, but it won't go anywhere, not when I'm thinking about *the plan* and what that means. I want to tell Eloise where she can shove *the plan*, that *the plan* has changed, but I know Eloise, and I know how she feels about *the plan*, and I know she doesn't think I'm smart enough to come up with a better plan on my own, but she's so wrong, and that makes me smile.

"Did you hear me?"

No, no, I didn't hear her because I stopped listening. But I swallow again just to make sure that lump in my throat is really gone and isn't coming back, and I respond, "Yeah."

"Good. So just lie low, okay? And I'll let you know when things are moving. I'll keep you in the loop, Ricky; you just have to keep the right phone on you and not do anything stupid."

"Right." I pause, thinking. "Wait, I want more money. I need more."

There's silence on the other end of the line; then Eloise sighs. "You'll get more money, Ricky, when this is all over. Don't ask again."

My mind races, but I can't think of anything to say that will make her do what I want. "Okay."

"Great. I'll talk to you later. Don't call me. I'll call you."

And then she's gone, and I'm left holding the phone for another moment before I put it back in the cupholder. I know what she wants me to do. And I know I should probably listen to her. She's the one who thought this entire thing out to begin with, after all.

But I don't like *the plan*.

There's no room in it for me to be with Tina, and that's the most important thing right now. Eloise is stubborn, and I don't think she's going to be able to get that through her head, no matter what I say to her.

But maybe Tina will.

My engine grinds as I crank the car. Without looking, I pull out into the road. There's a long honk behind me as I drive away, but I don't slow down.

Tina's at work. She'll be there all day, but I can wait. I don't mind sitting in my car and waiting until she leaves the daycare. I'll be there for her when she leaves, and while I wait, I'll come up with a new plan.

A *better* plan.

A plan where we can all get what we want.

A plan where I get Tina.

46

TINA

There's vomit on my shoulder.

Every time I turn my head just a little to the right, I catch a whiff of it. It's disgusting, and just smelling it is enough to make me want to throw up as well, so I keep my head turned to the left.

"I really need to go home and change," I say, poking my head in Bethany's office. She's at the computer, her readers balanced on her nose, and she turns to look at me when I speak.

"Oh, phew. That is... that is rank." Standing, she grabs the bottle of Lysol on her desk and sprays some in my direction. "Someone poop on you?"

"Vomit," I say, pointing to my shoulder. "I don't have a change of clothes. You mind hanging out in my room to keep an eye on the kids while I run home and change? It won't be long. If I don't, I'm afraid everyone else in my room will throw up at the smell."

"Please go." Bethany pinches her nose.

I have to fight to keep from rolling my eyes. She's acting

like it's so bad, but she's five feet away from it, not marinating in it like I am.

"And what kid was it? I'll call their parents."

"Taylor. He looked a little green when Mom dropped him off, but she assured me he was fine. He's not. And thanks, I'll be right back." I wave, then leave her office, letting her door shut hard behind me.

I feel like I could throw up. As soon as I get outside, I know I'm going to feel better, but inside, in the closed-in air of the daycare, I want to be sick. I have to beep myself out with my key card, a precaution Bethany put into place last year after we had a runner who always tried to get out the front door after his mom.

This time I make sure the door closes all the way behind me. The last thing I need is for it to catch on the rug or just not shut and to have a child escape because I didn't take the time to make sure it was closed. But as soon as I'm outside, even though I'm in the parking lot with the smell of cars and exhaust, I feel like I can breathe again.

My shirt sticks to my shoulder, and each step makes it rub. I didn't tell Bethany I'm also going to take a shower when I get home, but I have to. There's no way I can just put on a fresh shirt and walk around with any scent of vomit on me for the rest of the day.

But I don't have time to dawdle. I don't think she'll dock me the time I take to go shower and change, but she might, especially if another staff member says something. Nobody wants anyone else to get preferential treatment, which I totally understand, but I wouldn't judge anyone who needed to go home and shower and change after being barfed on.

Like the rest of the staff, I park in the back of the lot, making it easy for parents to find a spot closer to the building. I don't want to run, but I do pick up the pace as I dig in my purse for my car key. Halfway there, movement from the corner of my eye catches my attention, but it isn't until I hear my name that I slow down.

"Tina!"

I freeze. *Ricky.*

"Hey, Tina!"

The movement I'd seen from the corner of my eye was him getting out of his car. I should have seen it there and recognized it, but I'm just so focused on getting to my car and getting home that I honestly didn't pay any attention to who might be standing in my work parking lot.

Because, really, why would I think for one second that Ricky would be here? He doesn't have kids, and I don't think he has the ambition necessary to get a job, so why...

Because I'm here.

"Ricky, hi," I say. As I speak, I adjust my keys in my hand. Now my house key and car key both stick out from between my fingers. I'm the modern-day female Wolverine, the one we all turn into when walking to our cars late at night or when parked in a sketchy area of town.

Not that I think keys to the face would really stop an attacker, but it's better than nothing, and I'm not allowed to bring a real weapon, like a knife or even pepper spray, to work without getting written up.

"Hey, what are you doing?" He steps closer, then stops. Wrinkles his nose. "And why do you smell like that?"

"I have to go home." I keep my hand down by my side, but I'm gripping the keys so tightly I can feel the metal cutting into my skin. He wouldn't do anything to me, would he? Ricky might not be smart, and he definitely scares me, but I can't imagine him doing anything violent towards me, not in daylight. Not right here at my work.

I want to turn around and see if anyone is watching. The thought that Luke might be pressed up against a window, his eyes wide, his gaze locked on the two of us, makes me sick.

"I can drive you." His key dangles from his finger, and he holds it up to show me. "I know where you live. You don't have to go on your own."

Sweat beads on my brow. The top of my mouth feels filmy. "Thanks," I say, doing my best to smile at him, "but I don't want to make your car stink. And I have to hurry, or I'll be written up. Bethany is waiting on me." A moment of genius strikes me. "She'll be looking for me to come back and is probably still watching me leave."

I turn and make a show of waving to the building even though I know Bethany. She's not watching me. She's dealing with Taylor and probably calling his parents right now.

"But I can help." He's a broken record, and he takes a step closer to me. The look on his face tells me I still stink, but he obviously doesn't seem to be that bothered. "Let me help you. It's the new plan."

I blink at him. He's not making any sense, but I'm honestly afraid of what he might say if I tell him that. His eyes are bloodshot and red-rimmed. His hair, which isn't ever *styled*, exactly, looks more like a rat's nest than ever before. His clothes hang off his frame and are all wrinkled.

As I stare at him, he shifts his feet, shuffling a little to the side. It takes me longer than I'd like to admit to realize that he's now standing between me and my car.

"Ricky, have you slept? Are you feeling okay?" Maybe I can take a different approach with him. He's clearly not going to let me talk my way out of this, and I have to get past him. Would he grab me? Would he physically prevent me from getting into my car and leaving?

I don't know, and I don't want to find out.

And what plan is he talking about?

"I just want to help you." He holds his hands out to the sides. "Let me help you."

"I'm okay." Goosebumps break out on my arms. My mouth, which had been filmed with spit, now feels dry.

I feel my breathing quicken. My heart races.

"But you're not okay." He whispers the words, then looks around him like he's afraid someone might have heard him. "Let me help you."

Oh, God, what is he going to do? I've seen enough *Dateline*, read enough articles in the paper, and even listened to a murder podcast for half of an episode before getting so creeped out I had to shut it off and turn on some Mika to clear my thoughts.

Maybe it's engrained in women, this knowledge of when a man is going to be dangerous. Maybe we learn it, but whatever the case, I know one thing.

Ricky is dangerous, and I'm in trouble.

"I'm fine," I whisper back. A bird flies overhead, screaming its fool head off about something, but neither of us look up. "I just need to go home."

I have to get around him.

Fear prickles the back of my neck, and I feel the hair there stand up.

Ricky opens his mouth to say something, but he's interrupted by a jaunty tune.

A ringtone.

His expression changes, his eyebrows crashing together

in surprise. For just a moment, I stare at him, wondering what he's going to do, but then he breaks the spell by digging in his pocket for his phone.

"Not now," he mutters, but his head is tilted down, his eyes are no longer locked on me, and I feel like I can move for the first time since he appeared.

I run. It's probably silly and only serves to make me even more frightened, but I do it anyway, my arms pumping as my feet pound the pavement. My car is *right there*, and I'm closing in on it, my hand fumbling the key out from between my fingers, getting ready to jab it into the lock — *why don't I have a new car with a button I can just push so I can unlock the dumb thing as I tear towards it* — and now I'm here, and the key hits right in the lock and bounces to the side.

There's a scraping sound as it drags down the door, leaving a mark in its wake.

I try again and shove the key in the lock, this time getting it all the way in before I turn it — *do I hear him behind me, or is that pounding sound just my heart beating so hard it sounds like footsteps* — and then the door is unlocked, and I yank the key out, grab the handle and pull it so hard I feel like it's going to snap off in my hand.

I throw myself in the car, pulling the door shut behind me. The lock sticks straight up, and I bring my hand down on it as hard as possible, ramming it into place, ignoring the pain that shoots through my palm as I do.

I'm in. Panting, I jab the key into the ignition and crank the engine, only now stopping to turn and look out my window.

He's right there. If the window weren't up, he could reach in and touch me, could wrap his hand in my hair, his fingers lacing through my long strands, could pull me out —

I shake my head.

Clear the thought.

Ricky presses his hand up against the window, his palm towards me.

I have to rip my eyes away from him and slam my foot down on the gas.

47

ELOISE

One thing I remember my mom teaching me was that in order to perform your best, you have to look your best.

Growing up, that meant something very different than it does now. We weren't nearly rich enough to afford the clothing I wear as an adult, but Mom always shopped at thrift stores and managed to find decent clothes at rock-bottom prices. Her favorite belonging was her sewing machine, and I remember her sitting up late at night to make sure the clothes we had fit.

And her makeup might not have been high-end, but she always looked nice. She'd curl her hair with rags and paint a smile on her face, and that would ensure she looked and felt good, even though the only places she went were thrift stores, the food bank, and her job at the bar.

But things have changed. I might have started out in a similar boat as my mom, but I have money now, and I know how to make myself look the best I possibly can.

For me, this means regular trips to the salon. Perfect

makeup and hair every single day. Shoes and purses that match. I never leave the house without a full face of makeup and some heels, not because I think I'm a pin-up girl by any means, but because I know it's important for everyone to see you looking successful.

Even though I don't work with high-income clients any longer, I still want people to see me and think *money*.

Because that's what this is all about, isn't it? Money. Money and being able to do what I want without having to worry about Jared trying to tell me no or trying to stop me, or getting to spend his money the way he wants it — on women who will gladly fall into bed with him at a moment's notice.

I glare in my office mirror at the smudge of lipstick on my lip.

That's beyond annoying. "I need to fix that," I say, leaning closer to the mirror and lightly touching the edge of my lip. The more I mess with it, the worse it's going to look, but maybe if I just barely touch it —

It smears more. Heat rushes through me.

Stomping across my office, I open the bottom drawer of my desk where I keep my purse and yank it out. It's leather, of course, the feel of it soft and supple under my fingers, but I barely notice how nice it feels as I dig inside, my fingers searching for the lipstick I have on.

Coral Lover.

"Where are you?" It's not in the side pocket where I normally put my lipstick, and I start pulling everything out and putting it on my desk. My wallet. Keys. Phone. Second phone. Chapstick. Tampon. Breath mints. Planner. Three pens, four paperclips, a receipt from a bank deposit, and eyeliner.

No lipstick.

"Come on." Leaving the pile on my desk, I take my purse and hold it upside down, giving it a shake to see what falls free.

Nothing. Some lint, but nothing that matters. Nothing that will help me.

Closing my eyes, I try to remember where I put the lipstick. My purse was *right there* hanging on the closet door, and I slipped the lipstick in after putting it on in the bathroom. Then I'd gone downstairs and grabbed my purse and —

Wait.

I put the lipstick in my upstairs purse. Picked up the one from downstairs. Left the lipstick at home.

"Jesus, you idiot," I say, smacking my head with my hand. "You can't even bring the right purse to work, so how the hell do you think you're going to handle everything else that needs to be done?" Abandoning my purse, I start digging through the top drawer of my desk. "Maybe you have another color that's close that you can put on. You can change up your look; it isn't such a big deal."

The thought that I'm missing out on something eats at me. I feel like I'm forgetting something big, something I need to pay attention to, but I can't put my finger on what it is.

"Yeah, it's your lipstick, dummy," I say, but then I stop. My hand is wrapped around a box of tape refills, but my mind isn't here in my office.

It's on the purse hanging on my closet door. The purse with the lipstick.

I close my eyes.

I've been running on adrenaline and definitely not getting enough sleep while everything comes to a head. I think about the night Jared and Tina went out to eat at Postero. I'd done a great job hiding the box from 123DNA.

But where did I put the results?

A cold chill washes over me like I just took part in a polar bear plunge. It's hard for me to breathe, hard for me to take a big enough breath to not feel like I'm going to pass out.

I left them in my purse.

That fact hits me so solidly in the chest that it honestly feels like I've been punched. I gasp for air and plant both of my hands on my desk, hunched over it like that's going to be enough to help me get the oxygen I need.

My head hurts.

Over and over I'd told myself I'd bring the papers here, to my office, to hide them, and I left the little bastards right there in my purse, hanging in our bedroom, right where anyone could find them.

Right where Jared could find them.

I have to go home.

I grab fistfuls of the stuff that had been in my purse and shove it back inside, keeping my keys in my hand. As I grab the handle to my door, it flies open, forcing me to take a step back out of the way.

"Oh, good." Harrison grins at me, his eyes flicking up and down my body as he steps past me to my desk. "I need to talk to you about this little program of yours."

"Now's not the time." I grit my teeth and put a smile on my face. Even though I know I need to try to act as normal as possible, I want to scream at him to get out of my office.

"Where's the fire?" He leans back against my desk. From the look on his face, it's pretty obvious he's not in a hurry to go anywhere. "You have an appointment or something? There wasn't anything on your calendar."

Damn the online calendars. All they are is a way for him to keep track of what we're doing. He can't handle the thought that anyone in the office has something to do that doesn't include him or that doesn't bring money into Harrison Realty.

"I forgot to put it on my online calendar," I lie, pulling a face. My planner sticks out of the top of my purse, and I produce it with a flourish. "But it's in here. Doctor's appointment. I can't be late."

He doesn't budge.

"Women problems. If you want to know, I'm happy to tell you all about what's going on — "

"That won't be necessary. Just come see me when you're finished there. I talked to Jared, and he's not so sure about the stability of this program or if he even wants to keep funding it."

That catches my attention. In my mind I'm already halfway home, my foot mashing down on the gas, but I whip my head up to stare at him. "What?"

He shrugs. Casual. Completely in control. "We'll discuss it when you get back. The last thing I want is to be a distraction when you're obviously having problems. Drive safe, Eloise."

With that, he shoves off my desk and brushes past me. The man has doused so much cologne on himself that I feel it in my throat as he walks away from me.

For a moment, I just stare after him. Then it hits me that I need to get moving, get home, get the papers.

Then I'll be able to worry about what Harrison just said.

Jared knows something, that much is obvious. There's no way he'd just pull the funding on my project like that without some reason.

He knows about Luke, yes. I saw that on his face when we were on the deck. That's not what I'm worried about.

The only question running through my head as I race downstairs to my car is *how much does my husband know about what I've done?*

48

TINA

My breathing doesn't slow down until I pull into my driveway and kill the engine of my car. I sit still, gulping air and staring in my rearview mirror.

Surely Ricky wouldn't follow me home, would he? I know he knows where I live, and while that just seemed a little weird at first, now it scares me. Moving out was supposed to give me a chance to get away from him, but all it did was make it a bit more difficult for him to find me.

But he obviously can track me down if he wants to.

The memory of his hand pressed up against my window gives me chills. I get out of my car and run to the house, fumbling the key in the lock and throwing the deadbolt behind me once I'm inside. For a moment, I forget about what I'm doing and why I'm home; then I remember.

Taylor. The vomit.

While I'd wanted a shower, all I want now is to be back at the daycare with Luke so I can keep an eye on him. I yank my shirt off and toss it in the washer, then call Bethany, putting the phone on speaker as I run water in the sink. It'll take a moment to warm up, but then all I have to do is rinse my shoulder with a washcloth, throw on a shirt, and get out of here.

"Hi, Tina." Bethany has a great phone voice. She always puts a huge smile on her face before answering so everyone feels like they're the most important person when she talks to you. "Everything okay?"

"Hey, yeah, just rinsing my shoulder." I grab a washcloth and wet it even though the water isn't warm yet. "Hey, I just wanted to make sure everyone there knows Luke can't go home with anyone but me."

I have a terrible mental image of Ricky picking him up, lying through his teeth to get him, and then taking my son. To where? I don't know. I never would have thought that might happen before today, before he chased me to my car, before —

"Hang on." I hear her typing.

Go faster.

"Okay, I'm looking at his information right now. You're the only authorized pickup." She pauses, and I know her mind must be going a million miles a minute. "Everything okay?"

I hesitate. It would be easy enough to tell her the truth, to let her know about Ricky so she could keep an eye out for him. I don't know if he's still in the parking lot, just waiting for me to get back, but he didn't follow me here.

While I think through my options, I wipe my shoulder down. The water is chilly, and I shiver but do it again, wanting to clean myself from both the feel and smell.

"Tina?"

"Sorry, I was just thinking." Again I hesitate. Why don't I

want to come clean with Bethany about Ricky? It's not like I've encouraged him, have I? I don't think I brought this on myself, but I can't help but feel like I might have somehow given him the wrong impression. Still, there's a huge difference between accidentally picking up the wrong signals from someone and stalking them to their job.

"There's a guy in the parking lot," I say, leaving the washcloth in the sink and hurrying into the bathroom. I have to put the phone down on my bed while I pull my clean shirt on, but then I grab it again and hurry to the living room so I can look outside.

No Ricky.

"Is he dangerous?"

The last thing I want is to get the cops involved. Maybe that's stupid, and I'll wish later I had just called them, but coming to someone's place of work isn't a crime. Wanting to talk to them isn't reason to be arrested.

"No," I say the word firmly. "No, I don't think he is, but he is a little creepy. He's my old roommate, and I think he just... misses me. I just don't want him to try to take Luke."

Bethany's voice is firm. "Nobody can get to Luke without your permission, okay? You don't need to worry about a thing. Are you headed back now?"

"Yep." I grab my keys and unlock, then open the front door, hesitating as I peek out the crack to make sure he hasn't pulled up. "I'll be there as soon as possible. I'm so sorry about having to leave like this."

"Not a problem. Head on back, Tina, and then feel free to park up closer to the building. I don't see this guy you're talking about, but I don't want you to feel at all uncomfortable, okay? Just come on back."

"Will do, thanks." I lock the door and run to my car. It

feels foolish, especially since this is my house. My yard. My property. Nobody should feel afraid when they're at their house, but I can't help the fear nibbling at the back of my mind. "Thank you, Bethany," I say, trying to draw out our goodbye for as long as possible.

I just don't want to get off the phone with her just yet. Not until I'm safely in my car.

"Of course. Now, I'll keep a lookout for you, but like I said, I don't see anyone in the parking lot. And Luke is fine with Miss Debbie. Just drive safe; your kids at work need you."

"Thanks." I'm in my car now, the door locked. She hangs up, and I exhale hard, gripping the steering wheel with both hands to keep them from shaking.

This little thing with Ricky? Whatever he has in his head? It's his problem, not mine. Of course, when he brings his problem to my work, it does suddenly become my issue, but hopefully he's really gone now.

Right?

But at least I know Luke is safe. He's all that matters.

I back out of my driveway, casting one look up at the house across the road. Eloise's car is in the driveway, which is weird. Since I moved in, I've only ever seen her parking in the garage. For just a moment I consider pulling up her driveway and not only making sure she's okay but just getting some reassurance about what I'm going through.

But I don't. I keep my hands steady on the wheel and drive past her house, out of the neighborhood, away from Eloise.

Because, as much as I'd like to share with her what's going on, and as much as I know she'd be supportive, how can I?

Someone like her has probably never met someone like Ricky.

She wouldn't get it.

Her life is perfect and organized and wonderful, and, to her, mine probably looks like a hot mess. I'm just glad to have her as a friend, but I'm not dragging her into whatever craziness is going on.

I can handle myself. I have so far, without anyone there to help me out, and there's no reason why that has to change now.

49

ELOISE

When I was younger, I went swimming one time with my mom in the old reservoir north of here. It was early spring, and the water was much too cold to get in, but I'd been begging to go swimming in the summer, and she knew I wasn't going to be able to handle myself at a pool party without practice.

I'd stood on the edge of the water in a little floral bikini. It had gotten too small for me over the summer, but nobody had donated any recently to the thrift stores, so it's all I had to wear. At least, when people started going through their summer clothes and getting rid of what didn't fit, I'd probably get a new-to-me one then, but not yet.

It didn't cover everything. It rode up in the back. The frills along my hips were distinctly *little girl*, and I was growing into a teenager, but it was what we had, and, besides, we were the only ones there.

Just my mom and me.

She was up to her waist in water. We both wore shoes because you just never knew when someone would break a bottle and leave the glass in the water. The last thing we could afford was one of us getting cut up and having to go to the emergency room for stitches.

That just wasn't an option.

So shoes it was.

Shoes and a little floral bikini with ruffles on the hips.

"You can do it!" she'd called to me from the water like she was having the time of her life even though I knew she had to be freezing, I could practically see her shivering even from the edge. "Just jump in and swim."

And I did. Over and over, my wet hair sticking like spider legs to my skin as I surfaced, my bikini growing dingy in the dirty water. Each time I went under and felt the water over my head, it felt like all the air in my lungs was pushed out, like they were just useless sacks, empty balloons in my chest.

And I feel the same way now.

"Oh, God," I mutter, sitting down on the floor by my closet. "He knows."

Of course he knows. I'm an idiot. I left the proof of Luke being his kid *right here* where he could see it, but that's not what I'm worried about. It's more than that, more than just the fact that Luke is his kid, because he figured that out when he saw the two of them out for a walk together. It's proof that I know the truth. That I've been lying to him.

That I was in on it from the beginning.

Panic circles my throat, and I lean my head back, my mouth open, waiting for a scream.

It doesn't come.

The papers were in my purse. That should be good, right? That should prove that everything is fine, that Jared doesn't know a damn thing, but he does, and I know he does because they weren't in the pocket where I stuffed them.

They were in the purse's main compartment, the envelope crumpled just a bit like he'd squeezed it in with his fist, unable to stop himself, and now here we are.

And he knows everything.

My hand trembles as I reach for my phone. The last thing I want to do is call him, but I have to hear his voice. Jared can lie over text, we all can, we can make it seem like everything is fine, but if I get to listen to him and hear his voice, I'll be able to tell what's going on.

It's a battle to make myself push the call button. But I do; then I press the phone to my ear. My *real* phone, not my Ricky one, although that one is right next to me on the floor because I'm probably going to need it, aren't I?

To handle whatever comes next.

It rings and rings, the sound mocking in my ear, and when Jared's voice clicks on, a calm message telling me to leave a message, I hang up.

Wipe my hands on my skirt.

"His office," I mutter, tapping away on the screen. "He has to be there, and they can tell me if he's in a meeting, because that would make sense. He could be in a meeting, and that's why he can't pick up."

I know the number by heart, but I still find the saved entry for it just in case I misdial.

This time, there's only two rings, and Alice picks up. "JJones PR and Marketing, this is Alice."

Good, dependable Alice. Alice with three grandkids and gray hair and an ever-expanding waistline, who takes her job more seriously than anyone I've ever met. She'll tell me everything is fine, that Jared is just in a meeting, and I'll believe her, because she's Alice.

I exhale in relief. "Alice, hi. This is Eloise."

"Mrs. Jones." Her voice is prim. Proper. "What can I do for you?"

I relax even more. This is so everyday, so common. So normal.

Nothing to see here, folks. Just move along. You may think something's afoot, but you'd be wrong.

"I'm just looking for Jared, and he's not picking up his phone. He mentioned this morning that it hadn't been working right, so I don't know if it's even ringing through. Do you know if he's around?"

A slight pause. I might not even recognize it as one if I weren't listening for it, but it's there, and it makes my heart beat faster.

"He's out of the office right now, Mrs. Jones. Would you like to leave a message for him?"

It's difficult for me to think straight. I dig my fingers into my thigh, the pain helping ground me.

"I'm actually supposed to meet him somewhere. It's important. Where did he go?"

No beating around the bush, no pretending like I don't already have plans with my husband. Alice knows where Jared is, and she needs to tell me.

"Mrs. Jones — "

"Alice, Jared told me it was imperative we met up today so I could give him something. I don't know where he is, but I do know I need to get to him. Do you really want to be the reason we can't connect? I'm sure he'd love to hear that you're refusing to give me the information I need."

Silence. Then a sigh. "He's at Brett Larch's office."

Brett Larch?

I'm going to throw up.

"Thank you. I'll head there now to meet him." I hang up

before she has a chance to respond. Even though I want to scream at this news, want to run away from it, I can't do that.

Everyone in town knows Brett Larch.

He's the best lawyer there is.

My hand shakes as I put down the phone I just used. I hesitate for a moment, torn on what to do but knowing full well that I have to do something.

It feels like my hand is moving of its own accord as I pick up a phone.

Ricky's phone.

50

RICKY

I'm in bed when the phone rings, and even though I'd love to ignore it, it's not my personal phone.

It's Eloise's phone.

I roll over, yanking my covers along with me, then grab it from my bedside table. Thumb it on. Put her on speaker.

"What?" Anger washes over me at the fact that I'm talking to her, not Tina.

Tina, who was obviously so upset leaving work today. Tina, who drove away without saying goodbye to me, even though I was right there waiting to talk to her. If an old friend hadn't called and distracted me, then I could have walked her to her car, maybe even driven with her. I'd reach over, put my hand on her thigh, feel the muscle move there as she drove, and I'd know without a shadow of a doubt that the two of us were meant to be together.

But, more importantly, she'd figure it out, too.

Now, though, seeing her is just a memory, and I cling to it even as my cousin's voice fills the air. Her words are high-pitched and biting, and I wince as I listen. They feel like knives on my skin.

"He knows. Ricky, Jared knows. And he's at the lawyer's office, which means he's probably going to file for divorce, but I have to stop him. I have to finish this."

I'm silent. When I close my eyes, I see her, see Tina, and I don't like the fact that she's not here for me to see in person. I really don't like the fact that Eloise is going to mention —

"— the plan, Ricky. It's time."

I'm silent. The two words have so much weight they seem to press down on my chest like someone put a boulder there and is weighing me down, and I want to shift position and get rid of the pressure, but when I do, nothing changes.

"Ricky, are you there?"

I nod. Remember she can't see me. "I'm here, Eloise." My diary is next to me, open to the page I was writing on. I grab it and rip it out of the notebook, then shred the paper while I wait on a response.

Trash, trash, trash, it's all trash; it'll all end up there. I tighten my fist around the shreds, compressing them into a tight ball.

"I need you to move ahead with the plan. We're ahead of schedule. I really wanted the two of them out in public again together, wanted to make sure people saw them more so when this all comes to a head, everyone points their finger right at her, not at me."

Right at Tina.

"Right." I sit up, struggling against the boulder on my chest. My breath comes in hard bursts as I do.

"I need his phone," Eloise is continuing. "I need to be able to text her, tell her it's off. The police will see that, will see that he ended it with her, and she freaked out and killed him."

"His phone, sure." I'm still trying to wrap my mind around what she's saying. I thought I had more time. I thought I had —

"— more time would be great, but we have to move. He knows, Ricky."

He knows. He knows. He knows. The one thing Eloise was terrified of coming true has happened, and Jared knows the truth, and now it's all up to me to carry out the last bit of the plan even though — *what did you think was going to happen, what did you think was going to happen to Tina, you knew the plan from the word GO, yet you signed up, put your name right on the dotted line for that easy money, didn't you? And you didn't think things through, didn't think —*

"— she has to be framed." Eloise is whispering now, but hissing the words, and I picture them slithering out of the phone like snakes and wrapping around my neck. "You see that, right? You still see that? Everyone has to look at Tina. She has to be framed for this."

"Okay."

I need her to stop talking. She's still prattling on about something, about *the plan*, and I know I should listen to her so I can make my own plan, but it's really hard to focus when all I can see is Tina, and I need to figure out what I'm going to do. It's just hard for me to wrap my mind around it all, and she keeps asking me questions, keeps interrupting me, keeps asking me things like I'm an idiot, things like —

"— do you understand? I need to make sure you understand the timeline."

"Of course."

"Are you sure? We can go over it again." There's panic in her voice.

I sound perfectly calm.

"I understand everything." And I do. For the first time in my life, for the first time since Eloise and I came up with this plan — *although she came up with the plan, didn't she, you just signed on, a willing soldier who was happy to carry whatever weapon and do whatever needed as long as you got paid* — I understand what I need to do.

"Good. Then we'll meet up tomorrow and take care of it, do the plan, and I need his phone, remember that, Ricky. You can't forget that."

She always talks to me like I'm stupid, like I can't understand anything in this world, and I hate that about her.

"Then the money," she continues, like I'm not even thinking over here, like I'm not trying to work things out in my head. "Your money comes after. After everything is settled and it's all mine. Understand?"

I understand so many things. Things she can't ever understand. Things she'll have to wait to see how it all pans out, then try to wrap her mind around.

"Of course."

"Okay. I'll talk to you tomorrow. Keep your phone with you, Ricky. Don't mess this up."

I hang up. Stand up. Stretch. Keep the paper shreds in my hand so I can throw them away, just like always.

Then I walk out of my bedroom door. Out of the apartment.

Down to my car.

Without the phone.

51

TINA

A soft groan escapes my lips as I hitch Luke up onto my hip. He's getting big and growing every day, and while I used to be able to just pick him up and swing him around, I'm tired. Truth of it is, I think I've gotten a little more tired every single day since Ricky moved into the apartment.

And now, even though we're on our own, I'm still tired.

But at least I don't smell like vomit any longer, and at least Bethany was right and Ricky isn't here.

Still, I'm quick as I walk the two of us across the parking lot. My head is on a swivel, and I'm grateful Bethany told me to park up closer to the building so I don't have to walk all the way to the back lot. We make it to the car, and I put Luke on his feet, still holding his hand, while I fumble with the key.

"To the park today?" He squeezes my hand and looks up at me. Hope is written so clearly across his face that I almost feel bad telling him no.

"Not today, buddy," I say, pressing the button to unlock

all the doors. "Climb on in there, and I'm going to take you home. Let's make some popcorn and watch cartoons, what do you say?"

Yes, and we can stay inside, away from the front yard, away from any possibility of Ricky deciding to drive by my house again. We'll draw the shades so we can see what's on the screen better, but also make it impossible for anyone to see into the house.

His lower lip trembles, but he climbs in his car seat. "But the park."

"I know." I pull a face to try to show I'm on his side as I buckle him in nice and tight. "But it's going to rain, and I think cartoons are fun. What do you think?"

Luke sighs, and I get in the driver's seat, ignoring his theatrics.

He can be upset all he wants. As much as I'd love to go to the park and enjoy the gorgeous weather, I will lie through my teeth to my son if that's what it takes to get him to go along with my plan. After all, I'm the mom, and he shouldn't argue with me in the first place, but we all know how little kids are.

We're halfway home, and I'm lost in my thoughts before Luke speaks again.

"*Bunny Racer.*"

I glance at him in the rearview mirror. "That's what you want to watch?"

He nods. His arms are crossed and his chin lifted in a picture of defiance like I'm going to argue with him about the show we're going to use to rot our brains.

"You got it."

He's silent a little longer. The next time he speaks, we're pulling into the driveway.

"And ice cream."

"Of course." I park. Check all the mirrors. The car is still on, and I feel it rumble under me as I look around us, look to make sure Ricky isn't here. "Ice cream and popcorn and *Bunny Racer*. But we have to stay inside."

"Okay." He unbuckles himself faster than I do, and races me to the porch. My heart pounds as I unlock the door to let him in. Then, before I follow him, I look around one more time.

The neighborhood is quiet. There's a prickling feeling on the back of my neck, a tightening of the skin there, that tells me I need to slow down, take my time, really look around and make sure I'm not missing anything.

So I do.

I look up and down both directions of the road. No cars, no neighbors. Nobody walking a dog or pushing a stroller. It honestly feels like Luke and I are the only people left in the world, and the thought sends chills tap-dancing up my spine.

But look closer.

I leave the front door and walk across the porch, leaning on the railing for a moment to really get my bearings. Ricky isn't here, and that means I can slow down for a moment and make sure I'm not missing anything.

Nothing at my house. Nothing on the road.

I lift my eyes and look at Eloise's house. The sun's setting behind it, and the light in my eyes forces me to raise my hand and block it out. I do, but not before I see a flash of something in the driveway.

A car. But not just any car.

I know that car.

It's *Ricky*.

"What are you doing over there?" I lean farther over the railing, my eyes searching for any sign of movement at the house. I guess he could be parked over there so he has easy access to my house, but that's insane, right? Even someone like Ricky, who's obviously holding on to sanity with a very loose grip, wouldn't park at the neighbor's house to come over to mine.

He'd pull right up into my driveway. He'd saunter up the front walk.

But I'm sure that's his car.

For a moment, I consider calling Eloise and letting her know Ricky is there. I can't think of a single good reason why he'd be parked in her driveway or how he'd know her, but then I stop myself.

Just because I'm paranoid doesn't mean someone is actually out to get me. Just because I don't like Ricky doesn't mean someone else might not. Heck, he heard me talking about Eloise all the time in the apartment, and I wouldn't be half-surprised if he reached out to her to see about buying a house himself.

Yeah, right.

My jaw is tight. I can feel my teeth grinding together as I debate what to do.

Behind me, the screen door slams open.

"Mom, it's *Bunny Racer* time!" Luke grabs my hand and yanks it, trying to pull me back to the house. I should go with him.

I should stop staring across the street, stop worrying about what may or may not be going on over there.

It's none of my business.

Still...

I'll give it one episode of *Bunny Racer*, and then I'll check again. If Ricky is still there — *and it might not even be Ricky, right? Just because he has that car doesn't mean everyone who has that car is Ricky* — then I'll call Eloise and just let her know she has a visitor.

She'll laugh at me. Tell me she already knows. Tell me to stop worrying about what's going on in the neighborhood, but I'll still feel a bit better.

"Okay," I say, ripping my eyes away from the house across the street. It's always been big and made my house feel smaller in comparison, but today it feels like it's looming. Breathing. A huge, dark monolith overlooking my house, casting its shadow on me.

Chills race through my body. I thought I was cold before, thought I was nervous, but how I felt has nothing on how I feel right now.

"*Bunny! Racer!*" Luke stomps his foot.

I'd normally correct him and talk to him about how to better express his feelings, because nobody wants a little kid around who stomps their foot like that, but now I just let him drag me into the house. I lock the door behind me, double-checking that it's safe.

Relief floods through me once we're both safely inside. Still, I can't shake the thought that something isn't right. That I should be more worried than I am.

That there's a darkness about the house across the street that isn't usually there.

I shake it off. Microwave some popcorn like I promised.

By the time I sit down with Luke on the sofa, *Bunny Racer* blaring in our small house, I keep thinking I should be feeling better, but I'm not. One episode of pure little-kid fun and cartoon ridiculousness will take my mind off this. Everything will be fine — *I'm not stepping back outside on the porch, not until I know things are fine.*

Half an hour.

That's all. Even if something weird is going on over there, it can't get worse in half an hour.

52

RICKY

J ared stares at me, but he doesn't say anything.

It's been years since we talked, years since I've stunned him into silence, and I have to admit that I like my cousin's husband better like this, with his mouth open but unspeaking, his eyes locked on me like he can't wait to see what I'm going to do next. There's a look of surprise on his face, but that will disappear eventually.

Open and unseeing.

I bend over him, and when he doesn't flinch, I sit down next to him on the tile floor. It's cold, the tile, but it feels good on my legs. I'm hot, so hot, and while I'd love to take a cold shower or get a beer and relax for a moment, Eloise doesn't keep beer in the house, only wine and whiskey, and I need to keep moving if I'm going to hold up my end of the deal.

"Come on, Jared," I say, bending over and grabbing under his armpits. He doesn't respond, not like I really thought he would, although it would be nice for him to get up and walk with me to my car so I could get him out of here without breaking a sweat, but he doesn't help me, and he doesn't budge.

Blood pools out from around his body, the red liquid running in the grout between the tiles faster than I thought it would, spreading out, a spider's web.

The thought makes me giggle, and I clap my hand over my mouth to keep the sound inside before I remember that there isn't anyone here, that I can laugh all I want. Eloise and Jared can't stop me, and I throw my head back, cackling as the sound rolls out of me and bounces around their white minimalist kitchen.

Then I stop.

I still have work to do, but now the thought of trying to get Jared to my car is more daunting than before. He's losing so much blood, and that should make him lighter, shouldn't it? Shouldn't that make him easier to carry or drag or something, yet he's just as heavy as he was a moment ago.

I tug on him half-heartedly, then walk to the refrigerator and yank it open. I'm hungry and thirsty, and Eloise always has leftovers and bubbly water. That's what rich people drink when they're not downing alcohol, right?

Bubbly water?

"Black raspberry," I say, grabbing a can and popping the top. It fizzles like a soda, and my mouth waters for a rum and Coke, but then I take a sip. Spit it out. Put the can back in the fridge.

Disgusting.

When I'm rich, when this is all over and Eloise has given me the money I deserve for helping her out with her stupid cheating husband, then Tina and I can drink whatever we want. I won't want bubbly water, that's for sure, it's too spicy, but she might, and that's okay.

Tina.

I walk across the kitchen to the windows. My shoes squeak on the tile, and I glance down, not surprised to find footprints behind me.

I'm tracking everywhere. It's going to be a nightmare to clean this up.

The thought makes my heart race. There's no way I can, no way I'll be able to —

But Eloise will, because it's *the plan*, and then she'll be happy and rich, and I'll be rich, and Tina will be in jail for killing Jared and —

I shake my head to stop the thoughts.

"No," I whisper. "That's her plan. That's the old plan, not the new one I came up with. Tina's not going to jail. Tina's going to live with me. She can't live with me, can't fall in love with me, if she's in jail, and I have to do whatever it takes to keep that from happening."

I walk back to Jared. The knife is still sticking out of his gut, and I pull it out. Blood wells up around the cut — *how much more blood does this man have in him* — and then the knife is in my hand, and I'm standing over him just like I was when he first fell, only this time I'm remembering *the plan*.

Lure him out of the house. Get him to Tina's. Kill him there so the police look at her as a suspect.

Get Eloise his phone. Let her text Tina like he's breaking up with her — *like anyone would break up with Tina, they'd have to be stupid* — and then I remember that Jared broke up with her once because of *optics* and making sure his company was always presented in the best light, and I swing my leg back and kick him right in his ribs, and my toe sinks into his side, the feeling soft and relenting.

Where was I?

Get Eloise his phone so she can make it look like Tina did this in a fit of rage when he broke up with her. Only now I've gone and killed him in his own kitchen, not in Tina's kitchen, and there's so much blood, and I don't know how to get him down the hill and across the street.

"Hello, Tina, let me bring this body in and put it in your kitchen, and then my cousin is going to frame you for Jared's murder, and she and I are going to split all of his money so we can live happily ever after, and Jared won't, and you won't, and Luke won't, but that's *the plan*."

Eloise is going to be pissed off at me for already messing up the plan. My legs feel weak and give way. As I slump down to the floor, I scoot back, doing my best to keep away from the blood.

How in the world is Eloise going to clean up all of this blood?

I can drag Jared out. I can get him in my car and drive him across the road, but Tina won't let me in, not like that, she'll call the police and never give me the opportunity to tell her that I'm not a bad guy, that I'm just doing what Eloise wants me to, and I can't do that to her, not when she's so sweet and so perfect.

There's something in my hand, and I look down, surprised to see the knife still there.

I have to get rid of it. I stand and hurry across the kitchen. Yank open the trash. For a moment I consider dropping the knife in there and getting rid of it that way, but that's stupid, the police will look in the trash, and then they'll know I killed Jared.

No, no, no, do it right. I've seen enough police shows to know I need to do it right, need to be careful.

Blood smears on the oven when I grab the towel hanging there to wipe off the knife handle.

That's more blood to clean up.

But now the knife handle is clean. Dropping the towel, I spin in a slow circle, looking for a place to put the knife. I don't mean to hurt Eloise, but I don't want to hurt Tina — *can't hurt Tina* — so I run upstairs. Up the stairs with their white rug at the bottom.

My toe catches on a step, and I fall to the side, grabbing at the wall for support. Framed pictures clatter to the ground, but I push myself back up, leaving them there for later.

Another mess to clean up.

So many messes, and no time any longer, no time for me and no time for Eloise because I know if I leave the house now and leave this all for her, she won't be able to explain it all away, but if I don't leave the house and if I try to clean it all up on my own, then I'm going to run out of time, and I'll never have Tina.

And this is all for Tina.

I throw the knife into the bathroom sink. There's still blood on it, just a smear, and I turn on the faucet, letting hot water run over the blade.

Turn it off.

Now there's blood on the faucet handle.

"Think, think, think," I say. I make a fist and pound it into the side of my head. Sometimes there are thoughts in there I have to rattle loose, have to try to shake them out from where they're hiding so they can make sense again.

But right now, nothing, there's nothing, there's just emptiness and panic, and I grab the edge of the sink and turn the water back on, splashing it on my face.

Now there's blood on the sink.

It's everywhere. It's on my hands still, and my shirt and

my arms and pants, and when I lean over the sink, my shirt
touches it and smears the red blood on the white counter,
and I grab a fluffy white bath towel to try to wipe it up, but
now the towel is red, and there's still a pool of it downstairs,
still seeping into the grout, and I'll need bleach to get that
out because there's no way to get blood out from grout with
just hand soap, I'm not that stupid, everyone knows that,
even me, even though I just keep smearing blood
everywhere.

I hit myself again. Stare in the mirror.

I have to get out of here. I have to make sure nobody ever
thinks Tina did this because Tina *couldn't possibly*, she's just
so good, so I'll leave here, I remember where my keys are on
the kitchen counter, and I'll get them, and I'll leave, and
Eloise can clean up this mess for all I care, she won't want
me to have the money she's going to get, she'll probably keep
my half from me, but I'll have Tina, Tina, Tina, and that's all
I want right now.

I run down the stairs. Broken glass from the picture
frames crunches under my shoes, but I don't slow down
until I have my keys and I'm in my car, and I'm so sorry,
Jared, you're just going to lie there in your blood, and there
isn't anything I can do about it now because plans change,
and I had to change it even though Eloise is going to be so
angry at me.

I'm halfway to town when I realize I'm still covered in
blood. I pull over, park in the side lot of a gas station, and
there's a police officer now coming out the door with a
donut, really shoveling it in, and I sink down in my seat.

Can he smell me? Smell Jared's blood? Probably not, not
through the glass, but I still sink down, and then I realize
that just leaving Jared isn't going to be enough, that Eloise

will get there and take his phone and try to pin it on Tina, and I pull my phone from my pocket. Not my Eloise phone. My real phone.

"My cousin told me she was going to kill her husband." I rapid-fire the words at the woman who answers, and even though she sounds nice, like someone I'd like to talk to, like someone who would understand what I'm going through, I don't give her the chance to speak. I rattle off Eloise's address. Tell them her name. "You'd better hurry," I say.

And then I hang up.

Look around the parking lot. Watch everyone.

I'm good at watching.

The cop stops walking. He tilts his head to his shoulder, to his little radio sitting right there like a friend whispering in his ear.

Then he runs to his car.

53

ELOISE

Ricky won't pick up his phone, and if I know my cousin, that probably means he's doing something stupid. I've already left two messages, so I hang up when I hear the voicemail click on.

"Where are you?" I mutter, squeezing my steering wheel as tight as possible before forcing myself to relax. Then I take three deep breaths, apparently the magic number to help you get rid of whatever stress you feel, and I turn off the main road towards his shitty little apartment.

If he doesn't want to answer my phone call, then I'll just show up and talk to him face-to-face. He doesn't have to answer his phone, but he has to answer his door. If not him, then that roommate of his will.

Penny?

Patrice?

Paula.

The parking lot at his complex is surprisingly full, so I pull right up into a handicapped space, turn on my emergency flashers, and hurry up to his apartment. How this metal staircase hasn't fallen in by now is beyond me, but it holds, and I make it to the door, only pausing for a moment before banging on it.

"Ricky! I need to talk to you!"

There's silence, and I lean forward, pressing my ear against the door to try to hear what's going on inside. I hear sound, like maybe the TV playing, but nobody's coming.

"Ricky!" I pound again, hitting the door as hard as possible with the side of my fist to try to get through to him. "Come out here!"

This time, when I press my ear up against the door, there's footsteps. I step back, triumphant, ready to tell my cousin off for not picking up the phone when I called him before, but the door opens just a few inches before it stops.

"What do you want?" It's that woman, Paula, not my cousin, and I swallow my frustration.

"I need to talk to Ricky," I say, doing my best to keep my voice calm. In reality, though, I want to scream at her for causing a delay. "He's not answering his phone."

"He's not here," she's quick to respond, although why she couldn't get to the door in a timely fashion, I don't know. "His phone keeps ringing and ringing in his bedroom, but he's not picking it up."

"Maybe he's in the bathroom." I put one hand on the door, ready to push it open. "Let me come look for him."

She shakes her head even as I start to push my way in, but the door has a chain and catches on it.

"Please," I say, changing up my tactic. "I really need to talk to him."

"He's not here," she repeats. "Trust me. He left in a tizzy earlier and hasn't been back, so I don't know where he is."

I'm only half listening as I fumble my phone from my pocket and dial his number. It rings in my ear.

And from the apartment.

She cocks an eyebrow at me. "I told you. It's been ringing all day. Now, unless you want to rent the extra room we have, I'm going to have to say goodbye."

But before she closes the door, she stops. Stares at me. I watch with a sinking feeling as she snaps her fingers.

"I know you," she says, but before she can get another word out, I shake my head and back away from the door.

"Sorry, I just have that face."

"No, that's not it." She closes the door partway so she can unhook the chain and open it back up. "I know! You were here. You came to help move Tina out of here and into her new home. You're her friend. The Realtor." She pauses; then her eyes narrow. "But what are you doing trying to call Ricky?"

"He's looking to buy a home. We're meeting up this afternoon, and I tried to reach him but couldn't. I got worried," I lie. Still, even though the lie sounds good to my ears, I inch back from her. My brain screams at me to turn and run, to get as much space between the two of us as possible, but I'm frozen on the landing.

"Ricky is? And you're helping him? You must really work miracles." She relaxes, leaning against the doorframe. "I can tell him you came by looking for him if you'd like. He'll show up eventually, I'm sure."

I really, really need that phone. Ricky left it here, and I have a terrible feeling he's doing something stupid right now. I need to get it from her.

"Is there any way I could grab his phone?" I'm sweating now, and I know any person in their right mind wouldn't let me take someone else's phone. "That way, when he makes it to our meeting, I can have it for him. You know how scattered he can get sometimes."

She pauses. "You really think you're going to be able to help him move out?" There's a note of incredulity and hope in her voice, and I latch onto it.

"Definitely." I lean forward like I trust her, like we're close friends. "Between you and me, I think I found the perfect place for him. From what Tina said, she was really glad to move out away from him. It's okay if you feel the same way. I totally understand."

And I do. I know what kind of person my cousin is, and I don't judge this woman one bit for wanting him out of her apartment, even if that means she's going to steal his phone and give it to me.

"Wait just a second," she tells me, then disappears down the hall. A moment later she's back and holding out the burner I bought him. "Best of luck getting him out of here. Seriously. Then maybe one day you can help me buy a house."

Doubtful. "All you have to do is call me! I'd love to help you." I slip his phone into my purse. "And thanks for that. I'll make sure he gets it and get him out of your hair ASAP."

Now she grins at me, fully relaxed, just like we're two friends catching up.

"You have no idea how much I appreciate that. Seriously. He pays his rent, he's just..."

"Creepy?" I offer. "You know how men can be, but don't you worry. Everything will be just fine. Now, I have to go, or I'll miss our meeting later." I throw her a wave and hurry down the stairs, gripping the handrail to ensure I don't slip.

My car fires right up, and I tear out of that crappy little

parking lot as fast as I can go. I do want to hunt Ricky down, make sure he sticks to the plan, but there's something I have to do first.

It only takes twenty minutes to drive out of town to the reservoir. On the weekends this place is packed with families getting outside and enjoying nature, but right now it's deserted. I drive right up to where people like to put their boats in and get out with the two cell phones.

One for me. One for Ricky.

It's easy to pop out the batteries and SIM cards and smash those under my heel. I break the batteries, too, then throw them into a bush. The cell phones I lob as far as possible, watching as they splash about twenty feet from where I'm standing. The ripples expand, flattening and minimizing until they disappear.

That's done. Now it's time to go home. I need to talk to Ricky, need to make sure he's not going to jump the gun, but I have a very bad feeling that my cousin may have done something stupid.

That he may have done something I'll regret.

54

ELOISE

I'm sweating as I pull up into my driveway. Three police cars, their lights blazing, are parked in my driveway.

And I know exactly what happened.

What I'm going to walk into.

For a moment I strongly consider just driving on. Putting this place behind me. Jared is dead, that much is obvious, and I can walk away, let Tina win, but I won't. This is my house. I'm the one who stuck with Jared and supported and loved him. I'm the one he owes for all the trouble he caused.

I turn into my driveway.

Even without looking, I can feel the stares of neighbors as I park next to a police car. They're all watching me, I know they are, because that's what I would be doing. I want to walk up to the house with my head held high, but I whip around, fully expecting to catch Tina's face in her window.

Nothing. Her curtains are drawn tight, the house shuttered up. The thought that Ricky might be over there with her hits me, but I shake my head.

Who cares? Who cares if he goes off the deep end and

takes her with him? That wasn't the plan, but if he wants to change the plan a little bit and punish her even more than just sending her to jail, then I don't care.

If I'm being honest with myself, I'm really tired. I want this to be over.

Mostly because I need to pay Ricky off. I need to give him some money so he stops being such a loose cannon. He's more unhinged than I knew, but I'm cleaning up his mess. I got rid of the phones, so now there are only a few calls from him to me on our real phones.

And those are easily explained away.

He's my cousin.

Of course he calls me from time to time.

I'm standing on the front deck, and I reach for the door, taking a deep breath as I do, fully prepared to step inside. There's going to be commotion, I already know it. A dead body — *a dead Jared Jones* — is more than enough cause for concern, and I can only imagine what the police are going to say.

I compose my face.

Reach for the door.

It swings open before I touch it.

A man I've never seen before stands in front of me. He has a roll of crime scene tape in his hand, like I interrupted him from going outside and taping off the house. I stare at his brass name tag, *McMurray*, then force myself to look up at him.

He frowns at me. "Ma'am, you can't just walk in. This is an active crime scene."

"What's going on? I live here. This is my house." There's a tremor in my voice, and I mentally pat myself on the back for that one. I sound really worried, like I can't wrap my mind around the scene playing out in front of me. Like there's no reason why the police should be crawling through my house, and I need someone to make sure I don't faint.

"Mrs. Jones?" The officer in front of me is so big, his shoulders so broad, that I can't see past him. I try anyway, scooting to the side a little to try to take in the scene.

Not that I can see anything. The living room is pristine, like always. Most of the movement is in the kitchen. Through the door into the kitchen I can see someone moving around. He's bent over a bit, and it isn't until he turns to the side that I see he has a camera.

And then the smell hits me.

It's rusty. Coppery. I'd recognize the smell anywhere.

"Oh, my God." My hand flies to my mouth. There's fresh air outside, right behind me, but before I can move to the deck, the officer speaks again.

"Mrs. Jones, why don't you come on in, and we can talk?"

Yeah, why don't I?

"What happened?" I manage the words, my hand still pressed up against my mouth.

"I'm so sorry to have to tell you this, but your husband has been killed." The officer's eyes are beady. Sharp. I see how they dart up and down my body, obviously looking for any blood.

Not that they'll find any. My hands are clean.

"What?" I grab the doorframe for support. In high school I'd been in a production of *Much Ado About Nothing*, and while acting wasn't my passion, I like to think I still remember a few things from my time on the stage. "What happened to him?"

"I need you to come in and answer some questions for me. Why don't you join me here, in the living room?" He moves closer to me, but at an angle, like he's watching me and waiting for me to do something stupid.

Like run.

"What kind of questions?" A shiver dances down my spine. "You can't possibly think I had anything to do with this, can you? I loved Jared!" He raises an eyebrow, and I amend my statement. "Love him. I love him! Who would want to do this to him? He can't really be dead!"

I reach out for the officer, fully expecting him to loop his arm around my shoulders, talk to me, walk me to the sofa and sit down next to me. That's how this is supposed to go. I'm supposed to be at home when they come by with a death notification. I'm not supposed to be a suspect.

"You can either come sit with me and answer questions here, or we can go downtown and answer them there." His hand moves, just a bit, to his side.

To his handcuffs.

"I'm sorry," I say, sniffling hard. "I just don't know what to do. I can't believe he's dead. Are you sure it's him? Are you sure it's Jared?"

He doesn't answer. Instead, he puts his hand on my back and guides me into the house. I don't have a choice but to step away from the front door, and as soon as I do, he closes it behind me.

The sound of the latch slipping into place is very final, and I shiver.

"Mrs. Jones, where were you this afternoon?" There's no sympathy under those words. No kindness. Just suspicion. He puts the roll of bright yellow crime scene tape down on the entryway table.

"I was at work, and then I had some errands to run." I pause before turning and sitting down on the sofa, giving him the attention he wants. "You can't possibly think I had anything to do with this, can you?" I'm aware my voice is getting louder and louder, but I can't stop it. "Are you saying you think I killed Jared?"

He doesn't answer for a moment. I wish he would sit down just so I don't have to look up at him. As it is, though, he towers over me, his beefy arms crossed, his jaw tight. If he sat down, he might ruin the upholstery, but at least I'd feel a little bit more in control.

"Did you find a murder weapon?" I realize the mistake I just made as soon as the question is out of my mouth.

"As a matter of fact, we did." Turning, he yells over his shoulder, "Stallings, bring me the murder weapon."

A young officer with her hair in a high ponytail sweeps into the room. Her mouth is set in a grim line, but there's excitement on her face. I see it written there, and I suddenly hate her. I hate her for thinking this is fun, for believing for one second that I might have actually killed Jared.

But then she hands a plastic bag to the officer in front of me, and all thoughts stop.

"Do you recognize this knife, Mrs. Jones?" He holds the bag out to me like he wants me to take it, but I keep my hands clasped tightly in my lap. "Because it matches the ones in the knife block by the stove. And you have one missing from there."

"I didn't kill Jared." Four words. How am I going to get this through their thick skulls?

He grins at me, and I have the sudden mental image of a rabid dog closing in on a rabbit. I'm cornered, and I know it, and he just keeps coming, and he's so much bigger and is one step ahead of me.

But I'm innocent. I didn't actually kill Jared.

"The knife was in your bathroom sink, where you tried to wash it off. Blood everywhere, though, so that tells me you're not the brightest criminal in the world."

"I didn't do it." My heart flutters in my chest. It's hard for me to breathe. Is this what a heart attack feels like? How ironic would it be if Jared was dead, and I have all the money in the world, and I just keel over right here in my living room because this lunk of a human being can't put two and two together.

I have to make them look at Tina. This wasn't the plan, Ricky screwed it up royally, but I can still fix it.

I'm just grateful I got rid of the cell phones.

And Ricky's too damn dumb to speak out against me. He wants the money. He *needs* the money. And he's crazy, completely certifiably insane. There's no way anyone would believe his word against mine.

Just look at the two of us.

A giggle escapes my lips. The thought of someone having to decide which one of us to believe is too much for me, and the sound escapes. It's small, but it's a mistake.

"You think this is funny?" The man shoves the evidence bag back at the younger officer. "Go ahead and stand up, Mrs. Jones. Turn around. You're under arrest for the murder of your husband, Jared Jones."

"No!" I shriek the word, any other laughter in my body gone. "No, you're making a huge mistake. Trust me, it wasn't me!"

How can I blame this on Tina?

There's no way, not when Jared's dead in my kitchen.

But I have to do something.

"It was Ricky, my cousin! He killed Jared!"

"You have the right to remain silent," he tells me, grabbing me by the upper arm and pulling me to my feet. I stumble towards him on my high heels, and he catches me, but his grip on my arms doesn't feel kind. "Anything you say can and will be used against you in a court of law."

"I didn't do it!" I turn, teetering on my heels, not because I want to, but because he hasn't let go of me. "I'm innocent! You have the wrong person. It was Ricky!"

"Come on," he tells me, turning me back around. His grip has dropped to my elbow, and I stumble after him, casting one look into the kitchen as we go.

I see a foot. Blood. It's spreading out from the body in a pool, and even though I have other things to worry about, even though this is a terrible thing to think about it, there's one thought that launches into my mind and sticks there like a burr.

How am I ever going to clean it up?

But now we're on the front deck, and he's helping me down the stairs. If the neighbors weren't watching before, I'm sure they are now, and I lift my chin. Tighten my jaw.

They'll see. They'll all see.

I'm going to make Ricky pay for everything.

55

RICKY

I smell like Jared, like his blood, even though I killed him three days ago and even though I've showered twenty times since then. I still feel like he's on me, like his blood has soaked into my skin and is under my nails and in my hair, and this time when I shower, I take a bottle of bleach with me.

I have to get it off me. I have to stop smelling like Jared because if I do and I go see Tina, then she'll know it all. She'll be able to smell him on me.

Honestly, I'm surprised Paula can't. She can't smell the blood on me even though I can, and she didn't ask questions when I took five showers that first night, only told me I was going to have to pay for the increased water bill, which is fine, because Tina will help me pay when I tell her I did everything for her and that I love her.

And my diary will help. I pat the cover five more times, just to make sure it's still really there and on my bed and not in my imagination; then I take the half-empty bottle of bleach to the bathroom with me.

This will do it. This will make me clean.

Down the hall, I hear Paula watching TV. She's tired after working, and I get it, but I can't sleep. I don't know if I've slept since I killed Jared, and I'm not going to now, not when I can still smell him on me. It's disgusting, his scent, and the fact that I can't shake it, and this will do it.

It has to do it.

I run the water, but it comes out cold, no matter how long I wait for it to warm up, and Paula said that's another problem, that I'm using up all the hot water, so I'm not allowed to shower until she does, but she showered this morning and is nice and clean, and now it's my turn even though the water feels like icicles piercing my skin when I step in.

I gasp. My skin crawls. It feels tight on my body, like a suit I shouldn't be wearing because it doesn't fit correctly any longer, but this will help me get clean and make my skin loosen back up.

My fingers tremble a bit when I undo the cap.

The smell makes me gag. This is what Eloise will have to use to clean the floor and her bathroom and the stairs and towels and knife, and it's what I should have used when I killed Jared, but I panicked and didn't think about it, but it makes sense now, doesn't it?

Bleach makes everything clean. It'll wash me and clean me, and I won't have to worry about smelling like Jared any longer.

But the water will dilute it. I know you can clean with diluted bleach, but this isn't a job for that. I need the full-strength stuff to wash me, and I turn off the water. I'm dripping wet, but that should be okay. This will still work.

Outside the bathroom, I hear someone knocking on the

front door. They're banging, but the sound is muffled here in the bathroom.

It might be Tina. Come to get me. Come to tell me she knows she loves me now and she should have known from the beginning and will I forgive her for making me wait, and I'll tell her that of course I will because that's what love does and what we do for people we love.

And before I can think about it anymore, I take the bottle of bleach and hold it over my head so it will run down my body, and I dump it. It's half-full, just half-full, but that should be enough, and I feel the cold liquid splash on the top of my head, then stream down my neck, my shoulders, running down my body, and I drop the bottle with a loud thunk so the clean runs down my arms to my hands because that's where I still have a lot of blood.

Jared's blood.

And it drips off the ends of my fingers the way his blood did, and I can already see how it's making me cleaner, I swear I can see the blood leaving my body, and soon I'll be clean and ready for Tina.

I rub one hand down my arm. The skin feels slippery and wet, like I've soaped up, but I haven't soaped up, I've gone one step farther to make sure I'm really clean.

Now I'm excited, and I bend over, rubbing my hands all over my torso, my legs, even my feet. I feel the slipperiness, and I know without a doubt that it's working, that I'm getting clean, and then I straighten and rub my shoulders and my neck and my face and my head, rubbing my fingers hard into my scalp to get the bleach there just in case there's blood there I missed because this will get it out, and I'll finally be clean.

I'm tingling now, and the sensation is amazing. Do I

wash it off like soap? Do I keep it on my body so I can always stay clean? I like to think of it as armor I'm putting on, armor that will protect me from getting dirty again.

The tingling changes.

It's stinging now, like stinging nettles, like I've walked through a field of the gorgeous flowers and brushed up against them, and now they're touching me everywhere, and now there are bees stinging me, and I imagine my entire body covered in wasps, an angry nest of them that I've pissed off, and they're all stinging me.

And there's a loud sound, and it takes me a moment to realize I'm screaming. My eyes burn, and I rub them, trying to make it stop, but the pressure only makes it worse. I can't open my eyes to see, and I turn, falling into the shower wall as I fumble for the faucet to turn it on.

Who cares if it's cold now? I'll take anything over these angry wasps that are stinging me.

The water takes a moment to run, it always does, like it's on a delay to make sure you really want it to run, and that's never bothered me before, but now I can't breathe, and I'm still screaming, and the noise is punctuated by someone banging on the door.

I should tell Paula that I'm okay, but then the water starts spraying on my head, and it's freezing cold, but it's killing the wasps, and the relief is so amazing I bend over, bracing myself on the shower wall, and sob.

The door slams open.

Someone starts coughing.

"Police!" It's a man, and he sounds angry. The shower curtain rips back. I still don't look, not even when he yanks it so hard some of the rings pop free and hit me in the back. "We need an ambulance!"

I want to laugh at that statement, but instead I groan, turning around so the water can hit me on my torso. My skin is on fire, and my eyes don't want to open. I can't see the man. I don't care that I'm naked in front of him, that he can see me. I just want this to stop.

The sound of the exhaust fan.

People yelling.

I feel my legs start to give way under me, and even though I should be stronger now because I'm so clean, I don't fight it as I slowly sink to the floor.

56

ELOISE

My coffee cup is Styrofoam, and the sides press in when I squeeze it. I don't care if the entire thing breaks and coffee goes everywhere, it's cold now, absolutely atrocious. I just want out of here.

At least I'm back in my clothes. No more detention-center-issued outfits for me. My jewelry is back, too, and I can't stop staring at my engagement ring. It's so shiny, so bright and flashy after the dull and dark of sitting in a cell.

The door to the small room opens, and a woman walks in. She's dressed in a suit and has a file with her, which she drops on the table in front of me before sitting down. When she does, she sighs heavily, like even being here with me is a problem.

"How are you doing?" The question is so surprising I start. Nobody has asked me that since I was arrested for Jared's murder.

It didn't matter how many times I said I was innocent. How many times I begged them to look into Ricky. They sure took their sweet time on that one, and now they want to know how I'm doing?

I want to laugh, but the last time I did that, it got me in trouble, so instead I take a deep breath. "I'm doing better."

She smiles. "Right. Well, I want to go over some new information we have. Talk to you about it."

I know what the information is. Ricky. They finally followed up on Ricky, or I wouldn't be in my own clothes right now. I'm not stupid.

But I am worried because what if my idiot cousin ran his mouth and implicated me? I think I'm untouchable, I really think I am. But I won't know for sure until this conversation is over and I'm out of here.

"We looked into Ricky," she tells me, flipping the folder open and handing me a picture of my cousin.

I take it, because even though I know what he looks like better than she ever will, I still want to play my role. I know his beady eyes and weak chin and how he slumps over a little bit when he thinks the world is too much to bear. But this time, when my eyes drop down to look at his face, I gasp.

"What happened to him?"

He looks terrible. His eyes are swollen to the point where they can't open. His skin is red, splotchy. His hair is falling out. If I didn't know this man was my cousin, I honestly don't think I'd recognize him on the street. He's in a white gown, the front of it unbuttoned part of the way. I can see the red skin there, the angry color of it, how it looks like he has the worst sunburn I've ever seen.

He's in a bed. A tube runs down his mouth. His eyes are closed; there's oxygen to his nose.

"Ricky was showering in bleach when we went to his apartment."

"Bleach?" Surely I didn't hear her correctly. "He was showering in bleach?"

She nods. "We had to get an ambulance there immediately to take him to the hospital. He has a long road ahead of him, and honestly, there is a chance he might not survive. He breathed in the fumes and doused himself completely with it, so he has severe burns all over his body."

"Oh, my God." I put the photo down and push it towards her. I don't want to see it. Just like I pretended I didn't want to see Jared's crime scene photos, but those I was secretly happy about.

He deserved to die.

Maybe Ricky did too. But bleach?

"In his room we found clothes covered in blood. Bloody shoes, too. We're running tests on the blood to see if it's Jared's, but based on what he wrote in his diary, we're pretty sure he killed your husband."

I stiffen. "He had a diary?"

"Looks like it. Only most of the pages were ripped out. Maybe he was writing in it and then destroying the pages? We don't know. But we do know he wrote in it once before his shower and didn't destroy it."

I have to know what he was writing about.

But I have to sound like it won't affect me.

"What did he say in his diary?" Leaning forward, I take a deep breath. Can't seem too eager. But I have to know.

There's a slight hesitation before she answers, and I have the very distinct feeling that I might not like what she has to say. Slowly, so slowly I barely feel like I'm moving, I tilt my head a bit towards her.

"He was rambling for most of it," she finally says. "He

talks about killing Jared and now nothing will be able to keep him from being with Tina."

I realize I'm holding my breath. My lungs hurt. "Is that it?"

"It sounds like he was obsessed with Tina. Your neighbor. I know you helped her buy her home."

This is it. It's all about to fall apart at my feet, and just because I went about this the wrong way. Moving her across the street so I could watch her and Jared's downfall was hubris. There must have been a better way, and I just didn't see it, and now I'm going to regret everything.

"I helped her, yes. She's a lovely woman with a little boy, and they just needed someplace else to live."

"Because your cousin was creeping her out." She leans forward, so close to me I can see the pores on her cheeks. "He was creeping her out, and for good reason. I have to ask, Eloise, just between us girls, did you know Luke was Jared's son? Tina told us that was true, that she and Jared had had an affair years ago."

I freeze. This is the moment where everything matters, isn't it? There are two paths in front of me, each one leading to a vastly different future. I think back to the papers from 123DNA. There's no way they found them ripped up and thrown away in a trash can. No way they have any idea what I know.

"I suspected," I finally say, hedging my bets on what this woman already knows. "But what was I to do?" I feel tears well up in my eyes. "I love Jared. I always will. And Tina was so sad and hated living in that apartment, and I had no idea Ricky was so... crazy." My voice drops. "I didn't know he was crazy. I would have gotten him help."

She stares at me, and I have the intense feeling that she doesn't believe me.

Finally, though, she nods.

"Your cousin needs serious psychiatric help. I'd love to hear his side of the story."

"He hasn't talked to you?" The question is out before I can temper my excitement.

I catch the sharp look on her face. "You saw the picture. He's in the ICU. Intubated. I have no idea if he'll ever speak again."

"Oh, God." *Thank you, God.* "That's terrible." *That's the best news I've ever heard.* "Can I see him?"

"Not in the ICU." She stands and picks up her folder, tapping it on the table to organize all the papers. "I'm going to come clean with you, Eloise."

I stare at her. From what she's told me, she has nothing. Ricky is an idiot for bathing himself in bleach like that, but it might very well be the best thing he's ever done.

"I don't think for one moment that your cousin acted alone." Her words are quiet. She's dropped her voice and leaned forward, ensuring that what she's about to say is only for my ears. "He's not that bright, sorry to say it. He's off the deep end, and I think you put him there."

I don't blink.

"I know he's your blood, and normally you'd want to make sure your family was okay and was going to survive and get out of the ICU, but if I were you, I'd be praying that he didn't. Because if he does, Eloise, I'm going to be right there to interview him. I'm going to find out the truth of what really happened to Jared."

It's hard for me to breathe. This room is too small, and she's taking up all the oxygen. Still, though, I don't look away from her. It feels superstitious, like if I keep my eyes locked on her, I'll be able to make sure she can't attack me.

She's a snake, and I'm the mouse, and all I can do is keep my eyes on her. Refuse to break eye contact.

"So, no, to answer your question, you can't go see him. He's under watch to make sure he doesn't end up like your husband. You're free to go, Eloise, free to collect whatever money Jared left behind for you, but I'm not looking away. I'm watching. I'm waiting. As soon as Ricky can talk, I'll be there."

I rise. My back is stiff. "Are we finished here?"

She nods. "For now."

"Good." I sweep past her. Even though I want to scream, I walk down the hall in silence. Get my phone, keys, and wallet from the man at the front desk.

Step out into the sunshine and inhale hard, bending over and grabbing my thighs as I do.

I'm not a praying person, but Ricky had better die.

L uke clutches a bag of goldfish crackers in one hand
and my old cell phone he can use to play *Frog Run*
in the other. His eyes are wide as we walk through
the huge double doors leading into the law office. Under our
feet, there's a thick carpet, and I pause, letting my eyes adjust
to the dim lighting before putting my hand on his back and
ushering him forward.

"What are we doing?" he whispers, but still his voice
sounds too loud in the quiet, and I wince.

"We have to go see this lawyer," I whisper back, taking
his goldfish from him so I can slip his hand into mine. "So I
just need you to come with me and be a good listener, and
then we'll go home."

Brett Larch, whoever that is.

Home. Across the road from Eloise, who hasn't made an
effort to speak to me after Jared was killed, she was
arrested for murder, and then Ricky was charged upon her
release.

And then Ricky died a terrible death in the ICU, and

even though he creeped me out, nobody deserves to go like he did.

Just thinking about all of the moving pieces makes my head hurt. I can't wrap my mind around it all, around the fact that Eloise was Ricky's cousin, the fact that he would break into their house and kill Jared, and the fact that a lawyer reached out to me to tell me I had to be here at the reading of the will.

No, that's not entirely right, is it? *I* wasn't requested. It wasn't me who was wanted, it was Luke, but I had to drive him, and I'll act in his stead since he's so little.

The lawyer wouldn't tell me why we had to come to the reading of the will, only that Luke's presence was required. From that, though, I figured out a few things.

One, that Jared knew about Luke. He knew Luke was his and never said anything to me, which hurts a lot more than I want to admit it does.

Two, the lawyer knows about Luke belonging to Jared. Why else would we be here?

Three, that Eloise, if she doesn't know the truth by now, is going to find it out really soon.

I glance at my watch as Luke and I hurry down the hall. We're not late, exactly, but I didn't want to show up early and have to sit there in this stuffy room staring at everyone while they wondered who in the world I was. No, if Eloise is going to find out the truth about Jared and me for the first time right here in front of everyone, then I wanted to make sure there was space between us.

The last room on the right. That's where we're going, with light streaming out through the open door and the sound of low voices. I stop in the hall, turning Luke so I can get a good look at him.

"Just stay quiet, okay?" I whisper, cupping his cheek. He blinks up at me and nods, and I exhale hard.

Into the belly of the beast.

The room has a huge oval table with more than a dozen chairs around it. On one wall is a large credenza; the other has windows that look down over the city. Right in the middle of the table sits a man in an expensive suit, a file folder in front of him, a scattering of pens in front of that.

Next to him is a younger woman. I look at her and know immediately she's the secretary and he's who I'm dealing with.

And there's one other person in the room. A woman with her back to me. Her hair is perfect, her spine straight as she perches on the edge of her chair. There's a glass of water in front of her, and she reaches out, dragging her finger down the side and through the condensation.

Eloise.

Luke barrels ahead of me and throws himself into a chair, causing the man to look up at the two of us.

"And there you are. I was beginning to get worried. Have a seat." He gestures vaguely to any of the chairs across from him.

Eloise turns, a question on her face, but that changes when she sees me. "What are you doing here?"

My hand is on the back of a chair, and I freeze.

"Ms. Tina Miller is here by my invitation," the lawyer says. His tone is low and rough, and I have the immediate impression he's not someone who will lie down and take mistreatment from anyone. "Actually, her son, Luke, is here for the reading of the will."

Eloise goes pale. I swear, I see the moment blood drains from her face. Her hands clench into claws, and she clasps them together while she stares at me. "Why is he here for the reading of the will?"

Keeping a seat between us, I sit. My eyes are locked on the lawyer, but I can tell Eloise is still staring at me.

"He is here by request of Jared Jones." The man's voice is dry, and I hear the warning in his tone not to mess with him.

Next to me, Luke shifts in his seat, but he doesn't make a sound. I open his bag of goldfish and rub his shoulder.

"She's nobody." Eloise leans towards me, and I finally break eye contact with the lawyer to look at her. "Do you hear that? You're nothing."

"Mrs. Jones, if you can't be civil, I'm more than happy to ask you to leave. You are not needed here for the majority of the reading." The lawyer has one hand up like he's going to dismiss her.

My eyes flit between the two of them as I try to figure out what's going to happen next.

"No, that's fine. I can sit here while you tell her what sorry little bank account she's going to get. You do know who this is, right?" She looks at me and smirks.

Don't say it.

"This is my husband's whore." Eloise crosses her arms and leans back in her chair. "She already came after me to take my seconds, so let's just see how it's going to work out for her. I want to hear what second-place prizes she won."

There's a long silence during which I stare down at the table in front of me. I know the lawyer made it clear Luke needed to be here, but this isn't worth it. Jared never acknowledged him as his child when he was alive, so I have no idea why I would think he'd do it now that he's dead. Still, we're here, and even a few thousand dollars could go a long way towards paying for college.

"Then we'll begin." The lawyer clears his throat and flips open the folder.

Eloise leans forward, drawn by whatever information there might be in there.

It's alluring, sure, but I refuse to show that much interest. I sit still. Waiting.

Luke fidgets next to me but doesn't make a sound.

"The reading of Jared Jones's will, the most recent edition from last month," the lawyer begins, and I tune him out. I shouldn't, I know that, but I can't get over wondering why we're here. Wondering when Jared figured it all out. When Eloise figured it out.

"He didn't update his will that recently." Eloise is on her feet, and she slams her hand down on the table. "You're wrong. He didn't do that."

The lawyer glances up at her. "He did. He came to me, and I changed it for him. You're more than happy to check the security cameras if you'd like and compare his signature, but I assure you, Mrs. Jones, this is your husband's most recent will. Now sit down or leave."

She sits. Her anxiety is rubbing off on me, and I find myself bouncing my leg.

The lawyer clears his throat. "Now, if we're all ready. To you, Mrs. Jones, Jared left the contents of your joint account. He — "

"But a joint account would be mine regardless." Eloise is back on her feet. "Why would he feel the need to leave me that in writing when it's joint and it's mine anyway?"

"Because it wasn't joint with right of survivorship. Now sit down."

Eloise sits, but not before she turns and stares at me. It's a glare, her eyes locked on mine like she's never seen anyone or anything she hates more in her entire life.

I glance at her, then scoot forward a bit in my seat to make sure she can't stare at Luke like that. I don't want him to be the subject of her ire.

"And to Luke Miller, in light of recent events, Mr. Jones left the remainder of his accounts. His property, the vehicle in his name, and his business."

I'm so busy focusing on Luke and making sure he doesn't realize Eloise is staring at him like she hates him that, at first, I don't realize what he just said.

"Wait, what?" I lean forward, my heart and stomach seeming to switch places. I feel like I'm going to throw up, and it's not just because of what he just said.

Eloise has risen from her chair, and she's leaning closer to me now, her face twisted with rage. "What did you do?" She hisses the words and stabs a finger at me.

I wince back, looping my arm around Luke's shoulders. "I didn't do anything," I tell her, which is true. For the most part. I didn't do anything recently, although I'm sure she sees me having a child with Jared as the worst possible thing I could do.

"Mrs. Jones." The lawyer is also on his feet now, and his voice is so authoritative that Eloise stops and turns to look at him. "You may sit, or you may leave. But you may not speak to Ms. Miller like that."

Eloise blinks. Her mouth falls open, and she slams it shut. But she sits, collapsing into her chair.

"I don't understand." Grabbing Luke's hand, I stare at the lawyer. "What do you mean by that? He left everything to Luke?"

"Everything but the joint checking account. The rest of

his assets are frozen and will go to Luke as his only surviving heir. Obviously, he's too young to be handed things like a house or car, but that's where you come in."

"No." Eloise has her head in her hands. "This is not how it was supposed to go. I didn't think... I didn't think he had time." She lifts her face and stares at me. Tears run down her cheeks, mascara leaving black rivulets. "How did he have time?"

"Mr. Jones came to visit me and was very worried about having his new will drawn up immediately. I took care of it like he wanted me to." The man's eyes are steely as he stares at Eloise. She, for her part, doesn't blink. "You'll see that it's airtight."

"I don't believe it." Her voice is strangled, and she grabs at her neck like she's trying to adjust the sound of her voice. "He loved me. He wouldn't do this to me." She turns and looks at me. "You did this." Her voice is flat. Dark.

I'm shaking my head when the lawyer cuts me off. "I assure you, Mrs. Jones, that Mr. Jones came here of his own volition and was very clear about the changes he wanted."

Eloise shoves back from the table. Her hand shakes as she picks up her purse and swings it over her shoulder. "I don't have to listen to this," she announces. "This is ridiculous! I'll hire my own lawyer. Contest the will."

"You can do that." The man across the table from me sounds vaguely amused. "But I guarantee you, you won't get anywhere in court."

Eloise breathes hard. There's a huge red splotch spreading up her chest. She hitches her purse higher on her shoulder, then turns to stare at me. "I'll get my money."

Before I can respond, she spins away from the table. Rushes out of the room. It feels like she's taking all the air in the room with her, but then she slams the door, and I wince, the spell broken.

"Ms. Miller," the lawyer says, rapping his knuckles lightly on the table to get my attention, "you don't need to worry."

I swallow hard. Find my voice. "I hate to argue, but it really looks like I do."

He laughs and shakes his head before sliding the folder in front of him across the table to me. "No, Jared was very clear about what he wanted. He was thrilled to have a son and wanted him to have the best possible life. You — your son, actually — is rich. Neither of you will ever want for anything ever again."

Luke's still playing at the table. He's pulled a toy car from his pocket and runs it back and forth in front of him, making little *vroom* noises as he does.

I should be focused on the money this guy is talking about, but there's something else he said that I can't get out of my head.

"I'm sorry," I say, holding up a hand and cutting him off. "But you said he was thrilled to have a son? To have Luke? But he didn't say anything." My heart aches.

The lawyer stares at me for a moment. "He was thrilled. And maybe he didn't say anything, but he left everything to Luke." There's a curious expression on his face like he's trying to read my thoughts. "And before you ask, let me tell you again. Eloise can throw a fit as much as she wants. She's not getting her hands on this money. Or property. Or business."

I take a deep breath, trying to let it sink in.

Eloise knew everything from the beginning. I have to believe she did. She's dangerous, no matter how calm this guy might be when talking about her. But that's okay. I might have been blinded before and thought that she was a good person, but I know the truth now.

Which means now I can protect myself. Protect Luke.

"How quickly does she have to leave the house?" I suddenly want her out. I'm filled with desire to see her out of the house, to know she can't touch the two of us. "That sounds terrible, but — "

"As soon as possible. The house is no longer in her husband's name. She was never on the title, and now she's squatting. She can be removed as soon as you're ready. If she doesn't go quietly, then she might need to be evicted, but I can handle that for you, and you won't have to worry about whether or not you can pay the associated fees."

I never have to worry about whether or not I can pay any fees ever again. I take a deep breath and stare at the man across from me. Luke is oblivious to everything going on, and I'm grateful for that. I don't want him figuring out what just happened for a very long time.

I'll tell him the truth eventually. Of course I will. But there's no reason to rush it, not when he's still so young. So innocent.

"Do it." My voice doesn't tremble. My heart breaks a little as I think about the fact that Eloise was against me from the beginning. I didn't know this was a competition. All I was trying to do was make a better life for Luke.

But it was a competition.

And I won.

THANK YOU FOR READING

Did you enjoy reading *Her Husband's Secret*? Please consider leaving a review on Amazon. Your review will help other readers to discover the novel.

ABOUT THE AUTHOR

Emily Shiner always dreamed of becoming an author but first served her time as a banker and a teacher. After a lifetime of devouring stacks of thrillers, she decided to try her hand at writing them herself. Now she gets to live out her dream of writing novels and sharing her stories with people around the world. She lives in the Appalachian Mountains and loves hiking with her husband, daughter, and their two dogs.

ALSO BY EMILY SHINER

Made in United States
Troutdale, OR
06/08/2023

10511363R00224